HOME OF THE BODY BAGS

Terrell C. Wright

SenegalPress

Copyright © 2005 by Terrell C. Wright.

All rights reserved, including the right to reproduce this book or any part thereof in any form, except for inclusion of brief quotations in a review, without the written permission of the publisher.

Cover design by MZK

Design, typesetting, and other prepress work by
SenegalPress Venice, California.
Printed in U.S.A.
ISBN: 0-9758594-0-4
LCCN: 2005921592

DEDICATION

This book is dedicated to:
Anthony "G-Kev" Moguel, his friendship and memory will always live within my heart forever – B.I.P.,
Merrill "M-Dog" Vernon, my love and respect to him – rest in peace homey,
my dearest mother Sheryl A. Wilson, who stood behind me, encouraging me, and pushing me onward with the desire to achieve;
my children Shavon and Terrey;
my brother Charles and my sisters Virginia and Malinda.
A special thanks to my friend Tana Vernon, who has been an endless light at the end of the tunnels, I love you.
And a profession undying love for my dearly departed Aunt Mae, who will always reign supreme in my heart, and may she reign superior there in heaven with her creator – God bless her soul.

PREFACE

I wrote this book with the desire of wanting to share my experience and the truth of a gangster life with the American people, and to a larger extent, with the world. My experience isn't overly unique in a deeper sense, in fact, it's an experience that is replayed and repeated over and over again in many ghetto and inner city dwellings throughout the United States of America. To avoid the final outcome on my many journeys of being in and out of jail, I encourage the young reader to try as best they could to avoid the many pitfalls and obstacles I often experienced, and which are everywhere and plentiful. I encourage you, the reader, to prepare your future carefully, to stay focused and to remain determined to succeed. And as a final note, don't ever think about following in my footsteps because there is no such thing like perfect gangsterism.

Terrell Cortez Wright
a.k.a. Loko

ACKNOWLEDGEMENTS

Bulletproof appreciation is extended to my agent and publisher Elke Senegal for her invaluable inspiration with my project, and Teflon bullets are sent to all the haters – I'll holla!

LOS ANGELES
(1977-1981)

My earliest influence and experience from the gang world is an easy task of remembrance for me. My story begins when I was living on the east side of Los Angeles, on 116th Street between Main and San Pedro. The year was 1977, and I was attending a nearby elementary school located on 118th Street, respectfully called 118th Street Elementary. Most of the youngsters I knew and grew up with in the surrounding neighborhoods and I proudly and boldly displayed the gang banger's influence upon our lives. The scientists, who often analyzed our epidemic, labeled our experience an "environmental impact", but we simply called it "becoming ghetto fabulous". The neighborhood, in which I lived, was reputedly known as Crip territory. There were two local gangs: The first and smallest of the two were the 116th A-Line Crips (A-Line meaning Avalon Line), located on 116th and Avalon; the other and larger of the two was known as the 118th E.C.B.C. (East Coast Block Crips). As far back as I can remember I always found myself fascinated by the local gangsters and the war stories of their lives.

At the innocent and youthful age of eight, my friends and I were considered what everyone called wanna-be's (fake gangsters), but to us even that degrading title was okay. At the school I attended, there were two youth gangs: the one that I belonged to and another one, which hung out mostly around 115th and San Pedro. Neither groups had names, but my gang and its members were identifiable by the way, in which we wore our button-up shirts. Of all the buttons, the only one that would be attached was the upper most top one. Every day during the recess times, my fellow youths and I paraded throughout the school grounds mean mugging and harassing the other school kids; often time we'd never be chastised for our misbehavior. Every day there would be some after school entertainment; simply put there'd be an after school fight. Usually the opponents would be unknown youths from other nearby schools looking to make a reputation for themselves. As time would have it and combat skills acquired through plenty of squabbling, I developed a decent reputation from these after school brawls.

I would soon receive the honorable titles *King of the Block*, and the more appreciated one *King of the School*. I probably fought every youngster defending these titles. My style and choice of combat would prove simple and effective. I'd position myself dukes held high, and once I realized I had my opponent's undivided attention focused on my hands, and on our merry-go-around dance, I'd quickly and skillfully dive bomb for his legs, lifting him up and over my shoulders, dropping him head first to the waiting pavement down below. Dazed and half-conscious from the impact of the fall, my opponent would soon be finished off, and I quickly and confidently would add yet another victory to my title.

Eventually my fights in and around the school grounds would land me into trouble with the school staff, and soon enough with my mom. The more fights I had, the more detentions and suspensions I received at school; and the more ass whippings I received at home. Not much later, I found myself bouncing from school to school because of my disruptive behavior. From 118th Street Elementary, I would be transferred to 116th Street Elementary. After one too many troublesome situations there, I was subsequently transferred to Figueroa Elementary. But it would be the same attitude displayed at every school I attended fights, disrespect toward the teachers, and little or no interest at all in wanting to learn the much-needed knowledge that would help and possibly secure a decent life for me in the near future. Unconcerned at that time, and unknowingly to me then, my lack of respect for others would lay a future foundation that would eventually set the pace for my over all mentality in the world of gang banging. Memories searching, I vividly recall one particular summer afternoon.

I was enjoying myself skateboarding up and down the block, when I noticed a commotion in the far of distance. It seemed to me at first glance to be an uneven gang fight, but after further investigation I realized, it wasn't even close to a gang fight. The local A-Line Crips were stumping out a guy merciless. Rumors had it that somebody spray-painted the nearby walls with an insignia of a Blood gang, known as the Nickerson Garden Bounty Hunter Bloods, located in Watts. Since the Avalon Crips claimed 116th as their turf undisputedly, the banging on their walls was an act of war and had to be addressed immediately with a show of strength through the usual beat-downs. Most of the gangsters wore blue bandanas covering their faces like the cowboys from the wild-west movies; and in no particular order, they proceeded up the block chanting their call "A-Line Crip, A-Line Crip", and stumping guys out, who merely had the slightest resemblance of a Blood member.

The one particular guy they were harassing that day was known as Baby Huey. Huey looked like a typical L.A. gangster in demeanor and through dress, but to those, who knew him from the neighborhood, it was clear that he didn't give a damn about banging; whereas the A-Line Crips figured he was hooked-up with somebody, and due to that unwritten rule he was guilty as charged. And to make their point valid to any hidden rivals, they spray-painted their hood on the back of his t-shirt, took his much-admired ghetto blaster, and commenced to whipping his ass as an after thought.

From that one event in the 70's I had been exposed to enough rawness to develop a deep desire of belonging to a gang. I wanted to bang. The naked excitement, the untaught drama, the unquestioned power, and the gang bangers' respect were all things I desired as a young man growing up in South Central, Los Angeles. The gang influence started to become evident through my clothing, I soon chose and adopted an exact replica to the gang bangers' dress code: khaki suits, Chuck Taylor tennis shoes, Croaker Sacks tennis shoes, Pendleton shirts, golf hats, beanies, and Puma shoes. To the much experienced eye it was obvious I was imitating the role of a wanna-be gangster, but for the inexperienced and untrained people like my mother and others, I was just a youngster growing up with a simple desire of wanting to change my clothing style.

In the latter part of 1979, my fam-bam (family) and I picked up our lives and our few belongings, and decided to head west of Los Angeles. My mother figured it would be much nicer on the West Side, especially when in comparison to the gang-infested East Side; but little did she know the gang epidemic had already swept the Los Angeles County in its entirety; and the problem of the gang world she was trying to avoid, had already engulfed me. My thoughts, my desires, my emotions, and my near future were centered on the lifestyle of a L.A. gangster. Our new apartment and neighborhood were nice and a tad bit cleaner in comparison to the two-bedroom stucco house we'd just dearly departed.

47th and Hoover was now our new address, 5-Duce Hoover Crips were our new local gangsters; and a short time later Ronald Reagan would become our nation's 40th president. It was a beginning for us, Reagan promised an improved nation, and our new environment provided fresh opportunities. But as the years snail paced along, Reaganomics soon engulfed the entire country, as the gang world and its violence replaced our simple lives by misplacing them deep into a realm of an uncertain future.

I was totally craze ridden with our new neighborhood, and it didn't take me long to place names with the local gangsters. There was Mr. Chim-Chim, who lived up the block about three houses down. He was a short stocky dark skinned brother. Then there was Bam-Bam, who on the other hand was the total opposite of Chim. Bam was about six foot two with an approximate weight of two hundred pounds of solidness. Chim and Bam were considered roll dogs (best friends) and were always seen parading together throughout the neighborhood. Then there was Casper-Loc, who lived on the east end of 47th one house from the street of their self-titled hood Hoover Street. Casper was probably a year or two older than I was, and surprisingly we got along pretty good. He was considered a rarity when in comparison to the other young Hoover Crips: C-Dog, School Boy, Coke-Dog, and Bear, who were all young hoodlums. They were out for a gang reputation, for a reputation at anyone's expense including mine. I learned fast and quickly enough to keep them at a safe distance.

The new school I went to was called Menlo Avenue. Menlo was a far cry from the elementary schools I'd attended on the East Side. The only thing I truly and totally disliked about Menlo Avenue was the irritating fact of it being so far away. I grew up being used to walking only two blocks to school. Menlo Ave would definitely prove a challenge for the legs, being it was approximately eight blocks north of where I lived. But what I remotely appreciated about the distance was the freshness of the neighborhood, and the many unexplored scenic views that I readily absorbed with my young eager senses. Actually, I loved my new school, and quickly enough I developed new friendships. I enjoyed my new teachers, and at the youthful age of ten, I especially liked and enjoyed the girls.

It didn't take long for me to fit in; eventually I became a part of the new neighborhood and as the 70's passed, my new neighborhood and my new experience would become just another brick laid on my stepping stone journey through the City of Angels, soon to be labeled the killing capital of America. But to many throughout the South Central enclave it would be notoriously remembered as the home of the body bags. The gangs swept L.A. by storm, and my mother bounced us from neighborhood to neighborhood desperately trying to find some decency for us. Our new neighborhood after a year or two soon became our old neighborhood. From 47th and Hoover, we eventually landed ourselves on 41st and Main.

When 1981 had rolled around, I was graduating to the local district junior high. At that time, most junior high schools in Los Angeles were furiously becoming recruiting grounds for the Bloods and the Crips. The L.A. gangsters were systematically absorbing and claiming nearly every square block, corner, school, liquor store, park, and even the churches.

The 1980's would soon become the decade of the drive-by shooters; the decade of crack and the crack smokers; and sadly enough it would become the decade that would leave most of the South Central residents in a state of total confusion. Countless numbers of young men would die from the drive-by madness, and a countless many more would be murdered from the crack-slanging epidemic that would eventually blend itself and go hand in hand with the L.A. banging. The 1980's would be my turning point of not just graduating with good grades. It would also become the decade when I'd eventually graduate from my wanna-be status to become a notorious member of a gang calling themselves the "Neighborhood Rollin 20's Bloods", and soon I would be adding my own misery to the already miserable lives of the residents of Los Angeles, the home of the body bags.

INITIATION - REPUTATION
(1982-1985)

Becoming a front line soldier had become my aspiration as a youth, and to be put on the set was something I sought out. All around me in school, throughout my new neighborhood everyone seemed to bang and belong to somebody's gang, Blood or Crip. Every day during lunchtime my new friends T-Bop and Lil Moe and I did what we usually did every afternoon at school: eat coin machine burritos and talk gang talk. T-Bop and Lil Moe were brothers and both were members of the 29th Street Bloods. The 29th Street was a click of a larger gang located on the west side of L.A. notoriously recognized as the NHB's (Neighborhood Bloods) or Rollin 20's. From our daily lunchtime conversations, I absorbed and learned a lot about the surrounding gang world, like killings, fights, beefs, and parties. I was the pupil and they were my teachers.

About a year into hanging out with the fellows, I was completely influenced and totally infatuated; eventually I crossed the dividing line into the gang bangers' world and became a member in 1982. My initiation rites were validated through an armed robbery. It was an ideal night: A light mist blanketed the air, street traffic was slow in all directions, cars, pedestrians, and the annoying police cruisers were unseen. I wore all black and sported a trendy bomber jacket to fend off the encroaching cold and its misty air. Big D-Bop, my younger cousin by two or three years was also part of the initiation. Zig-Zag, Lil Moe, and T-Dog were across the street in the shadows to eyewitness the robbery, thus confirming its happening to pave our way into the gang world as 29th Streeters.

We walked up and down Vermont Boulevard looking for a victim that would assist us on our endeavor. Just as the mist condensed and visibility became murky and limited, a drunken Mexican happens to stagger by. As soon as we spotted him, we zeroed in to stalk him up the block from the opposite side of the street. He was sloppy drunk! If the wind had any more velocity to it, it would have blown him over without much effort. The mist obscured our presence, and we shadowed our way closer and closer toward the unexpecting overweight drunk. Within seconds, we had slithered within reach; our courage was caught in our chest, and just then, we pounced on him like two hungry and aggressive lions on the plains of the African Serengeti. We put hands and feet on him, knocking him off balance without much effort thus sending him to the slippery and wet pavement. Our strong-arm robbery and assault was topped in two minutes flat.

"Come on!" I screamed out as I sprinted across the trafficless street. We took a quick detour up 30th Street heading west making our exit from the main street a priority. D-Bop and I slowed into a semi jog allowing the council, who would either approve or disapprove us on our performance, to catch up. "Follow me!" Zig-Zag screamed as he sprinted passed us. He lived on 29th Street and Budlong, which made our exit off the street quick and desirable. All the merchandise from the robbery was turned over to and split up amongst the experienced members. Just that fast we were robbed of our efforts without no struggle or resistance to retain our goods we had just worked so hard for. It was the rules and a part of the initiation, so it was all good, as we were members of the 29th Street now, and that's all that mattered to us.

The next day we met our new comrades we'd heard so much about: Big Stranger, who was by far the tallest member of our click and had a reputation for his squabbling capability; Lace Dog, who was the click's highest ranking senior, and Buddha, an Asian from some country in the Far East, the only member of the click who wasn't black. Then there were the 29th Street front line soldiers: L-Bone, Kountry, B-Rock, Snipe, Zig-Zag, Hen-Dog, D-Rock, D-Bop, Skunn, Gumboe, Sparky, T-Dog, Dez, Tee, Lil D-Bop, Lil Flashback, Big Flashback, Bam-Bam, Joker, Lil Jerr, Low-Down, Big Earn, K-Dog, Big Spook, No-Brain, and Big Boo. Finally, there was me, now known as Mr. Loko, and my two roll dogs T-Bop and Lil Moe. Our click wasn't widely known yet, and we had approximately thirty to forty members total. However, as the gang drama intensified during the early 80's, so did our membership. Our borders expanded and our daily skirmishes with our known rivals along our established demilitarized zone of Jefferson and Normandie to Jefferson and Crenshaw became more intense.

Soon I developed a large reputation from our school and bus wars. During those days, most gang wars were mainly fought on the R.T.D. bus routes, or by visiting a neighboring school that was controlled and populated by the rivals. Every school in the L.A. geographical area was located in somebody's turf; and since the Crips completely outnumbered the Bloods three to one, there were predominately more Crip than Blood schools: Manual Arts High School, L.A. High, Crenshaw, Locke, John Muir, John Adams, Bret Hart, Forshey, and Gompers were all Crip controlled, whereas Jefferson High, Dorsey High, Fremont High, and Centennial High in Compton were in total control by the Bloods.

I earned new titles as being down for the set and being hard. Mr. Loko started to become a household name on the lips of members from our other clicks, who were hearing about me and my courageous forays into the enemy's territory with satisfactory results. All the things I'd heard so much about, dreamed about, and seen in the exciting streets of L.A., I was now living them. With my reputation development soon came a victory that all men desired, recognition from the girls. I was somebody, I was the new kid on the block, and unknowingly to me, I was widely considered fairly attractive.

Of the wide homegirl selection, I had my eyes set on one in particular, my homegirl Den-Rock, Denise Weston. She was quiet, relatively pretty with big bedroom eyes. About two weeks into dating her, my homeboys started sweating me, and asking about getting my dick wet. Since I was still naive too much of the gang slang, and since I didn't have the slightest idea what the hell they were talking about, I learned to jive and evade the question most of the time. I figured sooner or later I'd learn the meaning of the word, but to ask what it meant, would be admitting to not being hip. I was riding high at the time, and I couldn't afford to tarnish or damage my reputation. About six months later, I finally did get my dick wet, and I was really proud to be able to proclaim the fame to the fellows. Denise eventually became pregnant from my getting my shit wet too much, giving birth to a healthy little girl that we named Shavon.

I was a front line soldier finally, and I loved 29th Street and Vermont. I wanted to be the first to do everything in my click: the first to bomb on you (assault you), the first to shank you (stab you), the first to go to jail, and the first to kill. I banged on anyone and everyone. I always encouraged my homies into going to a Crip school with me for some drama. I wanted my stripes, and I wanted them bad; and the mean streets of Los Angeles had no problem giving them to me, but at a high and very expensive price.

Our gang, the Rollin 20's, had three sizable clicks: 29th Street, 27th Street, and 25th Street. In the early 1980's before the wars got out of hand, my click usually collided with the 5-Duce Hoover Crips, and with the Rollin 30 Harlem Crips. The 20's and Hoovers shared the same bus route which inevitably led to our beefs; but they were light compared to our war with the Rollin 30's and their three clicks Denker Park, 39th Street, and Avenue 30's. I considered them our most formidable foe (enemy). We beefed on site, there was no such thing as a compromise. From these early on-site seek and destroy missions, I developed a unique hatred-respect-relationship with two of my foes, Big Boo and Rick Rock, who were front line soldiers from the Denker Parks. We went from simple squabbling with each other over the years, eventually to the 1985 Saturday night drive-bys.

Shortly into the new year of 1983, my homeboy Kountry became one of my newest roll dogs. He was highly respected on both sides of the fence, and at times, his aggressiveness even over-shadowed mine. Throughout 1983 Kountry, Lil-Moe, and I terrorized many Crip schools together; and Forshey Junior High was always on top of our list. The 30's claimed the school as theirs, and since that was the case, we made it a habit to show our faces in its hallways, always looking for the drama. We also made it a habit to visit Mount Vernon Junior High, which was recently claimed by the School Yard Crips, who were growing and becoming more and more aggressive on the west side of our border. Eventually we made some very successful raids onto the school grounds of Mt. Vernon with shanks and screwdrivers, often with grave and fatal results.

The home of the body bags was living up to its creed, and as the 80's progressed, I found myself becoming more and more drugged up in the high, the city was giving me. I became addicted, and addictions are hard to break, as we all know, especially the addiction of violence. Violent activities became the norm for me, meaning there wasn't much mental contemplation into my harming of other people. My mind had become numb, naturally adjusting to the environmental impact of the gang world. Instead of grief and guilt after our violent sprees, we rejoiced and celebrated our brute ways, and congratulated each other on our violent tendencies. The more violent I became, the more recognition I received. I became anti-human; my actions toward mankind displayed my emotionless state of mind, and I soon developed a reputation for being ruthless and heartless in anything I did. Snatching purses, my earliest form of hustling, usually turned violent especially if the woman struggled with me; victimizing an enemy always resulted in me being ruthless; and eventually my relationship with Denise turned out to be heartless.

The O.G.'s (original gangsters) started paying close attention to our entire click, the 29th Streets. One such O.G. named Santa Klaus from the 27th Streets took a real liking in me. His reputation was wide in range, and widely respected. For me to be allowed to hang out with someone like him was undeniably a privilege of the highest honor. He became my new teacher and I became his eager to learn pupil. All the experience he had, I wanted; all the heart he had in dealing with the enemy, I wanted; all the ruthlessness he possessed, I wanted; and the larger than life reputation he had, I wanted.

In 1983, we became roll dogs and I consciously lived up to his expectation of being a young rider. For me to be seen with him was a statement in itself. It meant I wasn't a buster (a coward); it meant I was down for the set, and it meant I had heart. Santa Klaus and I had become extremely tight; eventually he announced to the homeboys and to me, that he wanted me to become Lil Santa Klaus, which quickly caused a verbal dispute among the 29th Streeters. They were arguing the fact that I couldn't become Lil Santa Klaus because I was a 29th Streeter already, he, Santa Klaus, was a 27th Streeter, and ones allegiance to his particular click was just as important as ones allegiance to his gang membership. But Santa Klaus was adamant; he wanted to break away from tradition. The arguments continued for a while, but the 29th Street eventually prevailed since they had tradition on their side. I could never become Lil Santa Klaus, that meant click hopping; and click hopping wasn't tolerated as gang-hopping wasn't tolerated. Gang hopping usually meant death to the perpetrator. I had a lot of love and respect for my homeboy Santa Klaus, but I loved my click even more.

During the summer of 1983, Santa Klaus and I could be found together hanging in the area of Western and Venice over to his girlfriend's house. On a particular night, the Fruit Town Brims were giving a gang party that we decided we were going to attend, and besides, word had been sent to me that the entire 29th Street click would be there. Santa Klaus and I departed from each other early, I for the reason of wanting to be with the 29th Street entourage when it arrived at the party, and he for the reason of not being dressed the way he desired, meaning gangstered up.

When I arrived at our headquarter, the entire click was there in gathering, smoking weed and getting drunk. As soon as I walked up, a 40^{oz} of Old English 800 was passed my way. I took a long and hard swallow, I wanted to be blasted by the time we reached the party; and there was more than enough weed and drinks to do the job on everyone. There was even some P.C.P. being passed amongst certain homies. I indulged in all the drugs that night, I figured the more buzzed I became; the more ruthless I would be especially if there was to be some unexpected drama.

By 10:30 p.m., we were ready to make our grand appearance. We mobbed up Vermont about fifty deep including the 29th Street Bloodlettes (homegirls) heading south to our shared border with the Fruit Town Brims on Vermont and Jefferson where they had an apartment complex, called University Gardens, the location of that night's party. As we reached the intersection of Jefferson and Vermont, we noticed two pretty well dressed females at the bus stop. My homeboy Bam-Bam immediately recognized the girls as female affiliates of the enemy, the 30 Harlem Crips. Both girls denied any involvement with the 30's, and they proclaimed complete innocence from the gang world, but we weren't convinced. Each one of them possessed enough circumstantial evidence to be found guilty. Both had on blue sweatshirts, blue barrettes in their hair, one had on some blue Puma tennis shoes, and the other some pink Chuck Taylor All-Stars with some blue shoestrings. They were guilty as charged. The 29th Street Bloodlettes were cut loose on them, and soon the individuals' squabbles turned into beat downs since our homegirls outnumbered the two Criplettes five to one. When my homeboy Stranger attempted to snatch one of the girls' purses, she for some odd reason was holding onto it for dear life. The reason soon became clear after a thorough search was done of the items inside.

She possessed some photos, but not just any photos, she had picture after picture of Harlem Crips posing at their park with gang colors and gang signs. The beat downs intensified and went into over drive, when an unmarked police car careered onto the scene giving chase and scattering us in all directions. I ran into the Fruit Town Brim apartment complex and found safety; and about an hour later at the party I started to notice all the familiar faces of my homies and homegirls. I knew then that everybody had gotten away from the police squad. The party was beginning to bump and the night was turning out to be a good one.

Santa Klaus finally arrived in full gang attire. I immediately pulled him to the side and briefed him about the incident with the 30's girls. Just as the party was in full swing, a voice ranged out over the noise: "The Harlem Crips are outside". The music stopped, everybody started shuffling around, many running to the window to get a look at them. "Get away from the window, they got guns". That really got the crowd going, and many of the partygoers ran out the back door to escape away from the violence that was sure to come. After the initial confusion, Santa Klaus gave us the order to follow him outside for a confrontation.

One by one, we gripped anything that could be used as a weapon: pipes, poles, bricks, and 2x4's, many of us had shanks and screwdrivers. We searched the apartment grounds and finally bumped heads with the enemy upfront near Jefferson. As on cue, they lined up on one side, and we on the other. Their entourage equaled in numbers to ours; I knew this was going to be a really good fight. Santa Klaus took center stage as was expected. He started pointing at individual 30's members: "I know you, I know you, and I know you". Unexpectedly he fired on one, and kicked off the biggest gang fight in our rival history.

Approximately one hundred gang members were going at it like wild cats and dogs, and due to the large disturbance, a large percentage of the Southwest Police Department showed up to break up the on-going gang fight. Upon the police' arrival most of the Rollin 20's ran northbound across Jefferson, and the Rollin 30's ran westbound up Jefferson, all trying to avoid the police. Gangsters from both sides were arrested that night; luck was on my side I guess because I could escape.

But as time would have it, and due to my increasing gang activities, eventually I'd be busted. The following year I was arrested some three days after my fifteenth birthday on May 19, 1984 for a gang fight that turned out to be a strong-armed robbery against some Venice Shore Line Crips. The judge hearing the case sentenced me to do camp time. The intention was to teach me a lesson for my disruptive behavior pattern with the hopes of me returning to society a changed young man. Unfortunately for me, the jail time didn't change me much. It actually made me worse. Jail to me as a young criminal was like going to college to learn about the many other criminal activities of the world. Thanks to jail, I returned to my community in a worse state than before.

In the short time of my absence, the usual gang fights from the shoulders became an old trade giving way to the massive drive-by shootings. When I was released on March 4, 1985, I was looking to make my name even bigger than before; and once again, I'd gotten my wish. The name Loko would become synonymous with guns and drive-by shootings. I was possessed. My homeboys figured I'd sold my soul to the devil, little did they know I did.

SATURDAY NIGHT SPECIALS
(1985)

A couple weeks after being home, I experienced the reality of the drive-by shooters. I nearly lost my life when a car turned the corner of Adams and Raymond Avenue with guns blazing and bullets flying everywhere. Literally, I froze where I stood. The drive-bys were new to me, and my reactions that night were counter-productive to life and to the street rules of survival. I believe the fact of me not running as the bullets zoomed by me probably saved my life. I had survived without any injuries, but somebody else wasn't so lucky. The screams I heard were unnatural; they were screams of agony and severe pain. Bone from Nickerson Garden Bloods slowly crawled from his hiding place, out from the safety of the bushes, he was hit. The bullet had entered approximately two inches away from his testicles and fortunate for him.

In the same night of madness, I met a young lady by the name of Yvette Gardner, a woman who I would later fall madly in love with. Despite all the commotions, sirens, and screams of retaliation, I automatically slid into a deep trance at the beautiful sight of seeing her, and when our gazes met for a brief and exiting moment, I told myself she would be mine. Thanks to Yvette, Adams and Raymond became my new stomping grounds, whereas Vermont and 29th Street turned into a distant memory.

Not soon afterward, the entire 29th Street click began to hang out around Adams and Raymond, and due to the drive-by intensity, we clicked up with the 27th Street consolidating our combined efforts and forces in our ever-increasing drive-by competition with the 30's. 1985 would become my turning point; quickly I absorbed the habits and skills of a drive-by shooter, and soon enough I scored on my first pistol, a two shot .38 Dillinger. My homeboy Rat from the 27th Street gave it to me as a gift.

About three weeks later Bone was out the hospital and showed up to visit on his way to work. He had on a crispy new security guard uniform, and I'm assuming the near death experience weeks before had undoubtedly convinced him to fly straight. He didn't stay long for his visit, and before he left for work, he handed me a bag full of .38 shells, regulars and hollow points. "Put 'em to good use", he said, as he stepped off, quickly departing out of sight. Immediately I sent my first reconnaissance team through the enemy's territory to find their location. Usually I'd meet my rivals in the field of battle, bus routes or school grounds, and even then, it may turn out to be a simple squabble with an occasional stabbing, but the drive-by madness of 1984 and 1985 took the gang wars of L.A. to another level entirely.

Anyway, Denker and Jefferson, on the east side corner of Denker, was where the rivals had gathered that day. The recon team reported there were probably eight to ten rival members posted out-front of the apartment complex on Denker. After arriving on the scene I reached the conclusion the best approach with the element of surprise on my side would be a rear-end attack. The apartment had a back exit that led to the adjusted parking lot. My homeboy Tall-Dog accompanied me on this particular mission; he wanted to see were my heart was. I'd also brought along an additional twenty extra rounds of hollow points, just in case of a possible shoot out.

As we approached the gate entrance from the parking lot, I could hear the closeness of my targets from their laughter not more than fifteen feet in front of me. Once looking over the back gate I was able to count nine heads sitting on a small concrete wall smoking and drinking. My presence was completely unnoticed, and not until I opened the gate with my .38 blazing with total accuracy did my enemies realize they were being hunted. "Boom, boom," the Dillinger had sounded much louder; the echo of the apartment rotunda amplified the sound ten-fold. The first two shots were solid hits; I was reloading, and within seconds given chase up Denker in hot pursuit of the remaining enemies, "Boom-boom", another hit verified by the same agonizing scream Bone released weeks prior with the intake of his bullet. It was time to retreat I knew, as the one-time (police) would soon be there. As stealthy and quietly as I arrived, I departed using an alleyway that ran east west, north of Jefferson. My first taste of blood was beyond anything describable. The naked excitement, the untaught drama and the unquestioned power reminded me of the gang excitement I visibly experienced and witnessed during the decade of the 1970's, then as now I knew my destiny would and was to be a L.A. gangster.

Tall-Dog from the 27th Street had become my latest roll dog, and we were relatively close especially due to the common denominator we both shared. I was dating Yvette, and he was dating Rochelle, Yvette's sister. Rochelle was the older version of Yvette, both possessed smooth dark skin, very intense eyes, and both had full luscious lips. They were the chocolate sisters on the block. About a week after my successful seek and destroy mission, I was visiting Yvette listening to some music, when all of a sudden from the kitchen area Tall-Dog and Rochelle could be heard arguing about his dedication to her.

I was listening intently to their loud dispute, and not that I was being nosey or ears dropping, but because the argument had also involved me. Rochelle wanted Tall-Dog to stop hanging around me for fear of getting into some gang trouble. She claimed his gang activities had noticeably increased since being around me. Rochelle didn't dislike me, by far that wasn't the case. Her only fear was that her man should slow his role on his gang involvement. Eventually her nagging, whining and legit concern would win. Tall-Dog slowed and soon stopped his activities with us altogether.

However, that didn't stop me, I was a front line soldier and soon enough I found myself another roll-dog, who was totally possessed in wanting to destroy and annihilate the Rollin 30 Crips. Even his name spoke his aggression toward the enemies, Mr. Tray-K (Tray-K meaning 30 killa). The first impression he gave was of a schoolboy preppy type person. He was always neatly dressed, spoke extremely proper English, and wasn't indulging in any drugs or drinking. But under his exterior image, there was a ruthless killer inside. Together we would give the 30's a dosage of the Rollin 20's aggression. We would go on countless seek and destroy missions, placing our turf on the map as an aggressive neighborhood that believed in gun playing.

Our first mission would come as a result of the 30's latest string of retaliations against us. They'd hit two locations throughout the neighborhood that day and so far there wasn't any casualties, but one of the targets they tried to eliminate was my cousin D-Bop. They had fucked with family and retaliation against them was now top priority. Report after report of enemy sightings was given to Tray-K and me when we arrived on the block, and from the description of one of the shooters, I made a field experience conclusion that it was none other than Boo from the Denker Park Crips. We immediately went to strike back.

I was heading toward 29th Street on my bicycle to get my heat, when out of nowhere a sky blue colored car slid up along side me. My survival instincts kicked in and automatically took over my action. Just as the passenger pointed his gun at me, I pulled on the brakes, and the first two bullets missed. I made a quick u-turn and paddled north back up Raymond Ave. toward 27th Street. The shooter then sat atop the passenger door frame to get a better shot at me, just as the speeding car closed the distance between us, Boo started blazing away, "Boom, boom, boom, boom", without doubt, I knew he wanted me dead, I knew he wanted the kill points against me and my reputation.

I nearly buried my head into the handlebars trying to keep as low as possible. I was pumping the pedals, as a professional rider would do in the Tour de France. Just as I crossed over 27th Street, I slammed into a large green bush, and the momentum from the impact flipped me up, over the handlebars, and onto my back. Ignoring my injuries fearing I was still in danger way, I jumped up and bee lined down the nearest driveway seeking safety from the bullets. I ran to the back of someone's house, and hopped over the back gate, and as quickly, as I did so a large dog chased me back over it. I felt Lady Luck had abandoned me. I then took refuge behind a grey colored camper truck standing on its large bumper. Footsteps were running up the driveway toward me and not knowing whom it was I was forced to finally believe it was over.

"Loko are you alright?" The voice was familiar proving that Lady Luck still had my back; I recognized the voice as being D-Bop's. After inspecting my bumps and bruises, I proceeded with him and Tray-K to get my gun. About fifteen minutes later, we were on our way to retaliate for the enemy's aggressions. We took the usual alley route toward the enemy's strong hold. This mission was important to me, and more than ever, I was determined to get close enough to an enemy, and without thought blow his brains out. As we crossed Kenwood, I happened to glance toward Jefferson, and to my complete surprise Boo from the 30's was standing there posted next to the car with his gun pointed toward me, damn he had seen me first, and he had the jump on me: "Boom, boom", I ran back to the alley for safety and cover. I reached for my gun but the hammer part was stuck on the interior of my coats inside.

As the seconds ticked away, life and death became precious, I began to panic. "Boom, boom", Boo was on a roll this day, and it seemed he was everywhere and God knows, he had brought more than enough bullets. Tray-K finally responded with the Magnum as he stepped from the alleyway blazing, "boom, boom, boom, boom, boom." I was still struggling with my gun just as I heard car tires in the distance burning rubber. I couldn't figure, if they headed our way for a better shot, or if there were running away. Finally, it was my turn; I stepped from the alleyway blazing just as their car was turning eastbound onto Jefferson. "Boom, boom," I figured I missed, but the fact that we answered with major gunplay was a message to Boo and his homies that we were as serious as they were.

We quickly retreated up the alleyway, reloading as we ran. I figured the cops would be there soon, so I took a quick detour into the back of some apartments. D-Bop and Tray-K kept running straight and within seconds, we were all completely separated from each other. Just as I reached the apartment front portion, Boo and his homies were coming up the block looking for us. He was already reloaded, searching for a target and looking to get the last word in, in our on-going gunfight. He spotted me and again he had the jump on me. I ran toward the front porch of the apartment for safety, and a split second later, he began blazing again: "Boom, boom, boom, boom, boom, boom, boom." I rose up, gun pointed straight ahead, seeking a target, but there was none; they were gone and most likely for the day.

Later that evening I met back up with Tray-K and D-Bop. We discussed our many mistakes made and how we could avoid them in the future. It was my first gunfight, and I gave myself props on my performances, but it also had taught me a lot. I was proven and tested as a gunner despite the obvious pressure of death hanging around. The only thing I chastised myself on was to never again have a gunfight, and to always find the enemy when he was most vulnerable, it was better that way. The element of surprise was something I soon mastered, and as a result, my enemies would be speaking my name with the respect due to a young rider who had no problem bringing the drama.

As the summer of 1985 inched nearer, the drive-by competition amongst the various neighborhoods intensified rapidly. The cocaine epidemic of the 80's also added to the already chaotic environment; as a result, many L.A. gangsters would be gunned down by the new and better automatics easily purchased with cocaine money. Neighborhoods would scramble to adjust to the new wave of weapons, which would sweep the gang wars to levels unseen before, and multiple body count casualties would soon become the norm. The early on traces of the automatic epidemic was widely published in 1984 in the *Los Angeles Times* newspaper reporting about a gang massacre that occurred on 54th Street; twelve people were shot at a gang party and five killed. It became known as the 54th Street massacre.

And evidently, the army camp of our enemy was becoming ever increasingly dangerous. Huckabuck (an O.G.) was one of their famous ghetto celebrities, and he was known to drive around in BMWs and massive Blazer trucks with 9-millimeters. Often times the enemy personnel would drive through our military encampments, flashing their gang signs and showing off their new cars. Their act of brazenness usually burned us up with anger, especially since knowing we lacked in the material possessions they had. For their latest show off, a recon team was being sent into their interior to scout out any weakness in their defenses.

I was a part of this team, as well as my homeboys Madd Ronald, Tray-K, and Rat. We rode in silence toward the bullet riddled apartments and houses of our enemies that were victimized and scarred by years of warfare. We drove past our last military position heading into the republic of the 30's. Our territories were miniature states complete with military personnel, an economical structure, and unwritten constitutions that governed our dos and don'ts. Geographically our republic was bigger than the 30's, but numerically in combat soldiers, I believe the 30's had a slight edge. It didn't matter to us, as we were front line soldiers bent on trimming their numbers to size.

We entered into the city-state section of the Denker Parks, as the street signs announced, traveled up Denker while checking out every crack and crevice searching for any enemy force movement. Tray-K and Rat were armed with butcher knives that looked menacing and deadly in appearance. Enemy, enemy, enemy; my heart thumped into an adrenalin pumping action at the sight of spotting troops from the opposing army. They were walking in the same direction we were driving, and had not recognized our threatening presence. They had to be amateurs, or freshly put on because they had violated rule number one in the field of battle: to eyeball every passing car, unknown person, and anything out of place in the killing field.

"Pull over! Pull over!" Tray-K was frantic, he wanted to keep the element of surprise we had. Madd Ronald slowed the car to a complete stop in the middle of Denker and 35th Street. Like robots of war, Tray-K and Rat bounced from their back seats quickly and stealthily looking to extend their hands in the design of life and death rotation. Tray-K was the first, pounding and thundering at the amateurs like Jason in Friday 13th. "Ahhhh!" the knife was buried deep in one of the field soldier's shoulder blade. His scream bordered between shock and total disbelief. The scream had echoed throughout their military compound, and enemy troops materialized out of every building it seemed. Rat and Tray-K slithered back in the car, and instinctive Madd Ronald smashed out. He completed a u-turn, and within seconds, we were heading in the direction of where the enemy had massed on our flank side.

Their troops began to scatter behind parked cars as we sped to within inches of their presence. They ran not knowing if we were heated or not, and Ronald's reckless driving spooked them into indecisiveness. Just as we were speeding by the last of the parked cars, a blurry figure materialized with something in his hand. A gun! Damn, I was about to die, he had a perfect shot at me in the passenger seat. I saw his hand draw back and lob the unknown object in his hand toward the car. I ducked, not sure what to think. The twirling object sped passed my head slamming hard on impact into the side of Rat's face. Glass and liquid splattered the car's interior. I kept my head low, and didn't raise it until I was certain we had crossed back into the safety of our neighborhood. Rat was a mess: Coka-Cola juice had soaked into his hair; he was pissed and complaining vehemently about his perm getting wet.

"Take me to my sister, Blood. On Blood gang take me right now!" He was carefully pulling shards of broken glass off his face and from his hair while swearing off steam about revenge. We headed to our new undisclosed headquarter on 27th and Budlong, called the decision porch. It was properly named, as all our retaliatory and military missions were decided there. The apartment barrack was deep with troop personnel; we debriefed on our enemy contact, and proceeded to plot and plan for another raid. Other homies of the republic readily volunteered their allegiance, but Madd Ronald, Tray-K, and I shrugged off their offers: We were front line soldiers, the enemy had assaulted us, and it was our problem to solve.

We waited for the cover of darkness; finally, the multitude of streetlights blinked into their nightly duty. That was our cue; and we made our way to Madd Ronald's old Lincoln Continental with the suicide doors. Tray-K and I each gripped our sixteen shot .22 semi-automatic pump action rifles. Our raiding party was ready and we were geared mentally for the imminent mission. In the cloak of darkness, we headed in the direction of our park, Loren Miller Recreation Center. Loren Miller was in the center of our stronghold, it was something like our capitol. Behind the park ran an alleyway southbound toward Jefferson that we drove up to its length while squeakiness reverberated off every inch of the old Lincoln thus taking our stealtiness away.

We finally came to rest at the back portion of some apartments which front part rested on Jefferson, but more importantly, the apartment's front section faced Denker. From the stairs of the apartment unit, one could see any and nearly all activities onto Denker. Madd Ronald executed the lights and stayed in the car whereas Tray-K and I brazed ourselves for the commando raid onto deadly grounds. There was no guarantee that we'd survive our Vietcong tactic of ambush and run, but as soldiers, there were no certainties in warfare. We scaled the back gate and trotted our way to the apartment's front area like some Apache Indians peeking over a mountain top, stalking General Custer looking to take some scalps.

Silhouettes of enemy troops could be seen in the distance moving about; we weren't able to discern how many of them we faced, so I devised a plan to draw the enemy out. I used the Sun Tzu strategy of "though effective – appear ineffective; when organized – appear disorganized; and although competent – appear incompetent". We secured the rifles against the gate, and made our way into the middle of the street. From where we stood, we could see the silhouette figures freeze and tense up. They had spotted us, and the element of danger swirled its head in all directions. "Are you ready?" I asked the question looking over at Tray-K. "Yeah", he responded nervously. His adrenalin was flowing as hard as mine was "Neighborhood Blood Gang!" I shouted my neighborhood at the top of my lungs, with the desired result of attracting the enemy's attention. "Rollin 20 Gang, West Side 27th Street!" Tray-K had joined in, and we were setting into motion our bait and hook strategy, it worked.

Enemy troop movement began materializing from all sections of their enclave, falling for our scheme. "Harlem Crips! Harlem Crips!" they retorted to our chant. Their words sounded off in unison, and the hardest part of our mission was accomplished. Now phase two could be executed. Without words, we both instinctively knew the time was at hand. I kicked the black gate open, reached in and grabbed my sixteen shot rifle; two seconds had barely ticked away, when Tray-K had reached in and grabbed his rifle. I didn't wait on him, and before the opposing army had time to react, my rifle was cracking its signature across the distance: "Pop! Pop! Pop! Pop! Pop! Pop! Pop! Pop!" By now, Tray-K had joined in: "Pop! Pop! Pop! Pop! Pop! – Pop! Pop! Pop! Pop! Pop! Pop! Pop! Pop!" I capped off my last eight rounds, and stood by while Tray-K laid down suppressive fire. Bullets banged and ricocheted off everything in the kill zone.

We expended all the shells in our rifles and bee lined our way back up the stairs making our get away. Tray-K mis-stepped, fell and his gun slid down the stairs back to the bottom. Damn, valuable seconds were ticking away. He retrieved it and we double-timed back to the car, which Madd Ronald had ready to go. No sooner had we slid in, he whisked us off down the alley that came to life as we thundered up its dense crevice. The wind was bouncing off my face as I sat there in silence thinking about my rise up the Totem Pole of the Saturday night shooters, I found out later we had made some direct hits against the Harlem Crips, the enemy I vowed to wipe away from the face of this earth.

The 80's definitely became the decade of a more violent and deadly level of gang activities that reached popularity among the youths from other inner cities throughout the United States, who began imitating and creating similar names of their neighborhoods. People like me would forever leave deep marks upon the hearts and minds of the terrorized citizens. Mothers, fathers, sisters, and brothers would loose a love one to the Saturday night specials and the street sweepers (Uzi machine gun), and the gangsters of all colors were to experience the meaning of the code: 664/187.

664/187
(1985)

By the summer of 1985 I had a total of four guns: two sixteen shot rifles, a .38 Dillinger, and an eight shot 22-millimeter long nose revolver. Many neighborhoods were in the possession of the better and heavier automatics; while most other turfs still dealt with their ancient home burglary revolvers because they were slower in catching the wave of cocaine hustling, and due to this fact, they would pay a grave and heavy price of lives lost in the drive-by madness.

The Rollin 20's lacked far and way behind. We were still driving around in stolen cars, while the cocaine epidemic assisted our rivals in purchasing the fresh new Blazers, and the sporty new Nissan trucks. But we still had an edge, we had something that most neighborhoods didn't have, or had lost: dedication, comradeship, and love for our neighborhood. We believed in patrolling our borders, we believed in mandatory retaliations, and we believed in watching each other's back.

The cocaine money craze split most neighborhoods up, broke old homeboy bonds, and subsequently to this many gang members were assassinated by jackers due to jealousy, and mostly from within their own gang. The Rollin 20's didn't have that kind of internal problems as we were consolidated as one. We grew from a few dozen that belonged to the 27th Street click in the late 1970's, to hundreds and hundreds of members as of to date, by adding the 29th Street, the 25th Street, the 2nd Avenue, the BZP 27th Street, and later in 1992 the Black Demon Soldiers, making our neighborhood one of the biggest Blood gangs on the west side of Los Angeles, numerically and geographically. And as a result of all the expansion, we found ourselves having more enemies to contend with: the Rollin 30's, the School Yard Crips, the infamous 18th Street Gang, the biggest gang in L.A. County, and the Mid City Stoners 13 with their allies the West Side Playboys 13. Even within our boundaries, we started to have beefs with gangs such as the Barrio Saint Andrews and the Harpys 13, who traditionally we've shared blocks and areas with. As a result of these gang wars on all our fronts, we've lost numerous homeboys.

The summer was slowly slithering away making way for the cold winter, and the drive-by shootings had slowed to a snail's pace largely due to the police's relentless attacks upon the many black neighborhoods. The L.A.P.D. was desperately trying to put an end to the drive-bys. When winter finally arrived the streets were relatively quite, and it would be in this wintertime period in the month of November that I would be arrested for an attempted murder charge, penal code 664/187.

Two months prior my cousin Big D-Bop was out with family members at the local swap meet in enemy controlled territory, when he was confronted by some rivals. Words were exchanged, identification and gang allegiance were spoken, and the wins and losses were established. My cousin was fortunate and lucky to walk away only with a swollen black eye. After the incident, he searched the entire neighborhood finally finding me at 29th Street and Walton, on the dead end.

I had been hanging out with some homegirls who I'd been teaching how to shoot my .38. The first thing I noticed as he rode toward me was his swollen black eye. Immediately I approached him with questions sliding off my tongue about who, what, where, and when. After being told all the relevant details, my reactions spoke what my heart felt: anger and revenge. I reloaded my Dillinger, jumped on my beach cruiser bike, and headed southbound up Walton toward Jefferson with D-Bop and Lil Moe following in hot pursuit. Our target was located deep into our enemy's territory, a place where I knew for sure I'd find a victim to rest: the capitol of the Harlem Crips, Denker Park. The nervousness was evident in the eyes of D-Bop and Lil Moe, each held their own private thoughts of my bizarre plan of riding on some bicycles to our enemy's stronghold, but neither spoke their discomfort.

As we neared Denker and Jefferson, I rode with one hand on the handlebars, while my other hand gripped the .38. Alertness, body intensity, awareness and nervousness all flowed through my body as I searched out an enemy troop. Surprisingly we rode all the way to the Denker recreation center with no altercations. It was in the middle of the afternoon, and not one enemy was in sight! We made a collective decision that it would be wise if we departed the area. It almost seemed eerie to me to be within their boundaries and not find a soul to take. When we came to the bus stop on Jefferson and Normandie, an idea hit me. I told D-Bop to go up the block about one block east and steal a can of spray paint at the neighborhood hardware store. I wanted to write our names and neighborhood on the Denker Park walls.

Thirty seconds later, it all happened. Everything went into slow motion, a City bus pulled up on the north side of Jefferson. Four enemies who were on the bus had spotted Lil Moe and me, and the gang signs began. Before they could exit the bus rear-end, I was up and moved toward my multiple targets, hungry and eager. I soon lost track of all objects around me I was zoned out. My mind was focused on my imminent mission that I planned to make successful. As I rounded the back portion of the bus, the four rivals were heading straight toward me, right into my line of fire. I played it cool up until the last possible moment, and then I drew the .38 and selected the biggest target. For a split second, I felt like the decision maker, wielding the power of life and death. Since retaliation was our mission, death was chosen and a second later, I fired: "Boom", the shot was perfect, and the bullet found its mark. It ripped through the white t-shirt of the person who I later found out to be Lil Bo Peep from Grape Street Watts Crips. "Boom", I fired again as the remaining targets ran in all directions desperately trying to avoid the slugs meant to take their lives.

Loud screeching tires and police sirens shattered my trance; the sirens were near, and I feared I'd be arrested right there at the spot... something in my mind said "run", and run I did. I ran as fast as my legs could move; the sirens were there again, the loud noise sounded like it was given chase. But the faster I ran the distant the sirens became. Later I found out the sirens sound were those of an ambulance, whose occupants witnessed the entire shooting incident. I bee lined up an alley, running as fast as I possibly could. I remember climbing gates, many gates. My adrenaline was flowing faster and faster; I was in somebody's kitchen, somebody screamed to my right. I started to panic again, I was zoning in and out of my mental trance, desperately trying to make sense of my unfamiliar environment, as I didn't remember snatching the back door off its hinges. Whose back door I wondered? The screams were there again, followed by a voice demanding that I should leave her apartment before she called the police. In my right hand was the .38, still wrapped in the red bandana.

"Please get out! Please get out", the old lady pleaded with me. I zoned out again, but I heard my voice calmly explaining to her that I needed shelter because some guys were trying to kill me. "Please get out of my house! Please leave!" The old lady wasn't buying my story and without thought, I quickly proceeded to the front door of her apartment. I glanced in all directions looking for a place to put the gun until later. One, two, three steps and I reached a large rock in the front portion of the yard. With one glance over my right shoulder to make sure no one noticed I sheltered the .38 beneath the rock. If I could just avoid the police cruisers for another ten minutes, I figured I'd have a total chance of escaping altogether. My homeboy L-Bone's grandmother lived one block north of where I was, if I could just get there. The sirens were silent, and my nervousness was gone. Right-left, everything was clear; I dashed across the green front lawn, bee lining up the sidewalk. In a matter of minutes, I was there... "Bang, bang, bang, bang, bang, bang," someone answered "Who's there?"

"It's me, Terrell, please let me in! Somebody's trying to kill me", I blurted out; the door opened. "Come in Sweety. Who's chasing you,

Baby?" I began telling her a long bizarre story that worked. A couple hours later, I was well rested, well fed and ready to roll out again. She'd given me a blue jacket to take with me, as the sun had fallen and the night lights had come on. Whatever danger had been hours before had now passed I believed. My destination was Raymond and Adams, and I walked three city blocks in record time. Once I reached Raymond, I noticed something different about my homeboys: Each had a devilish smile sliding off their lips. The news had spread, and everybody already knew, once again, I was greeted with the rising star status of a young gunslanger. My reputation was drenched in blood and deeply etched in many minds as being heartless and ruthless. "Where's Lil Moe?" I asked to no one in particular. "He's gone", somebody from the crowd shot back.

I needed a change of clothes. I knew the police cruisers were visible, and it was evident they had a tentative description of the perpetrator. My red sweats, red socks, red shirt, black house shoes, and 80's Afro were for sure a dead give away. I bee lined up the drive-way to my homegirl Tanya's house to change my clothes, and to have my hair put into nine neatly twisted corn roll braids. Advice was coming from everybody: "Leave town", "Go home and stay for a while", "Stay out the hood", but I wanted to find Lil Moe and D-Bop.

I headed toward the bus stop on Adams. Police cruisers were everywhere. Some driving fast, some slow. Some of them rode by and eye fucked me, but I remained calm and played it cool. I kept my emotions in check until I boarded the city bus, and a battlefield thought crossed my mind: retaliation and victory! I rode in silence the entire trip. Darkness had enveloped the vast sky, and the evening stars gleamed brightly. It was a good day to be a L.A. gangster, people respected me, girls threw themselves at me, and rivals spoke my name with awe. I liked that.

About an hour later, I approached the two-story stucco house on King Boulevard, where I could see dark figures moving about on the front porch. Relief and excitement crossed the faces of Lil Moe, D-Bop, B-Rock, and T-Bop as the outlines of my features came into view. Everybody started speaking at once, and from all the chattering I gathered the perceived thought they held was that I'd been captured at the crime scene. That night we celebrated the mission's success by smoking bags of marijuana and passing around 40^{oz} bottles of Old English 800.

I would never forget that day, how could I. It was 1985, September 13, Friday. Friday 13 was considered a day of bad luck, and most people I knew believed in bad luck. That day I was the bad luck to my victim Bo Peep. Initial rumors floated that he had died at the scene. But months later in November, that rumor would be dispelled. 1985 was an explosive year for me, and in the three short years of my gang activities, I was proven and tested as a cap peeler. Others even compared me to Santa

Klaus' reputation, but my gang stardom was briefly lived as I would soon come crashing down with my arrest for attempted murder and three counts of assault.

The victim I shot turned out to be the prosecutor's star witness against me. The ambulance drivers who had saved his life also gave their tentative I.D. of me. The case never made it to trial; quickly I took a deal for ten years for fear of receiving the maximum penalty if found guilty at trial. Not soon after my guilty plea, I embarked on a new journey in my life that would change me forever. I entered into the prison system, where the weak are weeded out and often times victimized, and where the strong boldly assert them displaying their animal kingdom of survival of the fittest. I learned quickly to block out my faith, I buried my head into many books trying to avoid the reality of my prediction at every mental corner. But nothing could have prepared me for the experience I was about to endure. I learned what most young men had learned once entering through the gates of the devil's den: mind over matter.

MIND OVER MATTER
(1985-1992)

Shortly after my conviction I was shipped off to L.P. (Los Padrino) Juvenile Detention; I wasn't there a second, and I already had to do some chin checking. A Crip from the Long Beach 20's had assaulted my homeboy Rat a day or two before I arrived. Some other Bloods briefed me in detail about the fight, I learned the Crip soldier was twice the size of Rat, and I was told he had justified his pre-emptive attack by proclaiming his turf was the original 20's, and that my neighborhood was the wanna-be's. Quickly I went about setting up a date with this cat. Not soon after I sent my message, buildings C/D and E/F were scheduled to a baseball match the following weekend; it was on.

I was fresh from the streets, and all the rowdiness of the asphalt jungle radiated off me, and just like the streets, I was looking to put my name on the map inside the juvenile system. The week past quickly, and when the weekend arrived, most prepared to play some competitive baseball, whereas I was in my room preparing for a battle with an opponent, who had dissed my homeboy, and more importantly, who had dissed my turf. After breakfast, we were marched to the recreation field to begin the weekly competition. Moments later building E/F was seen in the distance marching out, and the Crip from Long Beach was pointed out to me by some of the other Bloods as the unit neared the playing field. I geared myself for combat, and from where I stood, I was able to size him.

I took off my sweatshirt, and began my beeline in his direction. He tensed up as he viewed my sudden movement toward him. My heart thumped wildly and excitedly. My fists were clinched tightly, and when I was within striking distance, I released a barrage of face connecting blows, which had immediate results of victory for me and the home team. Within seconds, I had him on his back squirming in the dirt on the baseball perimeter. The counselors scrambled to intervene and stop the one sided fight. One of them snatched me hard off the defeated enemy, who now made his hood look bad. Without any delay, I was marched to the box (solitary confinement) where I was confined for three days.

The hole became my second home as my behavior went from bad to worse. L.P. was soon tired of me, and my fighting episodes, so they shipped me off to the East Lake Juvenile Detention, also known as Central. Since I had an attempted murder charge, I was placed in building E/F, which housed youths with charges similar to mine. From the moment I walked through the doors, I was greeted by the mad dog stares of the unit porters, and I knew then I was gonna be doing a whole lot of squabbling.

The counselor called me into the office and gave me the orientation speech; repeating the same rhetoric, I'd heard before. I wasn't even listening, as I was too busy eyeballing her nametag and looking into her mouth. Her tag read "Scott", and she looked like she was right up out the hood and given her present job just yesterday. "Are you listening to me?" She had caught me daydreaming. "Yea", I lied. "Okay then your room is the last door on the left hand side."

As I turned to leave, I was met by a host of stares from soldiers of unknown camps. One by one, I sized each of them: My stare, my walk and demeanor spoke the silent language of being a young trooper dedicated to his trade. I knew they wondered what camp I represented, but they looked hesitant to approach me. Finally, the biggest one stepped from the crowd to hit me up. "Where you from homey?" he asked me. "My name is Loko", I responded, "and I'm from the Neighborhood Blood Gang, why what's crackin?" I tensed, prepared myself for battle, and waited on his response, but his reaction told me right away, he was from my side of the fence. He walked toward me with hands extended for a handshake: "I'm Bad Boy from the Luther's Park Mob", at that we shook hands. I eyeballed the others and went to my room.

Moments later as I was getting settled in, Bad Boy came by for a visit. He briefed me on the active soldiers in our camp and gave me the names of some of the riders from the opposing camp. For the most part everybody respected everybody, he confidently informed me. "But you know how shit can get at times." – "Yea I'm knowing dog", I replied. "But it's all good though because this is West Side 20's on mine." I was letting him know then and there I wasn't gonna take any shit from no Crip, period! "White, come here!" Bad Boy shook my hand and went up the hallway to see what Ms. Scott wanted.

I lay in my bed thinking about my new surroundings, I don't know for how long, but when I awoke, it was already time to get ready for dinner. The counselors had changed shift, and in Ms. Scott's place was Mr. Franklin, who looked no more than eighteen years old. His voice roared up the hallway giving us orders to step out from our rooms and into the hallway. He gave a quick speech about being quite and orderly during dinnertime. One line at a time we marched up the squeaky-clean hallway, I studied every face for any signs of recognition, some I knew and others looked vaguely familiar, and yet some were non-combatants. I could tell Mr. Franklin got a kick out of his authority, the whole time we ate, he barked about everything he thought was of importance. With his attitude and obvious short man complex, I knew it was only a matter of time, before we collided head on.

I was placed into school and I soon learned that everybody and anybody who was somebody in the gang world went to school to be seen. There I met Romeo from the Black P. Stones Bloods, G-Rob from 30's Pirus, One-Punch from Pasadena Devil Lanes, and Demon from Bounty Hunter Bloods, all were young riders and all were facing time ranging from fifteen to twenty-five years to life in prison. They, like me, were caught up in the gang wars. As I became accustomed to the routine, I went about to eliminate all enemies of my neighborhood, since there weren't any 30's in my building; I went to school to find some potential targets.

My first squabble came with a Harlem 30's, whom I don't recall by name, but to this day I give him props on his courage to get down with me. In all the school books in my class I'd wrote my neighborhood on just about every other page; and to each page I struck up I was sure to diss my enemy's turf. A short time later, a Harlem Crip was checked into my class, and I knew the first book he grabbed and looked into, he got his eyes busted, but for two days his gang allegiance went unknown to me; that was until a Mexican named Thumper from El Monte Flores told me where he was from. But that wasn't the worst of it, Thumper also handed me a book and showed me where the unknown Harlem member had crossed my set out. He knew I would be all pumped up, and true to my bones and representing my turf to the fullest extent I slid into my gangster's mode.

"Me and ole boy got to get busy", I blurted out. In my mind it was never a case of okay, 'I crossed your hood out and now we're even', naw, I didn't play that kind of shit. 'If I crossed your hood out then we could get busy if you felt dissed', but he didn't approach me that way. Instead, he chose to whack my hood out, which was a declaration of war to me, and I took all invitations. I slid in between the chairs bee-lining toward my opponent, who looked up knowing already what I was there for as his face went from 'who-the-fuck-is-this-standing-over-me' to the recognition of his worst enemy of the class: Mr. Loko. I flipped to the back of the book and held it just so he could see what I was there for.

"Why you diss my hood homeboy," I asked, and I knew the answer was self-explanatory. But still I wanted to hear him say it. "Because you crossed my hood out, Loko." He spoke with the gesture of 'I don't want to fight you, but if you make me, I will.' I had no choice in the matter, by the rules and regulations of banging everyone knew I would be in violation of not taking up the battle stance. It would be a sign of weakness, if I didn't handle my business with a sworn enemy to the republic I represented. Instead of me knocking his head off right then and there, I opted to give him a chance to stand and defend himself. "We got to get down homeboy!" With the statement I backed away giving him enough room to take the challenge or to mark out. He opted for the former.

The whole time the teacher hadn't notice a thing. He was one of those people lost from the 1960's with long and stringy hair, hippy garb, and the hippy way of talking. The classroom watched intently as we squared off to do battle. Just as the teacher took notice of what was about to happen, I fought with everything I had in the vicinity of my opponent. I scored with a solid right and followed with a weak left. My opponent stumbled backwards into the chalkboard, and after regaining his composure, he bounced back with quickness, I had never seen before. I don't know if it was from fright or determination, but he regained his balance and was now zeroing in on me aiming to get a blow or two in to even out the battle.

I squared up and bee lined straightforward looking to finish him off, but I miscalculated, and he took advantage of it. I swung a hard right looking to connect with a solid blow again, but he was swift on his feet – side stepped my blow and stepped within my perimeter with his right foot, and all in the same motion he was counter attacking with a solid right that landed with results. I stumbled into the chairs behind me feeling the weakness in my knees. After recovering my balance, my determination pushed me forward. I was back on the offensive looking to retaliate, but just as we squared off again to begin round three, the teacher stood between us preventing anymore contact.

He was saying something about to stop it before we go to the hole, but I wasn't paying much attention as I had my radar locked in on my opponent still looking for some kind of advantage and for an opportunity to strike. When my opponent dropped his guards and began explaining some off the wall shit to the teacher, the hippy turned his head toward him to respond. That was the opportunity I was looking for, and it couldn't be wasted. I launched my attack with the swiftness of a fighter jet doing Mach 6 in space. My opponent's reactions were slow; his body lurched backwards, but somehow his head went forward. It seemed not to agree with its body's decision and it cost him.

I landed a solid blow to his jaw, he staggered back two or three steps, and before the chalkboard could impede his fall, he was already descending fast to the classroom's floor. Before I could put the stump down, the hippy had put all his weight to bear on me and marched me out the class, and straight to the hole. I really didn't give a fuck about the hole, as the only concern to me was I had shown my opponent that I was a trooper who believed in defending my turf from the shoulders or through the barrel of a gun. The victory over him made my whole time easier. I would lie in bed day and night replaying my solid blow against his dome thus giving myself and my republic a victory in the battle. No sooner would I be released from the hole, I would be sent right back for another fight. I was losing my mind over my seek-and-destroy missions in the Central Juvenile Facility.

After my fourth visit to the hole, the counselors warned me about not getting into any more fights or they would be forced to kick me out. Kick me out, they did, but not for a fist fight. I, my homeboy T-Dog, Do-Low from Blood Stone Piru's, and some other Bloods decided to kick off a riot by rushing a Hoover Crip who had dissed my turf. Both sides in unit E/F participated. The Bloods were so aggressive and violent that the staff made the decision that all of them were to be sent to the hole, and all the Crips were to be given immunity. We went in style, as we knew our consolidated army of many factions handled our business. We stayed in the hole for a month and from there we were shipped off to the old County Jail in downtown L.A., where we were placed on the 10th floor in the juvenile section.

Unlike the juvenile halls where Bloods and Crips were kept together, the Bloods were separated from all contact from the other inmates unless you were a juvenile Blood member. Each group had its own semi-module, which gave us a bigger desire to always try to get to each other. It wasn't about to happen as the many bars and gates kept us completely apart. I tried desperately to adapt to my new experience, I tried unsuccessfully reading books to kill time, I tried the mind over matter thing, but nothing seemed to be working. I soon found it much easier to gang bang whenever I got the chance; it made my time go by. Being in jail was like being on the streets: You had friends and foes.

I soon embarked on a downward spiral in gang activities. My continuous disrupting behavior pattern got me kicked out of the entire juvenile correctional facilities; it was just like when I was in elementary school; from Los Padrinos Juvenile Hall, I was transferred to Central Juvenile Hall. After one too many fights there I was subsequently sent to the juvenile section in the Old County Jail (H.O.J.J.). From there I was sent to a ninety-day observation to Norwalk C.Y.A. (California Youth Authority), but my attitude remained the same regardless of where I was. After a couple of gang fights in C.Y.A. the counselors tried unsuccessfully with a last ditch effort to put me back on track. For a while, I stayed calm, but then I'd explode all over again.

My ninety-day observation was over; I'd failed myself and the counselors who had tried to help me. Eventually I was kicked out and sent back to court to face a judge whose action displayed, he didn't have any time or patience with my disruptive pattern. The D.A. charged me with the crime of sneak attacks upon my enemies while residing in the California Youth Authority in Norwalk. My lawyer countered the attack and defended my actions, but after the judge viewed my history, he wasn't having none of it. Instead, he chose to give me the maximum time of two years commuting my original ten years sentence into twelve, and as if that wasn't enough punishment, he ordered for me to be transferred from all juvenile facilities, and without any delay to be sent to the men's penitentiary. I was devastated and shook up a bit. I thought about all the horror stories I'd heard about the pen. I was only seventeen years old, how could this be happening to me, I thought.

Two months later in the year of 1987, March 3, I was transferred to Chino's Reception Center for men. Chino was an intermediary location, where housing assessments were made upon arrival. I was given multiple school tests, multiple health shots, and I was seen by a prison counselor who gave his recommendation of where he felt I should be placed in the vast California prison system, which was Old Folsom State Prison. Old Folsom was like nothing I've ever experienced: Its outer concrete structure was menacing in appearance. The first thought that came to my mind at its sight it being a dungeon where prisoners were tortured, but once inside its vast complex, I was awed to speechlessness, it was awesome. Gun towers overshadowed every corner of its interior, even its old wooded gun towers from the 19th century were still standing where they were originally built. This place is old, I thought.

Since Folsom was a level IV maximum-security prison, inmate movement was strongly prohibited after 3:00 p.m. We arrived at around six o'clock that evening and all the inmates were housed away in their cellblocks. The grey goose (prison bus) pulled up to the R&R (receiving and release) patio location, where we were unloaded one by one like wild cattle branded in our orange jumpsuits. It took about thirty minutes for the bus to be unpacked, our prison records and few belongings were unloaded, and not soon after the bus departed on another state bound mission down the California golden coast.

I settled in for a long evening, as I knew from the Chino experience that the procedure of processing would be long and slow. A few hours into the orientation process, I heard a loud boom; it was distinctive and undoubtedly a gun blast. Minutes later, an inmate was escorted across the yard by four correctional officers. A sergeant followed behind the entourage with a large inmate manufactured weapon in his hand. I found out later the inmate stabbed somebody behind a drug deal gone bad, and hours later we were housed in the same building where the stabbing and shooting had just occurred.

The exterior structure of the building was massive indeed, but I couldn't believe my eyes, when I stepped through the doors. It was like a separate world existing inside the concrete structure hiding its existence: There were rolls and rolls of cells running in all directions, people were everywhere coming and going. There was music, laughter, screams, and the distinctive smell of an unfamiliar food all in the air. This was my new home I thought. It was something that I would have to get used to, inmate manufactured knives, stabbings, wars, lockdowns, small six by eight cells, and tasteless food. This was Folsom Prison and all the realities of Folsom life would soon become a part of me.

My cell was located on the upper third tier, and my cellmate was an old man named J.B. Once inside I immediately started unpacking and getting situated. All the prison garb I was given was brand new, and tucked inside I discovered a pouch of tobacco, which the state provided to all newcomers upon arrival. From my peripheral vision, I could make out an unknown number of dark images gathering in front of my cell. I turned to face them, it was the welcoming party coming to find out which side of the fence I stood on: Blood, Crip, 415 (Northern California Black Gang), B.G.F. (Black Guerilla Family, a California prison based organization), or non-affiliate.

They were Crips. "Where you from homey?" the short dark-skinned one asked as he eyeballed me intensely. "I'm from N.H.B.", I heard myself respond. I looked at them to see if my words of identification had been registered. "We're from the Hoover Criminal Gang", the short dark one spoke again, "You've some homies here", he went on. The intensity they originally arrived with when they first approached my cell gave way to a much friendlier atmosphere after finding out I was a Blood member and not a Crip.

I soon learned respect in this prison was a rule, and a way of life behind the walls. They even offered to give me a care package, which I declined for fear of being in depth to some men, I hardly knew. A short time later, the Bloods arrived at my cell, and some of their very first questions were about the Crips' behavior. I informed them that everything was okay and that no disrespect was involved. Again, I was offered a care package containing food, cosmetics, extra clothes, and drugs. This time I accepted it. The hospitality was overwhelming and reassuring that I was in good company and amongst friends.

After a while the psychological effect of being in Folsom started to wear on me. It wasn't visibly noticeable in my outer appearance, but when I went to bed, I had terrible nightmares. I was stressing, and I was desperately trying to adapt to an environment that was the home for broken men and cast away souls. The stress and nightmares finally took its toll on me and reluctantly I put in a form to be seen by the prison psychologist.

About two weeks later, I had a 10:00 a.m. appointment. The psych was an old white man, about fifty, and dressed in a brand new white colored robe. The interview started immediately upon arrival: "Have a seat young man, and please tell me your problem." His voice was rich and thick, and it sounded like an angry and raging waterfall. I was nervous and my voice shook noticeably. "My, my nightmares are bad", I explained. "Umm huh", the doctor responded prodding me with eyes that encouraged me to continue. Again, I began to explain: "I, I, I dreamed that I killed my little sister by throwing her into a pit of fire." The doctor shuffled in his seat at the bluntness of my confession. "Go on", this time his deep throttled voice startled me. He began asking me a list of questions: "Do you hate your sister?" – "No" – "Did you and your sister have lots of fights?" – "No", I responded again. "Has your sister ever done anything to you that you've never forgiven her for?" – "No" The questions were making me uncomfortable. I loved my sister, and we were friends, and if we ever had a fight in the past, I didn't recall.

At that moment his office phone rang from somewhere in the back. "Excuse me", he said and departed quickly to a back office. I didn't like this interview, I didn't like the questions he was asking me about my sister, and I didn't like him and his irritating voice. I scanned the entire room and thought to myself, how it looked nothing like a psychologist office, which I thought, had to have all kind of weird things and gadgets. The doctor's voice traveled from the back and broke my daydreaming trance. I didn't want to continue this interview anymore, I wanted to leave. I wasn't crazy, I was just stressing a little, I told myself. With a quick glance toward the doctor's office back area, I was able to confirm that he was still on the phone. I bounced out the chair and bee lined out the front door, down a corridor, which was lined with offices on both sides that looked like the psych office I'd just left. I was cool, and I convinced myself that I didn't need to see no psych.

Days went by and the psych never re-inducted me for another interview, and I never placed another form in to be seen either. Like any other environment I'd ever been in, I soon adapted and learned to get used to my life traveling experiences, experiences that threw all sorts of obstacles and crash courses my way, and with each one I endured, I learned something new. The one year I spent in Folsom before I was put up for transfer to San Diego State Prison was everything I'd heard it would be: prisoners successfully escaping, prisoners stabbing correctional officer, prisoners stabbing each other, and prisoners being nothing more than hard core convicts. For the most part, I spent the entire year of 1987 on lockdown, and when I finally departed out of Folsom Prison, I took with me a part of its being. Folsom was a living thing, a culture, a way of life, and it was me.

San Diego on the other hand was new in every way; it wasn't even five years old, when I arrived in 1988. The prison yard was twice the size; we got to walk outside to the kitchen area, and we had night yard, meaning we were able to stay outside up until 9:00 p.m. It was still prison, regardless how you looked at it, but the freedom through movement made the difference. When I was finally cleared and housed in a regular building with the general population, some of my homeboys immediately greeted me: Karate Dee from the 27th Street, Big Snake and Big Loonatic from 2nd Avenues.

Just like the streets, the Crips outnumbered the Bloods three to one, and just like the streets, gang banging was a plague that was spreading and getting out of hand, because it was only loosely monitored by the older convicts, who usually kept things in check. Due to that atmosphere, it wasn't even quite two months before a minor incident occurred. A Crip was getting at me in an irritating and aggressive manner. We exchanged words, threats were made, and a date was set for violence with the result that the fight was prevented by the C/O's (correctional officers), and I was marched off to the hole. I had been busted with an inmate-manufactured knife.

The hole was terrible; being it was my first time to the hole in prison. It was a prison inside the prison. The inmates were much like wild animals, and the day and night noise level was unbearable. Respect was far and non-existent. The worst part for me was being confined to my cell with only a few hours for recreation in a secure and gated up area, an area, where the gun tower had complete surveillance over us. Some time later I was seen by a prison committee that reviewed my case, found me guilty and sentenced me to a ten months solitary confinement term. From the San Diego hole, I was transferred to the San Quentin's S.H.U. (segregated housing unit) program.

Upon arrival at San Quentin, one of the oldest California State Prisons built around 1830, I developed an instant case of claustrophobia. The cell seemed to have closed in around me from the exact moment I walked into its confinements. It was small. It was so small that I could sit on my bunk with my back against the wall and place my feet on the opposite wall with no problem at all. I lived like this for at least eight months and was left no choice, but to adapt or to go crazy.

One late night when sleep evaded me, I tuned into an on-going conversation over the tier. Instantly I thought I recognized one of the voices. One of the person's talking sounded like Keith Fudge a.k.a. Ase-Kapone from the Van Ness Gangster Bloods, who was convicted for the 54th Street massacre, where twelve were shot and five died. After listening a little while longer, I felt confident that it was Ace, and I decided to intervene on the conversation: "Uno, is that you?" Uno was another name we called him. The conversation upstairs abruptly stopped, and I repeated my statement: "Uno, is that you?" – "Yea, who's that?" – "It's me, Loko, from NHB." Instantly he recognized my moniker and my republic affiliation.

"What's up Loko Blood?" He was overexcited that I was there, as we hadn't seen each other since 1984 at a gang picnic at 2nd Avenue Park. We talked into the night and covered old and new subjects in the gang world. For half my stay in the hole my boy kept me company and I did the same for him. I tried to keep his mind off a reality that he lived with everyday, although it was an impossible task: Ase-Kapone was on San Quentin's death row for the massacre of the Hoover Crips.

I finished my time in the hole, and was now ready to be released back into the mainline population. The hardest part for me was my re-adaptation. I'd become anti-social and hadn't realize it. When my homies spoke to me, I didn't respond, or I ignored them completely; the hole-time had affected me. It was like being forced to live in a dark cave for a year, then abruptly placed back into the mainstream of society, there's bound to be some kind of adverse affect. My first month out the hole was the worst part of my experience. When people gathered around me, I'd sweat profusely, and my speech was like chattering teeth. Usually I found my peace of mind within the seclusion of my cell at the end of the day. But like all obstacles I had encountered on my life journey, I soon adapted and conquered my problem.

From San Quentin Prison I was transferred to New Folsom Prison that became my home for the remaining three years left on my sentence. New Folsom was built sometime in the late 1980's, some hundred and thirty years later than Old Folsom. The only two similarities they shared were continued violence and the name Folsom Prison; other than that, they were different. New Folsom was much larger in every aspect. Its cell space doubled that of Old Folsom; Old Folsom had one main yard for the entire population, and New Folsom had three separate yards.

It was there in New Folsom, I decided to embark on a path to reeducate myself: I received my G.E.D. certificate in 1989; I enlisted into the Sacramento City College taking such courses as English, Political Science, Physical Geography, and best of all Philosophy. I held important jobs throughout the prison, which also added to my new and changing experience, and I mastered typing skills with up to seventy-three words per minute.

When I finally paroled, I was ready for the world. I was a different person, and I had been gone for seven years. The day of my release I gave my good-bye's, my take-care's, and with me I took words of encouragement and words of warning of how the world had changed since my absence. On March 4, 1992, I walked away a free man into a world with an uncertain future. The odds were stacked against me, percentages dictated I wouldn't make it, and statistics soon became my enemy. But I was determined to succeed. I wanted to succeed.

A month after my release, everything I dreamed of doing would change. The "not guilty" verdicts of the police who had beaten Rodney King would alter my courses of aspiration. Los Angeles would respond to the injustice of police corruptness that plagued the city like cancer, and like cancer, it had to be removed. I came home to a city that was about to explode, a city that turned itself to a living volcano with enough lava to blanket the entire county. The 1992 riots made history, and I was there in the depth of the volcano's anger, making history with the rest of the citizens of Los Angeles, who had changed the name to Los Scandalous, I was there when the block was hot.

THE BLOCK IS HOT
(1992-1994)

There was a light drizzle in the air that morning, and it was cool out and winter like. I promptly reported to the watch office, and from there I was escorted to R&R. Since I was the only person being released that day altogether, I was sure I'd be a free man in a minute, but that wouldn't be the case. It took them all and nothing short of three hours to process me. I couldn't wait to feel the winds of freedom floating against my skin, I couldn't wait to gloat in the sun that I believed shined differently on those who are free compared to those who are confined, and I couldn't wait to have my first Mac Donald's Big Mac, especially after doing seven years.

It was over finally, the longest tedious three hours of my life were over. I was taken to an awaiting van, which drove me through the prison double gates and dropped me off a few more yards out past the gated area in a vast parking lot filled with cars belonging to the institution employees, I assumed. I exited the stale smelling van and felt like the astronaut who was the first man to place his foot on the moon. I was giddy with joy and the excitement of accomplishing a seven-year goal, going home.

My baby sister Malinda and my cousin Bobby were standing in the distance waiting for me. We embraced each other, spoke a few words and they immediately sensed that I was ready to depart. As if my confinement was nothing more than a dream, I was whisked down the highway, leaving behind all the realities of what I'd been subjected to for the past seven years, wondering was it true or not. My sister and I conversed about everything, trying to cover the time lost. She'd missed me I could tell, as she was my favorite when she was small and young in age. Our chitchat ran its courses, then silence ranged supreme and sleep soon followed.

When I woke up, we were within the Los Angeles city limits, for the first time excitement rushed through me. I was empted, and I scanned every bush, tree, passing car and building. L.A. excited me, and once entering back into its grasp, I was instinctively revived. It had taken eight hours until we finally arrived at the parking spot in front of my mother's home. The first thing of importance to note was where she had now moved, 58th and Figueroa. We were in the midst of Hoover-Crip-land; across Slauson was the 59 Hoover battleground, and behind us were the 5-Duce-Hoover Gangsters, my mother lived somewhere in between. I exited the car feeling out of place, desperately trying to control my many uncertainties; it was going to be a long up hill battle. From the front door of the yellow and brown house, my mother was making her way outside. We hugged it seemed for an eternity, and it seemed we were going to get stuck together, if she didn't release me anytime soon.

Finally, we all headed into the house, and after a few hours, the entire family showed up to see what and how much I'd changed in the past seven years. It was like a freak show on display as each family member took their turn eyeballing me thoroughly; some looked at me as if I'd grown a tail on my ass since my departure. But the real love of my homecoming came from my Aunt Mae, my second mother. You know how everyone has that special and favorite aunt or uncle; well that's what my Aunt Mae was to me. From as early as I can recall, she always overshadowed me with her love and motherly ways. I loved her unconditionally, and she loved me just the same.

The house was soon loud with voices and laughter; I sat in the distance on the far side of the room, soaking up each sound that traveled throughout the house, I was free, and I was learning to get use to it; I was having patience. Later that evening my sisters Virginia and Malinda threw me a surprise welcome home party in Compton at my Aunt Mae's newly decorated home. I had a ball, as we had a live D.J., and we partied all night long. I was introduced to drinks I'd never heard about: Pink Panties, Sex on the Beach, and Orgasm. Before I realized it, all the sexual drinks had me stumbling and tripping all over myself. If it weren't for my aunt cam cording the events and activities that night, I would have never known just how much fun I really had.

I woke up the next morning lying next to a female I didn't recognize at first; it was Denise, my teenage love. I guess she arrived at the party sometime after I was already too intoxicated to remember much; when she finally shook off her somber sleep, she was shocked to find out, I didn't recall any of the sexual acts, she had performed on me the previous night. She made up for it, as she performed them again right there and then, and man I tell you, the girl knew her shit, and she knew how to do it well.

When all the excitement passed, the task of taking care of business was at hand. A week after being home, I was immediately confronted with the duty of decision making over a family problem. My baby sister was three months pregnant, and my mother left the ultimate power in my hands, whether she should or shouldn't have her baby. When dealing with my enemies, I quickly decreed their life to be forfeited without a second thought. But this was different, this was my baby sister, we were talking about. My mother was obvious indecisive about the pregnancy or maybe she was upset altogether. I was the oldest of four, and I was like the supreme ruler of the land, wielding the ultimate fate of the less fortunate souls. I loved my baby sister greatly, but more importantly, I had a positive philosophy on the issues of life. To me procreation was important to mankind, but more important; I made the decision that would make her happy. I ruled that the family should get ready and prepare for the coming out of our niece, or nephew, and grandchild, as we didn't know the baby's sexual orientation yet. Six months later my sister gave birth to a healthy and beautiful baby girl, she named Sade.

After squaring away the issue of my sister's untimely pregnancy, I went about looking for some employment. My homeboy Kenny, K-Dog, hooked me up with a Temp-Agency in the Wilshire area. They quickly located a job for me in the City of Torrance; the job description was something like a clerk. The work was mediocre, but the pay was okay. I was making six dollars an hour, and I needed every penny. Every morning my mother would have my lunch set out for me for work, and every morning I would make my way to the bus stop located on the freeway's upper deck, and every morning my mother would watch in the distance making sure, I got to the bus stop safely. When April rolled around, I was set into a daily program: one-hour ride to work, boring work, ride home, marijuana session, dinner, sleep – repeat. That was my life my first month out. I was taking my time and taking each day as it came. I wasn't in no rush to jump into the mainstream of things; I was still recovering from the shock I experienced of coming home. It took a lot of mental work and focus to stay on track. Everything had changed, the world had evolved drastically, but mentally I still remained in the 1985 days of long past. I had seven years of distance to overcome.

On the evening of April 29, 1992, I was with my homeboy E-Dog doing what I usually did after work, having my marijuana session. We were watching the evening news, reporting about the trial against the three officers who had teased and beaten Rodney King. Charge after charge was wiped away by verdicts of not guilty. I wasn't up on the Rodney King trial, as I had my own life trial to deal and contend with. But E-Dog knew enough about it because he had followed it all the way to the end. I was buzzed off the marijuana, but I could tell, the news had disturbed my homey. "Ah Blood", he began in his old man voice, "I'm about to take you home, the city is going to go crazy about the verdicts." When I'm high, I don't talk much, but I responded to his statement by standing and dusting my pant's legs of the lent that wasn't there. It was a gesture that I was ready to go whenever he was. He put the TV back inside the house, got rid of the mess we'd made on the front porch, closed the front door, locked it and we were off.

We rode with the topic of discussion being centered on Rodney King; he knew something I didn't. All the time he kept saying the city was on the verge of rioting. I kept looking around me for any signs of his conviction, people looked normal to me. He dropped me off at home, we shook hands, and he departed. Soon nighttime rolled in, and true to every word he spoke, the people drew their battle lines, and in no time, the city was ablaze, thus starting the 1992 Los Angeles riots. I had never been in a riot before, but it was an experience almost indescribable: One minute there was calm and normalness, the next minute there was chaos and disorder. The city had erupted; the people were angry which they expressed through the multiple fires that ravaged throughout the blocks. Businesses, houses and cars were all looted. You could smell the thickness of violence. Death was in the air, and it traveled for miles unchecked by the law. Every positive thought I held prior to release went up in the orange and red flames of the riots. The block was hot, and people were angry and upset about the verdicts, the city was driving deeper into unstableness as the rioters ran rampant expressing themselves.

The first day of the disorder I rationalized that it would be safer, if I stayed home, but when I awoke the next day, I was blasted with every news station reporting that the rioting had continued throughout the night, and had now traveled wide in range. I couldn't believe what I was hearing. The civil authority wasn't stopping the killing, looting, and destruction. People became encouraged by these signs of anarchy, and the momentum continued on moving faster and faster going unchecked. It was getting more chaotic and violent.

I gave in to the excitement, and soon I found myself participating. I hastily ate breakfast, got dressed, and headed toward the neighborhood that I vehemently vowed to avoid. It was unbelievable at what I witnessed on my way to my old hangout area. Blacks, Mexicans, and even some Whites were stealing everything that wasn't tacked down. The killings and the robbery victim related shootings were unbelievable and staggering. We were well on our way to breaking all the records and statistics of the Watt's riots twenty-seven years ago.

I finally reached the block of my old neighborhood, and like days of past, my friends were there in gathering. I was warmly greeted, and the surprise look that I was hanging out again could be seen on their faces. Drinks and marijuana were passed around as usual and long before we all departed into the hot inferno of the city to add our own thievery and violence. That day we looted and stole, we survived and killed, and we were making history, and history was recording our anger. The experience we all endured would be etched in our hearts and minds forever.

Out from all the mayhem and violence, a flower of peace began to blossom on the horizon: The Bloods and Crips had declared a citywide truce;

an agreement was reached amongst the many factions to put an end to the on-going gang violence. Rivalry between neighborhoods that had been at war with each other for years was wiped away overnight. It was amazing how the violence had abruptly ended. The gangs held many peace treaty parties with thousands of gangsters in attendance. I went to one of these parties in the P.J. Watts Crip territory located on Imperial Boulevard and Mona Avenue, and what I saw was beyond all my experience. Usually the P.J.'s were at war with the infamous Bounty Hunter Bloods and the Grape Street Watts Crips, but since the peace treaty, they invited their most hated enemies, and any other partygoer who wanted to attend.

The party was in full swing when we arrived, and it was the first time I had seen so much respect and courtesy given by so many different gangsters from various sides of the fence. Red and blue bandanas were tied together to symbolize the peace that everybody wanted and desired. It was good to see, the blood baths from the gang wars came to an end, and in its replacement were the peace treaty parties, the peace treaty picnics, the peace treaty relays, and the peace treaty football games. The gang peace traveled throughout the city just as the riots of 1992 continued on unabated.

Finally, the National Guards were sent in to replace the chaos with order. They went from block to block reclaiming the blazing city. Soon a curfew was put into effect with the orders that any violators could be shot. The enraged citizens who had disagreed with the court's verdicts, soon returned to their normal lives, and the rioting was over after three days of intense disorder. When the smoke had finally cleared from the countless property fires, it was said from some of the politicians that it was going to take a miracle to rebuild and replenish the devastated city. Property damages exceeded deep into the tens of millions of dollars. The city was badly scarred, and it was going to take a lot of help and nurturing to bring it back to health.

And like anything in life, everything is bound to change, either for the good or the bad. With no exception to this unwritten law, the gang truce began to crumble and fell apart not soon after the riots had ended. It first started on the West Side, when my roll-dog Lil-Moe was shot eight times at close blank range. The shooting had enraged our entire neighborhood, which prompted us to take revenge on all our rivals and enemies. We hit everybody and anybody who we thought had something to do with it. Soon the blood bath was in full swing, and as a result, the homicide statistic again began to rise.

By the time summer had rolled around, I was in total disarray. I was jobless, I was broke, and I was back hanging out. The environmental impact had swerved me hard from my original path of goals; eventually I did what most black men would have done, when hardship was dragging them through the streets like a bum, I hustled. I was determined to pull myself up by my bootstraps, so I started engaging in an activity, I'd only heard about, selling cocaine. I learned fast and quick about the do's and don'ts of slanging, with the result of finding myself playing catch up to most of my friends, who had been pushing for years.

When I left the streets in 1985, we were on bicycles and driving around in stolen cars; but upon my return most of my homeboys had nice cars, and some even had new ones. I couldn't believe how fast the money was coming in from pushing rocks, and not soon after I had hustled enough to buy myself a 1980 brown colored Oldsmobile Cutlass. I added a few more hundreds to the upkeep of the car and decided then to sell it. I invested that money in a 1980 grey colored Cadillac Coup Deville and was really styling now, as most of my friends had also Cadillacs.

For a while, I tried hustling rocks, but I soon found out, I didn't have the patience, and I wasn't prepared for all the gives and takes that came along with it. Therefore, I made the decision to put my life back on track, and enrolled myself into Trade Technical City College. I wanted to do something positive with my time by taking courses such as business management, business science and math. For a while, I stayed on track, before the financial monster started to eat away at my stability, once again I started hustling. I pushed marijuana on campus to help me through the hard times. It worked out as I planned; I completed my summer courses successfully and decided to take some more in fall. I was happy and content with my progress. I had money in my pocket, I had a nice and clean car, I was in school pushing my books, and I was free. But all it took was one small mistake to throw me off course, one small mistake that would derail my momentum of progress. And that's exactly what happened to me in the following year.

I was arrested on January 31, 1993 for a charge I thought to be a bullshit charge in general; nevertheless, I was sent back to the penitentiary for receiving stolen property. My homeboy Lil Loko had carjacked a Crip from the Gardena Based Shot Guns, and after stripping the car of its music equipment, he told me I could have the rims for my Cadillac, that's where my problems began. I should've declined the offer, but the temptation was overwhelming. Needless to say, but totally expected of the outcome, I received the maximum penalty: sixteen months with half time based on good time behavior; that time was to run concurrent with my twelve months mandatory parole violation. It would be my first violation and I had barely stayed out for eleven months, I was disappointed.

Upon my return to prison, I went through the withdrawal stages like a heroin addict; I was kicking the habit of being addicted to freedom. I was trying to keep the junky monkey of failure off my back, but somehow it always seemed to find a way to hitch a ride. After leaving Men's Central Jail, I was sent to Tehachapi State Prison. In the early 90's Tehachapi was the place where parole violators from Southern California were sent to.

Everything was going as typically expected, then the unexpected happened. Out of nowhere, a curb ball was thrown my way: Two correctional officers showed up at my cell door with restraints in hand. At first, I thought they were coming for my cellmate, but that notion was soon dispelled, when stainless steel was placed around my wrists. I protested and without much explanation, I was hauled off to the hole, given a lock-up order for the reason of being in the hole. The write-up stipulated I had been locked away because I was a threat to the safety and security of the institution.

The charges against me were overzealous and unbelievable. I figured, if I didn't have bad luck, I wouldn't have no luck. It was nothing that I had done on my present incarceration; they were locking me away in solitary confinement for my past behavior. I was soon seen by the prison committee who told me that I would remain in the segregated unit, until my impending transfer to Pelican Bay State Prison. I couldn't believe it, I was being sent to California's hell on earth for no other reason than my past. My past was haunting me and the prison system was about to make sure I'd never forget it. The punishment was a tactic they used to try and break my spirit and determined nature.

If you were labeled a threat to any California prison, you were literally singled out, separated from the general population, and housed in a maximum-security solitary unit. Once there, all your privileges like the comfort of yard time and contact visits are taken away. The treatment of inmates by the prison administration usually goes unchecked, and the inmates are subjected to any kind of punishment the C.D.C. (California Department of Correction) system deems warranted. I was about to be subjected to this inhumane treatment which left me mentally scarred and would bleed its injustice on my life forever.

My stay in Tehachapi Prison was somewhat pacified. Once housed in any solitary confined unit, inmates are normally restricted to possess such items as cigarettes, matches, and extra food; but I was flooded with them. I was on walk alone that means I had yard by myself, and the C/O's paid me off for the use of my yard time, so they could play handball. They also used to gamble, and I heard their matches were for high stakes. It was cool with me, as I didn't mind giving up my yard time for the cigarettes. I soon became the man, as everybody started sending me commissary for the thin rolled papered cigarettes I was now selling. During my entire stay at Tehachapi, I probably received yard only once or twice; instead, I was on fat status from my hustling. But like every good thing in life, it must come to an end.

I was transferred to Pelican Bay on June 5, 1993, and the environment there was nothing like the atmosphere of Tehachapi. I was going to the belly of the beast, as most inmates would say. Pelican Bay was maximum security at its best. The person who devised and drew up the designs for the construction of that prison had to be related to the devil, as the maximum-security confinement unit was beneath the earth. It was a reality right out of some Stephen King novel. I was taken from the grey goose with my hands and feet shackled tightly; once the chains were removed, I was shuffled down a long tunnel. To my left and right was granite rock, but right above me, directly over head, there was a metal structured catwalk across the entire underground, which enabled the gunner having access to any part of the complex.

I was taken to a location called the pod. There were eight cells in each pod, and each of them had its own shower and mini concrete yard, with a camera safely secured in the upper portion of the structure. I was placed into the cell that was nearest the pod shower. Once inside the cell one of the first things I noticed about it was that everything was made of concrete, straight out of the Fred Flintstone days: the bed, the shelves, and the dinner table. The only thing that wasn't, was the iron gate with the food slot that separated me from the outer section. The cell size was like none I've ever seen before. It was large enough for at least five inmates to lie side by side, and there was plenty of room for exercise.

Pelican Bay's library was one of those things that left an immediate impression on me: It was the best I'd ever seen with sections like Western, Mexican-American, African-American, Mystery, Philosophy, History, et cetera. I buried myself into the variety of books until my mental satisfaction was established.

It wasn't long after my arrival that I was given a prison television to make my stay in such harsh conditions more pleasant, I assumed. One of my favorite stations I recall was the all black station B.E.T. (Black Entertainment Television). Black show after black show was aired with the best part of having no commercials.

When I arrived at the Bay, as it is sometimes called, I had eight months left on my total term. Around the six-month's mark, I was given a roommate named Dooley. Dooley was cool, we became tight right away and not soon after the best of friends. Usually it would be hard for men to live in such close quarters for so long, but we didn't mind. We were on the same level, as we had a lot in common, and we made plans to kick it together upon release. Dooley's release date was a month or two after mine, and we planned far ahead.

Time flew by with Dooley as my cellmate, and before we realized it, I was released. We said our good-byes, gave each other our last hugs, and spoke our last words of encouragement to each other; I vowed to wait on him on the outs, a promise that was made by many inmates upon release. But I had given him every possible address and phone number, so we'd keep contact if he wanted.

It was the first day of February, 1994 when I was on my way back out into the world of the unforgiving. From the prison complex, we were led away on a prison van to the local area Greyhound station, where we were watched by the eyes of the overseers while we bought our seventy-five dollars one-way ticket to L.A. The bus arrived and not soon after, I was whisked off down the California coastline back into a city that held the mysterious keys to my uncertain future.

UNCERTAIN FUTURE
(1994-1995)

The ride from Pelican Bay State Prison to Los Angeles had taken me a little over twenty-four hours, and my legs and buttocks were completely numb and fast asleep from sitting in one place. But it was well worth it for the beautiful feeling to be out of prison and back home. Before grabbing a cab I decided, I was going to get something to kill my ever-growing hunger pain. The moment I stepped from the bus my appetite for food kicked into overdrive, and I wanted to buy everything in sight that was food related.

I purchased myself a double cheeseburger and fries with a medium size soft drink and headed in the direction of where the cabs had massed on the perimeter of the Greyhound station to jump into the first one I came upon. Inside I took a big adult size bite into my meat patty, if that's what you could call it, and gave the driver instructions of my destination. I rode in silence as most of my thoughts were focused around my future: I had a total of one hundred and twenty dollars left out of the original two hundred I had departed with. I knew I needed some money, and even more and equally important, I needed a car.

The day of my unwarranted arrest and despite the promise from the police that it wouldn't happen, my Cadillac had been towed away; but that wasn't the worst or the last of my problems, I didn't have a girlfriend to come home to. During my stay in Tehachapi, a letter-mishap destroyed my relationship with Yvette. I don't know if it was a mistake I had made, or if it was an intentional act of cruelty by the prison guards, but somehow the letters to Yvette and my friend Dara were swapped; the outcome was predictable, as Yvette wrote back talking plenty of shit, speaking about how I had turned her into a monster. It was then and there that our relationship ended, and I was coming home girlless. Most men would love to have the opportunity to start fresh, to find another girl, but not me. That was something I was afraid of. I wanted things to remain the same as change spooked me. It made me feel uncertain.

The cab driver's voice startled me, as I was so deep in my personal thoughts, I hadn't notice that my time of travel was up. I walked the short distance to my mother's house, braised myself, took a deep breath, banged on the door three times, and waited. Seconds later, I could hear her rumbling about inside; I knew it was she because she was the only person in my family, who stomped around like big foot. I could tell she had been fast asleep from the way her voice sounded, when she answered the door.

"Who is it?" It was one of those half woke, half asleep 'who is it'. "It's me, Mama." Within seconds, the front door was opened. From the way she hugged me, I was able to tell that she had missed me. Without words, she kissed me on my cheek, turned and headed back to her bedroom to finish her beauty sleep. The moment I walked in my room, I plopped onto my bed with complete exhaustion rushing out my bones, and within minutes, I was fast asleep.

I woke up hours later, somewhat disorientated by the sudden change of my environment; my senses were desperately re-aligning and re-adjusting past images and replacing them with new ones that were presently dominating me. I slid of the bed, pulled the curtains back, and the bright sun rays danced around the room filling it up instantly. I trotted over to the pink colored stereo that was donated to me by my youngest sister, and put on some Al Green, whose sweet tunes of love and happiness started me on my day.

I began rumbling through my closet to check out the few clothes I owned. They looked to have been untouched. Everything was still clean, and I quickly made a mental match between a nice looking shirt and pants, which I ironed with some heavy starch before I took a bath; I wanted to scrub myself clean of all the micro cells and any other thing that may have been Pelican Bay related.

After bath and breakfast, I faced the hardest part of my homecoming: What should I do with myself? I didn't have the slightest idea of what I was going to get into that day, as I didn't have no car, so my travel would be limited, and I didn't have much money, so my spending would be conservative. I was at a lost with my life, and I needed to figure something out, I needed a game plan. I ventured outside to soak in the sun; maybe an idea or an ingenious plan would brainstorm into my head. There I was, all dressed up, fresh out no more than twenty-four hours, and I didn't have a damn idea of what I wanted to do with myself.

A truck was coming up the street with two men on each side in the back part; each was sitting on a bundle of newspapers in which they were throwing into the front yards as they went up the block. The truck had covered the entire block in a matter of minutes, before it was out of sight and on its way to another location. The paper thrower was good, as the paper had been thrown within inches from where I was sitting. I picked it up, and at first, I was browsing and breezing through it, then I figured I'd look through the job section to see, if anything of interest might jump out at me.

I soon found myself seriously scanning the employment pages: warehouse workers needed no experience; clerk wanted; typist wanted, et cetera. I figured I'd call some and see what would come of it. Soon I had a list of appointments and dates set for interviews with people all over the city. The hundred dollars I had left, would be drained and quickly depleted, but my searching wasn't all in vein, as it turned out I landed a job placement in two days paying five dollars fifty cents an hour.

The description was photographer/receptionist: I worked at Avon in the reception area processing information, taking photos for ID's of all newcomers, who wanted to be able to buy Avon merchandise at wholesale prices. I was required to wear black shoes, black khaki pants, and a stripe shirt the business provided. I learned fast, and soon I had mastered my job chores. I worked around the clock and saved every paycheck. Even my employer was so impressed with my work ethics that I was given a promotion to a different section of the building paying seven dollars an hour. My new job was different in a few aspects: I went from taking photos and processing them into identification cards to having to operate my own computer, processing and fulfilling orders, restock, keeping the costume jewelry display current, and working in the lingerie department. The experience was fulfilling and exciting, as I really liked the pleasure I received in satisfying the customers.

For four months I held the new position up until the day, I called in sick. I was explaining to the receptionist Lydia that I wouldn't be able to make it, but unknowingly to me, I was already laid off by the company. Lydia went on to explain that I was no longer needed as an employee at Avon. I dug my heels in immediately and demanded an explanation for my relief. In so many words, she explained to me, it had to do with my being an ex-convict; they had done a background check on me. I was infuriated at their decision to relieve me based on my past. It didn't make any sense to me. Here I was, trying to do something constructive with myself, staying crime free, feeling good about my job, reporting to my parole officer, keeping him content with my progress, only to be rewarded with my dismissal based on my past, what luck! My first reaction was to vandalize the business, and my second was to seek out a lawyer that could help me file a lawsuit for discrimination. Needless to say, I acted on neither. Instead, I chose a third option, back to the block, hustling full time as a rock slanger; it never occurred to me to get another job, I just gave up right then and there.

I had saved enough checks to get what I needed. Within days, I bought a 1979 Ford Fairmount. It was clean and ran good, real good. My first drive was to the local swap meet, where I bought myself the cheapest pager they had on sale. From there I went to the neighborhood to seek out a homeboy, who would sell me a sack of rocks at a reasonable discount of the original price. It didn't take long to track down someone, who understood my predicament, and who decided to reach out and help me.

My homeboy Tank, who I was responsible for putting on my click, wanted me to help him to push some cocaine, but we had to find an apartment to push from. We rented one out on Cinmarron and Venice, furnished it with some cheap furniture, and devised up an economical plan of payment and percentages, of how the money was to be distributed with the sales of each sack of rocks. Initially it was fun and lucrative, the money was rolling in, and everyone was content and happy with the amount.

But the spot soon became hot. The local police department started staking me out as well as our clientele that stampeded to the apartment all hours into the night. It was time to abandon the ship and anchor somewhere else. My homeboy insisted that the location was still okay, but that was easy for him to say, especially since he wasn't the one, who was under the constant glare of the narcotic task force. We soon had a fallen out, and I made the decision to go it alone. My new spot was at 27th Street and Kenwood Avenue. I purchased myself a sizeable sack of rocks, and within hours, I had flipped it with my profit and re-up money fully accounted for. To be solo was more rewarding and beneficial. I was totally independent, and my hours of hustle were, as I wanted them to be; there wasn't that pressure of paying my homeboy hanging over my head.

Things were looking up for me. I had solved some of the problems that troubled me when I first came home; the only thing I hadn't accomplished as of yet was finding myself a stable girlfriend. I was dating, but none was serious, only one even came close to being a relationship, it was a long distance affair. Every other month I'd been lucky to see her. When she wasn't in L.A., re-upping on some dope, she was there in the cold city of Chicago pushing it. Her name was Rockelle, and she was one of those Belizean girls who liked to hustle and carry guns. My homeboy and soon to be best friend G-Kev encouraged me to date her; he'd told me she was loaded with cash from her international hustling. In the beginning, the relationship was mostly based around convenience, but after awhile the long distance left a strain on the love affair. It started deteriorating, and it was only a matter of time, before the erosion took its total effect. I was cool though, I mean I pretty much enjoyed my semi-bachelorhood. That was until I met Sheila.

Sheila was completely beautiful and attractive. She had been hanging at her girlfriend's house on a daily basis on Kenwood between 27th and 29th Street, the exact same area I was hustling in, and we were destined to bump heads sooner or later; it was sooner. I pulled up to the local market to buy myself some Zig Zag's, when I first noticed her. She was leaving the store with her girlfriend. "Excuse me", I jumped out my car just as she turned to face me. "You", I pointed to her to clarify I was demanding her attention. I extended my index finger and told her to come. She smiled at my suggestion and began bee lining between the parked cars heading in my direction.

"Where you on your way to?" I asked. "I'm going to my girlfriend house." She spoke with an accent that sounded like music to my ears. I had to control myself as my heart was thumping fast; I looked at her face wondering what kind of soap she used on her skin to keep it smooth and pretty. I was daydreaming, and without realizing, I asked her the first thing that came to my mind: "Can I have your number?" Damn, I thought to myself, I'd probably just blown it with her, but surprisingly she said "Yeah". When she in return asked me for mine, I didn't wait a second. I quickly jotted all the numbers I had and knew onto a piece of paper and handed it to her. I had no plans of losing contact with her. Then she totally surprised me, when she asked me, if she could wear my bright red Pendleton shirt. As insurance, that she'd see me again. Man I have never taken a shirt off that fast like I did that day. She put it on and gave me a lovely smile that could have melted the entire continent of Antarctica. I watched her walk away, turn the corner, and blend out of sight.

I stood there for a second, lost in thought damn near forgetting what I'd come to the market to get. After gaining my composure from the trance of her beauty, I ran inside, bought the Zig Zags and rolled myself a big marijuana stick. Two days passed before I hooked back up with her. When I arrived to pick her up, she was outside on the sidewalk patiently waiting for my arrival; I still was astonished by her natural beauty. "Hi", she spoke as she reached over to lock herself in. "How you doing?" I responded, desperately trying to keep my voice in check. My anxiety level was high, and one slip off control, I would be a total mess, and for sure, my date would be completely ruined. "I'm doing okay", she replied with that smile. So far so good, I was doing all right.

"Do you smoke weed?" I was hoping to God she did, as I needed to get high and feel the affects flowing through my body, soothing me plus relaxing my nerves. "Yeah, I get high. Why, do you got some?" I reached into my ashtray and pulled out a marijuana stick, lit it, dragged on it hard and passed it to her. I began driving aimlessly through the neighborhood with no destination in mind. Our conversation was on every subject we could think of; we soon discovered that we had a lot in common. We were both new hustlers, we were both semi-single, as she was dating a Blood from 30 Piru's, we both had one kid each, and we both were looking for love. After that first date, we realized, how much we enjoyed each other's company, and soon we were seen throughout the neighborhood hustling together. We were giving each other, what the other one desperately needed, comfort, attention, and love.

After a couple of weeks, the desire of lovemaking was evident within each of us. I remember that day as if it was yesterday; it was beautiful and pleasant. We eventually fell madly in love with each other and were soon totally inseparable. We became the Bonnie and Clyde of the neighborhood, and we loved it.

Her becoming pregnant a few months later slowed me. I was serious in making her comfortable with my baby, and it was my job to take care of her. We moved into my mother's new apartment in Torrance, a little city southwest of L.A. My plan was to give her a heaven of comfort from the street life she was living prior to me. I hustled day and night, so I could save enough money to get our first apartment and another car, a four-door Cutlass; and immediately we ventured together apartment hunting which was fun, but time consuming. After two weeks, we had found one in a run down building deep north of Torrance. How deep? My mother lived on 204th and Normandie, and we were on 9th and Normandie! That was a big difference of travel.

We made the initial arrangement of payment with the landlord and began our move-in. The New Year of 1995 was about two weeks away, and I wanted to be situated by the time it arrived. I rented out a medium size moving truck and gathered up a few homeboys to help. My mother was very supportive, as she donated everything she could find, pots, pans, chairs, tables, bed sheets, and a rollout bed, she even gave us food. About a week before the New Year, we were happy and cozy, and deep in love with our new first apartment together, and regardless of how it looked, we loved it like a newborn baby.

The building we lived in was called the Fox Normandie Apartments. But although it looked more like the Garbage Normandie Apartments, it was home to us, and we planned to make the best of it. There were five stories in the building with eight apartment units on each floor. Our unit was on the third floor with probably three other tenants total; most of the units were inhabitable as they were filled with piles of trash, broken plumbing systems, rodents of all sorts, and completely in dire need of a major clean-up. Despite all the ills of the building, Sheila loved our home, and she made it into something special, it was her little project.

The New Year rolled around and we brought it in with spaghetti and meatballs, and some new resolutions for the future that we were going to get paid through hustling and to wear green to clarify our goal and destiny, but we were broke. The apartment and the car had completely depleted all the funds we had saved up. I had to come up with a plan, and I decided to seek the assistance I needed in the neighborhood. Somebody would help me I rationalized. I deserved the help, I convinced myself. We finally found assistance from my homeboy G-Kev. I fed him my sob story of hardship, and in return, he blessed me with enough rocks to get me going.

Within two weeks, I had an instant clientele that I had started from scratch. In the beginning of making our new apartment into a crack house, I sold rocks of every value. I had twenty-five cents rocks, fifty cents rocks, dollar rocks, and up. All day and night, I had a constant flow of people beating down my door to get their fixes. After awhile the clientele was too much for me to handle, as I was the only person in the neighborhood who was selling rocks so cheap.

Since my plan was a success, I figured it was time to implement plan number two, which was to cut the clientele in half and inform them I only had five dollars rocks now. The transition occurred without many problems, and each sack of rocks I bought was flipped within hours. Soon I was selling ten dollars rocks only, the money was good, and it rolled in non-stop. I even had lookout men who sat on the apartment balcony directing the traffic to and from the building, but more importantly, they kept an eye out for the narcotic units that were always looking for a target to hit.

By February, I decided to have a little fun to celebrate my success. I threw a Valentine's party and invited all my homeboys and homegirls. Sheila cooked so much barbecue and other food that day, she had to borrow a neighbor's kitchen to keep up with the hungry mouths that kept coming and coming. Before I realized it, I had a full-scale party going. We shot dice in the hallway, people were eating and licking their fingers everywhere you looked, and poor Sheila was ripping and running around trying to keep up with the orders that were flowing in all around her. I worried myself and became major concerned about her health, especially since knowing she was six months pregnant. But she reassured me that she was fine when she glanced my way with her heart-stopping smile. I relaxed and we both continued our hospitality to our guests up until the party ended late in the evening that day.

The good times were rolling in, and in the same month of February 1995, I moved Sheila and my unborn daughter two blocks east on 9th and Fedora. I was trying to be responsible by choosing a building that was cozy and comfortable for her and our child, and the new apartment was the ideal place, plus drugs were prohibited. Smokers of crack were warned with harm of violence not to tread on my safe heaven; still they were some persistent people. I found myself shuffling from one apartment to the next; I was bringing home the bacon, I cooked, I cleaned, I comforted Sheila, I went to the doctor's appointments with her, and I somehow managed everything in stride.

While I was riding high on my good times, my boy G-Kev was feeling the affect of hard time and despair. To help him out, I agreed for us to rotate the days of hustling in the first apartment, only if he would pay half the rent. After the agreements were reached, G-Kev was soon wreaking the benefits of my goldmine. He bounced back and was able to regain his financial composure. But then the problem started. My homeboys migrated in numbers to the area. Soon the five-story apartment building was totally occupied by members of my neighborhood on all floors and levels, except for one. On the fifth floor, Lil B-Rock and his girlfriend moved in; on the fourth floor G-Kev had his apartment, where he rested; on the third floor was our rock house; on the first floor was my homeboy Kountry and his mother, and two doors down from him were my homeboys Lil Boo, Baby Boo, and Big Timebomb.

The problem wasn't that they had moved in, the problem was they had moved in on me and G-Kev's clientele with the result that my clientele I had worked so hard to establish had been systematically divided up amongst me and my homies. And there was another problem: With their arrival the building also became something like a frat spot, parties, domestic disputes, noise continuously, and disagreements with the tenants and the landlord. The local Narcotic Division began their 'round the clock surveillance of the building and its massive traffic. I was spooked out of my wits upon hearing about the police presence. They were asking questions to my neighbors about us, they even went so far to arrest a youth for driving around in a stolen car, and promised to release him, if he could provide them with some adequate information about us. Fortunate for me he didn't know anything about me, and I was also fortunate to have known his sister who had informed me of the police's drilling of her little brother. I was ready to abandon ship, I told G-Kev, he could have the apartment, and that he was on his own. I took my few belongings and washed my hands completely of the goldmine that had given me a sense of comfort and stability.

I had to revise and regroup, and come up with another brilliant plan, something that was going to be financially rewarding like my first apartment, but I was cool on the goldmine. I couldn't run the risk of going to jail, especially with the knowledge that I was being watched. G-Kev stayed and tried to tough it out, but that was completely suicidal, and soon enough the inevitable happened. The Narcs had enough information, and they were ready to make their move. Instead of the typical bust-the-door-down method with them storming in and fanning out, they simply went to the landlord, asked him for the keys to unit 304, walked in unannounced and arrested G-Kev, while he was asleep on the sofa. He was hauled off to jail, arraigned and charged with possession of marijuana, P.C.P., rock cocaine, and unregistered handguns. I lay real low for a good while after his arrest; I knew they were wondering what had happened to me. To them I had vanished, but little did they know, I was still in the neighborhood, just two blocks away.

Shortly after all these problems, another one popped up. My homeboy Lil D-Kapone had died, while chasing some Crips up Crenshaw. The car with him, Baby-Snake and Q-Ball from the Neighborhood Pirus was side swiped and went into a complete spin. They lost all control, slammed into a large pole, and the impact was so great that D-Kapone went flying out the back window and subsequently died from his internal injuries. Baby-Snake and Q-Ball received minor injuries. If that wasn't enough bad news already, more was on its way. I soon found out that my homeboy's family didn't have any money to bury him; they looked to us for help. Like many neighborhoods in similar situations, we raised the money thru car washes, bar-b-queue sales, and donations, so we could give Lil D-Kapone a respectable and decent funeral.

Days after things blended back into the norm, everybody went back into their private lives with their personal problems. The problem of me to readjust and find a decent location to push my rocks was harder than I'd expected to be. I was trying to find a place that didn't have much competition, a place that the Narco Division wasn't too familiar with, but that the crack smokers were over familiar with. After a few days, I found something close, but not exactly, of what I had in mind. It was back to Kenwood and 27th, the same location where I met Sheila.

Although I knew the Narcs were present in that area, I avoided them completely by venturing out at night only. I knew from experience they were rampant in the day light hours, setting people up with their carefully orchestrated buy and bust stings; during the night only the regular black and white units were out, and they were seen coming a mile away. I set up shop and my hustling began at 6:00 p.m. up until I finished with the entire sack of rocks. Every night I took a hundred dollars worth of rocks to sell, and as soon as I accomplished that goal, I returned home immediately.

When I wasn't out pushing I was at home tending to my pregnant girlfriend making sure, she was okay. She was eight months now and large as hell; the full affect of her pregnancy was riding her back: she was grouchy, always irritated, usually tired, and she had some weird and bizarre eating patterns like pickles, ice cream with cookies and chow mein, yuk! Chow mein was too slimy for me, but she loved every spoon full. During the latter part of her pregnancy, our sex life had slowed completely. It wasn't that I'd lost my attraction to her, I was in love with her, and I still desired her. But the baby-in-the-stomach-and-sex-thing didn't seem to work for me. That was until we went to the doctor for her annual check up. He gave the advice that it would be better for her and the baby, if we had sex in the last months of her pregnancy because it would make the delivery of the baby easier. Sheila looked at me with wickedness glowing all around her, and eyes saying 'I got you now, sucker'. It was the doctor's order and the doctor said it was good for the baby; she had me and she knew it.

The drama unfolded as soon as we got home. She began by telling a story about how she was so horny, and how it would be good for her and the baby. Here she was repeating the doctor's words of advice, playing her trump card early, and betting everything on it. To resist her urgency for sex would be suicidal to our relationship, so I struck a deal that I would do it, if she agrees on our sex position. Before I realized it, I was naked in bed lying on my back. Sheila was possessed, she couldn't contain herself, and she was about to make me pay for all those long months of abstinence.

I lay there motionless, watching her as she undressed, within seconds she was fully nude, and I looked about her with a hidden desire. Her eyes glow a hunger and lust that devoured me on a level purely immaterial. Her breasts were beautiful; they sat on her chest like two swollen watermelons with two large dark brown eyes. They looked like they were living and breathing separate from control of her other bodily functions: up and down, up and down they went. Her stomach was full and all but ready to drop her load. A load that we had created together, a load that we would love and care for, a beautiful load. Her legs were her prize position; they were beautiful and perfectly shaped and fitted her body just right. All this loveliness of a woman I loved was inching on her hands and knees crawling toward me, and instantly I became aroused.

To this day, I would never forget the sexual self-possessed look Sheila had in her eyes as she eyeballed my erection. Then she gave a little laugh that spoke her desire level. She was happy and she wanted me. She straddled me, reaching beneath her; I could feel the softness of her hands as she gently handled me. Skillfully she guided me to her entrance, she was wet and it made the penetration easy. I was aroused more than I believed I would be. Soon we were in full physical intercourse, and in her every motion on my manhood, she was being carried away deeper into ecstasy. She was handling her business atop me, and the thrill finally overtook her.

"I'm coming, I'm coming!" She was gasping and moaning the pleasure she felt. I wanted it to be good to her, so I began my rhythm of pushing up inside her. That did it as she went over the edge in her cries of joy and pleasure, she had finished. Boy was she a happy camper, grinning and looking down at me. "Did you come?" she asked with sweat perspiring off her forehead. "No", I responded, "but I ain't tripping", I continued. "As long as you're happy, I'm happy." – "I love you", she replied, bent down and gave me a sweet tenderly affectionate kiss. "I love you, too Baby."

It wasn't all that bad sexing her, my train of thought was off, completely off. I had convinced myself of making love to her during her late pregnancy period as being taboo or something. Actually, it was rewarding in a certain way. She became more relaxed immediately there after; she cooked more often; she was less irritated, and she was happier, which helped major when it was time to deliver our daughter. In her ninth month, she seemed to have blown twice the size she was a month ago. Her stomach filled out any clothing she wore, as she was that big. She was ready to drop her load, and any person, who happened to see her in traffic, would say the same thing.

Two weeks until her date of delivery, I ran into a little problem, a problem that would last for two years. It was check day May 1, 1995, and money was going to be flowing in the streets. I prepared ahead of time for that day: I had spent five hundred dollars on an ounce of rocks, knowing full well it wouldn't last through the day. That bright morning I got dressed with all the energy in the world not knowing it would be my last day with Sheila who headed for an appointment she had at the local A.F.D.C. (Aid for Dependant Children) to seek the eligibility of welfare for our unborn daughter. We kissed each other and left the house in different directions.

I had a hundred rocks on me at the retail distribution price of ten dollars each. I was looking to make a five hundred dollars profit. Within the first few hours, I had nearly made my re-up money back. The sales were rolling in: twenty, forty, fifty, even one hundred dollars sales. The users wanted to get enough to last them at least a few hours at a time. But they would spend throughout the day; actually, they would spend until they couldn't spend no more. The day was good, I was nearly out, and it was only three o'clock in the afternoon. Since I had a few rocks left, I figured I'd go to 27th and Kenwood, where I probably could get them off quickly.

As soon as I hit the corner of 27th, a twenty dollars sale came my way. I knew the smokers, but there was a guy with shades on in the distance that had my attention. "Who is that Mexican right there?" I asked. "Oh him? He's with us". Something was wrong though, I sensed it. Smokers would tell you anything to get their hands on some rocks, and they knew I was the paranoid type, so they skillfully and quickly put my nervousness to rest. My years of experience in the streets spoke against this sale, and the way the Mexican was acting was unusual. He kept peeking at me from around the street pole he was leaning against. Still yet, I decided to make the sale. I took the money and from my mouth out flew two ten dollars rocks wrapped in their individual plastic. There, the sale was done, but I was still nervous and uncertain about that Mexican on the corner. I walked away from the smokers, giving myself some distance.

I trotted up 27th toward Normandie, alert sounds thundered across my built in warning system: Narc! Police! Narc! Police! An unmarked brown police Caprice materialized on Normandie. The driver was white, clean shaved, and looking my way. These were all tell tale signs of an undercover; I was headed straight toward him, and he was waiting to make his left turn on 27th in my direction. I waited and tensed up. He stopped and bounced out; I walked faster and shuffled the few remaining rocks in my mouth into a swallowing position in case of a possible chase. He had a plug in his ear; someone was talking to him. He listened and pointed in my direction. Every fear I had of being set-up in the buy and bust stings had just snared me in its trap. My heart was thundering in my chest, and my freedom of fresh air unrestricted movements was slowly vanishing before my eyes.

Before I realized it, I was running in full stride, as if I was making a prison break. "Stop, hey stop!" I ran that much faster. More police cruisers dropped out the sky it seemed, bearing down on my every move. My lungs were burning, and my throat was dry, I was scared. I remember thinking to myself, "Maybe I was having a nightmare." I zoned out briefly, and when I zoned back in, I remembered I had forgot to do something very important; I had to dispose off the five remaining rocks in my mouth. I tried to swallow in one big gulp, that wasn't going to work. My mouth was like the Mojave Desert, dry and depleted of moisture.

I continued to run up Normandie, zig zagging and dodging the long arm of the law. One by one, I swallowed each rock. The plastic they were wrapped in served two purposes. It guaranteed I didn't have to taste the numbing effect of the rock, if it was allowed to touch my tongue, and it protected my stomach in case I had to swallow the evidence upon my arrest. But there was a draw back, the plastic made it difficult to swallow, especially if your mouth was dry. Finally, I stopped running and gave up, after my last piece of evidence was on its way into the interior of my stomach.

The police surrounded me from all sides and made any further attempts at running futile. I was ordered to lay spread eagle on my stomach, with trained guns on me. I didn't resist, I was too damn tired. They cuffed me, snatched me off the ground, and rushed me to the paddy wagon. I was sick, not from illness like the common cold; I was feeling wheezy about being captured just two weeks prior to my daughter's birthday. I'd failed myself and my family. I took the chance of gambling, and I crapped out. I was shuffled into the dark colored wagon, where I sat in silence, feeling disgusted as the buy and bust team filled the empty seats. They were snatching other fools like me who had fallen for the same entrapment scheme.

The news had reached Sheila, and she was hysterical. She cried for days. Two weeks after my arrest, the love of my life entered into my world. Terrey was born May 17, 1995, a day after my birthday. I on the other hand was going through the rituals of processing deeper into the L.A. County Jail's interior, before I was shipped to the Honor Ranch of Wayside, East Max. East Max was just a portion of the vast compound called Wayside, known for its violent riots between the Cholos (Mexican gangster) and the Bloods and Crips who shared the same close quarters together. All it took was one spark, and the flames of violence would erupt into a do or die life-taking situation. Environments like Wayside brought the Bloods and Crips together to face off their common threat of harm from the Mexicans.

I was vigilant in protecting myself from all harm, and by aligning myself with combat troops from other Blood republics, we collectively provided protection for each other in the face of so many of our sworn enemies. I had been banging about thirteen years, and my experience geared me for the psychological warfare that raged in my head. It also stirred my mind frame to scan and process information about my new home in Wayside, East Max, which atmosphere at that moment was peaceful and content, but when violence was on the horizon and traveled unchecked by the mediators, it could be smelled in the air like a raging out of control wild fire.

"Terrell Wright, you have a visit! Terrell Wright, prepare for your visit!" I was beaming when I bounced out of bed. I hastily got dressed, slapped about five hands full of water on my face, brushed my teeth quickly, slicked my baldhead free of lent and tucked my shirt. I was given a visiting pass, the gate was opened, and I bee lined down the ramp rushing toward the visiting area. I wondered who it could be who was visiting me. My mother? Naw, she hadn't come to visit me since the juvenile days. My sisters possibly? Naw, neither had ever come to see me in jail before. The only person left was Sheila. But naw, the doctor had given her strict instructions to rest and stay off her feet.

I handed the young looking deputy my visiting pass, he wrote some numbers on it, and directed me to where I was to sit. Once the visiting roll was filled and occupied to capacity with inmates of all shades from different neighborhoods, I waited and watched as each visitor walked by my window looking for his or her love one. The roll was nearly completed, and I still looked at an empty window. Maybe it was some kind of mistake, I thought. Maybe the computer misprinted and accidentally printed my name; and just when I was nearly convinced of my train of thought, Sheila turned the corner with the baby in her arms, smiling the joyful grin of love and admiration for me. She held my bundle of joy, which was busy squirming and twitching. Very few things made my heart jump, most of the time gang violence was the cause, but at the sight of seeing my sweetheart, my heart beat out of control. The visiting phone came to life and Sheila managed to shuffle my daughter with one arm, and balanced the phone on her ear in her other hand.

"Hi Baby", she began, giving me that smile that always made my heart thump. "Hi Sweetheart", I responded, rotating my stare from Sheila to Terrey. "Isn't she beautiful?" Sheila commented, "She looks just like you". Like a mother in love with her baby's father, Sheila accredited all the young features of my daughter to me. She was on a roll: "She got your lips, your nose, your eyebrows, and she even sticks her tongue out her mouth like you do". Any and everything my daughter did, it reminded Sheila of me. I sat in that chair glued to the beautiful images in front of me, knowing it would be awhile before I touched either. I was facing sixteen years, and I was still feeling sickish from my arrest.

A Dove Will Get You Eighty Percent
(1995-1997)

When I was being shipped back to the L.A. Men's Central Jail, the first thought that came to my mind was maybe the D.A. had concluded the case was weak, and thus so decided to dismiss all the charges pending against me. But that hopeful thought was soon dispelled. As soon as I reached the downtown jail, I was separated from the group of men in blue, and under escort by three deputies who marched me to booking front. My mind raced a thousand miles per hour; I was frantic with fright, as most times when you are taken to booking front, especially after already being in jail, you'll be re-booked in for an additional charge. In my line, those additional charges would be more than likely for murder, and they could stem from any incident in my distant or recent past.

Once arriving in R&R I was given an orange jumpsuit and a High Power wristband. "What the fuck is this about?" I enquired to the three non-speaking deputies. "We just following orders". The deputy that answered had to be a new recruit, his jumpsuit was greener than the other two, his boots looked to be fresh out the plastic, and his facial features were still soft and friendly. He knew he had fucked up by satisfying my curiosity, as he received some hard and wrinkled face stares from his more experienced comrades. They escorted me to the first floor module 1700, High Power, where I was given over to some real looking brutes who were some of the deputies that gave the County its reputation as being violent.

I entered Able Row, cautiously eyeballing everything in sight; it was eerie quite and squeaky clean, unlike any other part of the County. They removed the metal restraints, before I was given a bedroll with all the material I was going to need. One of the brutes then directed me to go and to stop in front of cell number nine. I walked up the tier like a lion stalking its wounded prey, cautiously, slowly, and quietly; analyzing the occupants of each cell while holding my solemn features in check as some of the tenants were up when I arrived.

I stopped in front of cell number nine and waited. "Watch the gate", the brute screamed over the module P.A. system. The gate then went through a serious of bangs and booms, slid open, and I slowly stepped through the dimension and the reality of being in High Power, a jail inside the jail. A shadowy cloud of depression blanketed me once the row lights dimmed for the night. I needed sleep because my emotional and mental condition was bruised by my new placement. I needed to recover and went about making my bed preparing myself for a long night.

When I woke up the following morning feeling out of place and grudgingly, I stirred in my bed stretching my muscles into life and flipped onto my side to find a comfortable lying position, only to be met by an entourage of brown, black, and albino roaches. Damn, I thought to myself, I got to do some major cleaning and scrubbing. The roaches sat huddled together, barely moving at all; at first glance, they appeared to be asleep, but upon seeing their antennas twitching and twirling, I knew they probably were in gathering like they were to keep each other warm, what the hell did I know about the roaches' habits. But I knew one thing for sure, I was about to declare an unconditional war on them with the only conventional weapon I had, my shoe. I threw the blanket off me, slid from the warmth of my lying position, grabbed my shoe from the filthy floor, and dropped my first of many bombs onto their wall position stronghold.

Pop! The remaining roaches that avoided the devastating blow scattered, dodging my precise guided shoe missiles. Pop! The sound amplified off the wall throughout the cell as broken and badly mutilated bodies splattered everywhere. The one sided war waged for another thirty minutes, before the roaches had vacated from every section on the wall, and if any had still existed, they kept their presence from me for my remaining stay. It took me another thirty minutes to scrub, deep clean, and disinfect the entire cell making it a livable place.

Breakfast was announced over the loudspeaker, and in the distance I could hear the bang and boom noises of a cell opening from somewhere in the back. An inmate trustee was being let out to feed us. I gave myself the once over to see, if I looked up to part, I was cool. I geared myself to my thug gangster mentality, so whoever the trustee worker was, he would draw a quick conclusion that I was a serious, battle experienced brother, I waited. The moment of truth had arrived as I could see the reflection through the one-way mirror of a large looking inmate coming up the tier. Damn he was big, really big. I knew him, I knew those features and that face was shot into my identity files for comparison to decide, whether he was friend or foe, he was friend. The six foot four, two hundred and fifty pounds, with twenty inches arms was none other than Ant Dog from the Black P. Stones Bloods. He glanced my way and broke into a wide cool aid grin, "What's up Loko Blood?" He had recognized me immediately. "What's up Ant Dog?" I responded bracing myself and reading into his face for any signs of tension.

Ant Dog and I had had a show down with each other five years ago on the C-Yard in New Folsom Prison. Even back then in 1990 he was huge like he was now. I was only on my last two years, when he returned back to Folsom on a parole violation. During my three years stay in Folsom up until my parole release in 1992, Ant Dog had been violated and came back at least four times, so when he asked me one day to wear my jewelry on a visit to floss (to show off), I obliged him on his request. I was over familiar with him, and we had never had any problems with each other. After the visiting hours had ended, he returned to the yard where he was met by my roll dog Condo from Bounty Hunter Bloods who was looking to get my jewelry back for me, as I was at work that evening in the P.I.A. (prison industrial authority). When he approached Ant Dog about my nugget ring and gold chain, Ant promptly turned over the gold chain, but gave a bizarre but possibly true account about a K-9 had confiscated the ring. Condo took the chain and left the explanation on the ring to be analyzed by me.

The next day when I approached Ant Dog about that issue, he went on to explain in great dramatized detail about a K-9 named Wilson had taken the ring being it wasn't a wedding band. Not once did I think of foul play on his behalf, the ring wasn't a wedding band, and an asshole K-9 could take it and send it home, if he chose to. Ant Dog dropped my guard of suspicious against him when he apologized, and when he volunteered to pay me a hundred dollars to cover its expense. Cool, I thought, a real homey would do just what he was doing. I wrote my name, C.D.C. number and housing on a piece of paper, and handed it to him. We shook hands and that was the end of our business, at least in theory.

Two days later, I approached the accused K-9, and the weirdest shit happened. When I challenged him, he vehemently denied any knowledge of a ring being taken by him. "What the fuck you mean, you didn't take my ring?" I was now shouting at him who I believed was lying. "I want to send the ring home to my family", I demanded, looking at him with eyes that spoke the tension building inside me. "Look man, I don't know what you talking about. I don't know who told you that shit about me taking a ring, but the motha fucka lied." I scanned every wrinkle and crease in his face looking for any signs that would betray his convincing reply. There was none, he held his facial composure steadily and gave nothing away I could use. I stormed away pissed as hell. The idea of someone gangstering me fucked my psychic up. I'd have to chalk the ring up as a lost and be thankful for the hundred dollars Ant Dog promised. But somewhere in my mind I believed the K-9, he was too sincere; on the other hand why take his word over Ant-Dog's, he was a K-9 and K-9's weren't to be trusted, fuck him!

Patiently I waited for the money from Ant-Dog. One week passed, two weeks passed, three weeks passed, and right before the fourth week rolled around, I had a sudden and unexpected run-in with my ring. It happened when my building and building number four were being released simultaneous for yard time that I noticed a ring on the finger of one of the inmates from the other building. From where I stood, the ring looked just like mine. The more I stared at it, the more convinced I became it was mine. I decided to pull him over, and asked him in person. "Ah homey", I shouted loud enough over the noise of the rising voices of activities by the other inmates on the yard. He knew I was speaking to him; he stopped suddenly and turned to face me. I mobbed on him with my typical L.A. gangster walk.

Without delay, I poured it on: "Where you get that ring from?" My voice was strong and accusing. He froze up right away, and scored poorly on his return answer. "Why?" He was hiding something, I could tell. After cutting loose my verbal barrage, he cracked and spilled everything to me. He had bought the ring from Ant-Dog for a cap of weed (a Chap Stick cap is used to measure marijuana in prison). Damn! Ant-Dog had swindled me and had me looking like a fucken fool. I told the unknown inmate to erase anything we had just talked about. He agreed and we departed.

Immediately I plotted my revenge on being played by Ant-Dog. I was gonna make him pay dearly for his unworthy actions against me. The unknown inmate didn't keep our conversation a secret, he ran back to Ant-Dog first chance given and spilled the beans on our conversation. Shortly thereafter Ant-Dog approached me with the truth about the ring and how, if I wanted to settle the dispute. We could go in the prison boxing ring and deal with it like men. I couldn't believe my ears, there I was weighing in at a buck seventy and he out weighted me by at least eighty pounds. There was no way that I was going to get into the ring with him. I shrugged him off, told him I was cool, and that I tossed it up as a lost. He took the bait like a hungry fish in shallow water, whereas I plotted his destruction for three weeks straight, watching his every habit, stalking his every move, and looking for all his weaknesses.

After three weeks of heavy surveillance, I knew the time had arrived to make my move. The day I'd chosen was perfect for violence, the wind blew lightly, the sun was giving off long warm rays, and the yard was packed with inmates and convicts. I sat in the distance watching Ant-Dog like a hawk in the sky. His habit had not changed in those three weeks. Every day he walked to the weight pile, looked around and began his workout routine. That was his weakness, the weight pile.

I bee lined across the populated prison yard, zeroing in on my target. I felt alive and aware; the thought of violence and mayhem gave me energy like nothing else. My killer instinct was put on autopilot; my body guided itself perfectly without flaws. I was zoned in and focused. As I neared my target, I skillfully eyed all the gun towers that posed the imminent threat of sabotaging my mission. Everything was cool; the towers were looking about the yard, but not at me. I was within fifteen feet of Ant-Dog making my move, when he sat up abruptly on the weight bench. I froze and squatted where I was; he stretched his limbs and lay back down.

Now I had a new problem on my hands: I had violated a prison rule by entering the Mexican side of the weight pile. The Cholos eyeballed me angrily, and I quickly tried to reassure them that everything was fine, and that I meant them no harm. They still remained tense, but I had a mission to accomplish, before it slipped away. I looked in the direction where Ant-Dog was, and just like the fool he was, he hadn't noticed anything amiss. I still had my advantage, and I didn't waste another second; I grabbed the nearest dumb bell bar handle in my left hand and palmed the top part with my right, Ant-Dog had never seen it coming, I was like a dark cloud that covered his entire presence, and I was definitely about to rain on his parade.

Just when his mind realized it and began its first phase of computing my face to his possible life saving body reactions, it was already too late. I was dropping the sixty-five pounds dumb bell onto his face. It was all in one swift motion, even the gun towers missed it, but most of the inmates had seen it, and a distant silence swept across the yard. B.O., Al-Dog, Krazy-Ray, and Green Eyes, all from the 6-Duce Brims Bloods, scattered out the weight pile getting away from the mayhem they had just witnessed. I was given mad respect and kudos (prestige) from that mission. Later that night I was rolled up and placed in solitary confinement for assaulting Ant-Dog's other homeboy, who also had been involved in the selling of my ring. Ant-Dog and I departed from Folsom back then on that note from the weigh pile incident.

Now here he was standing in front of my cell some five years later. Immediately into the conversation he apologized about the Folsom incident, he said he left it back in Folsom where it had occurred. It wasn't like I was tripping though; I had closed the weight difference between us drastically as I had an easy two hundred and twenty-five pounds and muscles bulging from the body. I wondered was this the real reason why he was cool with me. A few more words were exchanged between us, and he went to pass out the cold County Jail breakfast.

Right after breakfast and clean up, Ant-Dog and me chopped it up for almost an hour, and I soon realized he had been up to his same old bag of bullshit. Before my arrival in High Power, he had already robbed two inmates on the row of their money. One of his victims was a Crip from the Rollin 60's which usually meant bad business due to the potential of warfare, but the other Crips didn't back him because they considered him to be a buster. The other victim was a Mexican from a gang calling themselves the West Side Rebels Trece, and unknowingly to Ant-Dog, the Mexicans had been plotting a move against him since the day of his disrespect.

Ant-Dog worked in the morning time feeding, cleaning, and passing out supplies, and once he was locked away in the evening, a Hispanic porter was let out taking up where he had left off. A week passed, and all the time the Mexican shot caller prepared and geared his troops for a possible war with the Blacks after the hit on Ant-Dog, depending on how we reacted. The Mexican trustee who worked the evening shift was designated to put the hit down; he had found Ant-Dog's weakness after only a week of observation. He was taking naps with his head facing the bars of the cell.

The predator had waited until the chanced opportunity arrived. Ant-Dog was taking his typical evening nap. I had been busy cleaning up my cell, then I stopped suddenly upon hearing footsteps thundering up the tier. Initially I was confused, and it took a second for my danger radar to compute what was happening. But as the footsteps picked up speed and suddenly stopped with a loud screeching sound, I knew then somebody had been hit. The hitter used a broom handle as a spear with a knife tied on its end to use its length as his advantage in case Ant-Dog had tried to run. In the few seconds after the assault, Ant-Dog was telling me that the punk ass Mexican on the tier had just speared him. "What's up Blood?" I inquired already knowing the answer. "Are you okay?" His response relayed his faith, "Naw Blood, I'm bleeding from my head." He babbled on about all kind of stupid shit while he was packing all his belongings into his pillowcase getting ready to make a speedy exit from High Power the first chance given.

I didn't buy any of his sad shit; actually, I became infuriated with his plans to leave. I wanted to fight with the Mexicans behind them hitting a Blood, regardless if he was wrong and despite our past experienced run-in. I was down to have his back because I am a firm believer in Blood-love, they fuck with one Blood, they got to fuck with all Bloods. We were the only two Bloods in High Power, and I was gearing myself for war. But my adrenaline rush was short lived, as Ant-Dog didn't share in my same aggression. He had made his mind up already that he was leaving period, now I was really pissed off. How in the hell were we supposed to maintain respect from so many opposing troops, if he wanted to leave in disgust with his tail tucked between his legs? I didn't want any parts of it. I made one last ditch effort to give him some of my courage.

"Ant-Dog", I began, "what's up, Blood?" – "What's up Loko," he responded with no aggression in his voice, he wasn't even mad at the assault against his being. "What's on your mind, Blood?" I asked seeking out any light of toughness he might still possess, "I'm outta here, Blood," he shot back defiantly. I was hot now, and I expressed it uncut: "What the fuck you mean you leaving, Blood?" I was shouting by now. "You go make me look bad, Blood!" I was ragging on and on about his ill decision, but nothing was working, and when his gate opened up for showers that evening, he walked off the role with his belongings and his head low. I looked at him with contempt and a lack of respect that was the last day I laid eyes on him. I was later told the court had given him a life sentence, and somewhere in the system of prisons, he had been swallowed up forever lost in the state's hungry appetite for cheap souls.

I stayed another two months in High Power. After they had dropped my charges from sales (sixteen years) to possession of drugs (two years), they shipped me out to the Delano Reception Center on the morning of September 15, 1995. My treatment of being singled out remained with me even at Delano; straight from the bus I was hustled out to the hole. I was been told by the administration that I was still a threat to the safety and security of the institution. I had heard that bullshit so much I was beginning to believe it myself. The harsh and bleak environment of Delano's solitary confinement unit was mind depressing, and the one and only thing that gave me a sense of hope and inspiration was the steady and weekly visits from Sheila. She brought the strength I needed to carry on to the following week. My stay at Delano Reception Center ended on December 19, 1995, and once again, I was hauled up the state on my way back to the devil's den of California, Pelican Bay State Prison.

My mental stability went from bad to worst. I hated Pelican Bay. I tried to fend off the stalk reality of my depression by working out rigorously, reading books, and writing poems and articles to the *Los Angeles Sentinel Newspaper* that was publishing my work. I became an avid and dedicated reader of Philosophy, Geography, English Literature, and History. I dissected all philosophy books of worth, one such book called *Seven Theories of Human Nature* left an immediate and lasting impression on me. I read other books on Socrates, Plato, Aristotle, and Hegel. Physical Geography also became a subject of interest to me; soon I was able to place national capitols and national flags with countries far away. I subsequently became more aware of the world around me; but History would be the love of all loves; it possessed me: the Roman Empire, the Egyptian dynasties, Alexander the Great of Macedonia, and the ancient and old civilizations of Candace Ethiopia.

When I wasn't buried in some books, I was working out faithfully, or I would be writing some heavy poetry based on reality, which both helped release, a lot of the tension that steadily rose from within. Before I realized it, I had written hundreds of poems. I was becoming a new person in the inside, a philosopher, a theologian, a historian, and a writer. I had plans upon release to do everything possible to become recognized as a poet and writer. I was ready for the world. I was gonna make it this time, and nothing was gonna get in my way, or so I thought.

The nightmare of Pelican Bay was being left behind again, as I rode the Greyhound bus in silence. I was deep in thoughts on the things I wanted to do: visiting my parole officer, getting all my clothing in order and cleaned up, and visiting the office of *The Sentinel Newspaper*. I made it to L.A. some time around three o'clock in the morning. The cold air hit me like miniature icicles the moment I stepped from the bus. I walked through the terminal and without any delay I waved an old looking cab down, "27th and Hoover", I shouted to the driver from the backseat. Since traffic was light, twenty minutes later he had me safely in front of the new apartment Sheila had gotten since my absence. I paid the driver and exited back into the cold air. I was looking for apartment number three, I knew she would be asleep, and I knew she didn't have the slightest idea of my time of arrival. I walked the length of the driveway, and to my right apartment number three jumped out at me. The air was unbelievably crisp, and I had had enough of it.

I banged on the door and waited a few seconds, nothing. For a minute, I thought she wasn't home, then I remembered that she was a heavy sleeper. I banged louder, the whole door rattled. I'd probably waken the other tenants from their sleep, but I wasn't in a caring mood, I was cold, and I wanted to be in bed. Finally, Sheila's voice came from the other side, "Who is it?" – "It's me!" I responded shivering from the cold that was robbing me of my body heat. "Clink, clank, donk", the door was opened after a serious of locks and bolts being removed. "Hi Baby", she smiled at me, waking up at the sight of my presence. "Good morning", I responded, bent forward, and kissed her full on the lips as I walked through the door into a warm, cozy, and dark living room.

"You like it Baby?" She was shadowing my every move throughout the house, "Yes Baby, I love it. It's so big and roomy." I ventured to my daughter's bedroom where she was fast asleep. She was two years old, and I had a lot of catching up to do. She looked like the angel she was, so beautiful, lovely, and peaceful. I walked closer and kissed her lightly on her puffy cheeks. I was so in love with her, and in her sleep, somehow I felt she knew. I walked out the room and quietly closed the door behind me. Without delay I grabbed Sheila by her hands, led her to the bedroom, closed the door, and without any foreplay or much kissing I made love to her vigorously. I tried to sweat every thought, residue and microscopic fiber of Pelican Bay from my being.

The next morning I woke up feeling fresh and alive, I was ready for the world. I looked over at the digital clock on the dresser drawer to check the time. My eyes adjusted to the dim lit room, and the clock read

6:15 a.m. Sheila hadn't budged, she was knocked out, and her breathing confirmed she was deep into her sleep. I put some underwear on, and went into the bathroom to run some bathing water, before I trodden over to the kitchen to take out some semi-frozen bacon, a pack of sausages, and four eggs. On my way back to the bathroom, I gave the house a once over and thought how much I liked it. I eased myself into the warmth of the water, soaking every inch of my body, I sat there reminiscing about my scarred life, and all type of thoughts bounced into my head. Some I liked, others I didn't care much about, and yet some were of severe concern to be answered by myself.

I was analyzing my past, present, and future. One part of my mind chastised me about cutting all ties with my homeboys and the gang atmosphere, another part argued about to never abandon my extended family, and to remain a loyal and dedicated trooper. Other wars raged within my head about getting a job and keeping one, while the con side of this argument went on about how I'll be fired anyway, so why bother. On and on these pros and cons weighted in my head trying to influence my decision, I stepped from the comfort of the lukewarm water and grabbed the biggest bathroom towel in sight. I felt good to be home, my stomach growled aloud, reminding me that I was still hungry. I quickly dried my body and put on some fresh and clean boxers.

On the way to the kitchen, I glanced into the mirror, and the reflection that stared back looked nothing like me. I was twenty-eight years old, but I looked more like fifty-eight. The wars, the battles, the jailhouses, the funerals, and the up's and down's in my life took a heavy and burdensome toll on me. My face showed every sign of a rough experience, a street life experience undoubtedly. I was a veteran, I was skilled and equipped for the streets, and I was an O.G. now. I'd been banging for fifteen years, and most of my homeboys gave me my due respect, but as I looked into the mirror, I wondered was it all worth it? Was it worth the jail time? Was my reputation drenched in blood worth it? I never gave myself an answer and shrugged the thoughts away. I took one final look in the mirror and banged on myself, I extended my pinky finger and thumb. I looked at myself, and the gang sign that meant so much to me; I smiled. I knew then as I always knew for so long that I would remain a faithful and loyal member of the Neighborhood Rollin 20's Bloods. My destiny was to bang, to become ghetto fabulous, and I knew in the process more blood would be wasted on my journey.

CAN'T STOP – WON'T STOP
(1997)

Without any delays I quickly went about consolidating the entire neighborhood. I was briefed and updated about all the current activities. The latest money scheme, the foot soldiers were into, was the organized robbery of credit unions. The enemy situation was that we were lightly at war with the Harlem Crips, and seriously at war with the 18th Street gang; and we had two losses: Kay Kay from 25th Street, and another member named Ant-Dog from the BDS (Black Demon Soldiers Avenues). To make sure we were successful in our endeavors, and to bring some structure in our actions, I went about to establish the three things that ran governments: an economical system with all its echelons; a constitution of do's and don'ts, written or unwritten; and a military equipped with a chain of command, in our case Y.G.'s and O.G.'s.

Within three weeks, I had changed my neighborhood into a solid unified war machine with branches of intelligence gathering, double spies (usually females), credit union robbers, professional car thieves, cadres of assault troops, and workers who pushed crack to bring in a considerable amount of funds that kept everything functioning and running smoothly. We were almost ready. I made a hundred flyers and hit every location throughout the turf to invite everybody to a meeting scheduled on June 20, 1997 at 2:20 p.m.

When the meeting day arrived, I left the apartment early to ensure Sheila and myself enough time to cook all the food for the homies. We went about grilling chicken, hamburger patties, and hot links. Soon after, crews of soldiers started arriving, and before long, we were deep. Immediately I began barking orders. The soldiers who had straps (guns) on themselves were stationed in and around the park in strategic positions, and the sentries were expected to keep a watchful eye out for the rollers (police). At 2:20 p.m. I began my oration:

"I've been told there's a lot of jealousy going around throughout the hood. I've been told that some homies are jealous because others are having money due to their hard work, and others are looking for handouts, that's not fly. I've been told that homies are withholding their heats from other homies who are eager to put in work, but for the most part, they are strapless. I've been told that the Harlems and 18th Streets are waging a war against our republic without suffering due punishment our hood can issue out. Today is the day we will bring all this shit to ahead. My gun is your gun, and if any homey denies another homey his heat to put in some work, he will be disciplined, period. We are the Neighborhood 20's, and motha fuckers don't like us no way. If we don't respect ourselves and our turf, no one will. Each one of you represents the 20's, and it's your obligation and duty to represent it at all times. With a show of hands, how many of you want a gun?"

Hands from all around the crowd were raised, "I'm taking my hat off, and I want everybody to put what they can afford into the hat; the big homey K-Ray got a connection on straps, and the money we raise today will be taken to purchase guns. For all you Y.G.'s who want guns in defense and offense of the turf meet me here next week, and I'll be sure to bless each one of you with a heat. Before I end this meeting, does anybody have anything they want to add?" A few hands rose about homies doing stupid shit, some warranted discipline and others received verbal abuse about refraining and consequences. After we were finished, the energy of unity was flowing hard throughout the park.

When everyone was about doing their own thing, I took liberty to call some of the battle ready soldiers into a private meeting, and briefed them about my plans for a pre-emptive attack against the Smiley Drive 18th Street Cholo gang. We were presently winning our war against them with two casualties on our side, and three casualties and two wounded in action on their side. My homeboy Lil Flashback and Lil Krazy-Boy were facing the death penalty for those multiple and attempted murders. Tonight I planned to further tip the scale in our favor with the mission prepared at the first sign of nightfall. When the picnic came to an end, as the evening wind chill took its toll on the jacketless participants, I packed and bagged all the extra food and drinks, and headed toward my apartment. It was 8:45 p.m., and I had a scheduled meeting at nine o'clock on 64th Street and Normandie with the cadre of troopers who were specially selected for the impending mission.

At 9:00 p.m. sharp, everyone arrived. Bullets were cleaned, guns were wiped spotless of all fingerprints, and everyone was issued garden gloves, known to us as brownies. The briefing included routes of attack and escape, and the intended targets. Recon intelligence reported enemy sighting in and around the area of Hauser and Gear Avenue. We packed into two cars, both manned with two gunners each. I drove one of the cars with two of our up and rising ghetto stars looking to prove their allegiance by putting in some work against the biggest gang in the county. We drove through the back streets of the city heading deep west, all the time keeping a watchful eye out for any police cruisers. When we finally reached the Redondo and Adams area, the gunners knew to take all the heats off safety, and to prepare for the elimination of any 18th Street troopers. We drove past Redondo in silence looking and searching for any movement of enemy forces.

Enemy! Enemy! Enemy! My inner voice yelled out, a lone Cholo was spotted at a phone booth on our left hand side two blocks east of Hauser. The troopers in my car instinctively jacked rounds into their chambers without any commands. The seriousness of the mission was at hand, as I eyeballed our enemy target. I turned up Hauser heading deeper into their turf; at that point, any target in our path would have been suitable for elimination. I took another left turn down the first block looking to take advantage of the enemy who was slipping. We drove full circle and were now heading back toward Adams Boulevard. I pulled the car to a halt, and killed the lights, the second one pulled in behind me. The assault teams bounced from each car walking toward the soon to be dead 18th Street trooper. I watched, as the action was unfolding, and thought about the overkill I had orchestrated. The cadre was closing in; they were thirty seconds away from the target; the unknown enemy unaware of the imminent threat descending on him continued his conversation with a person who was fifteen seconds away from getting an ear full of automatic gunfire.

Just as the kill squad drew their weapons on their target, a C.R.A.S.H. unit (community resources against street hoodlums) came to a streaking halt directly in front of the Cholo whose life they'd just saved unknowingly. The assault team froze in their steps, and without delay, they u-turned and walked back to the cars to leave the area down the back streets. The next night we succeeded in our efforts, thus adding another victory in our war with the biggest gang in the city.

Baby Tray-K had also made some progress in locating a small credit union, suitable and structured just the way we liked them. I was briefed by a barrage of information relating to the bank; and an hour later, I knew about its weakness, its camera count, its location, and its strong points. A date was set for myself and the 211 crew (211, penal code for robbery) to take a first hand view of the credit union that was reported as an easy take over. True to Baby Tray-K's account, it would be like taking candy from a baby. We stayed on the scene for an hour looking for escape routes nearest the freeway, and checking the credit union perimeter for undisclosed cameras. A week later, we were ready; the squad was staying at my safe house with the orders to avoid any other neighborhood functions that could possibly get them into trouble.

Although when the day of the robbery arrived, we ran into a small problem. The homegirl who had been selected to drive one of the get away cars had chickened out at the last possible minute. I was in disbelief; maybe she was scared of money. We were four short hours away from our scheduled departure, and time wasn't on our side. I left the safe house at 5:30 a.m. that morning smashing as fast as I could through traffic without drawing too much attention to my erratic driving, and headed back to my apartment that I shared with Sheila to wake up my homegirl Mooky. My plan was to offer her a sizeable cut out of the credit union proceeds if she agreed to drive one of the get away cars.

I pulled into the driveway recklessly nearly colliding with the apartment wall. I had called prior to leaving the safe house, but nobody answered the phone. Maybe all girls slept hard as none of them obviously had heard the multiple phone rings. Mooky finally answered the door after the second round of my thunder knocking. "Blood let me talk to you." My words whisked passed her ear as I walked into the house waiting for her attention. "What's up, Loko?" – "Look dog", I began, "Lil Porky had a change of mind to go on the lick, and I wanted to know if you would be down to take her place for a decent cut?" Mooky was tall and of medium build, and in her eyes I could see I had assaulted her dedication: "On Bloods I'm down to drive the get away car". She spoke with conviction and allegiance to the turf. I asked her had she ever driven the Pasadena Freeway before. She hadn't, and we had three and a half hours until our due time with the credit union; we didn't have a second to waste.

The Pasadena Freeway has multiple twists and turns that could easily wreck havoc on an inexperienced driver. I wanted to nip that in the bud before it became a problem. I sat in the passenger's seat and gave Mooky instructions to head up Adams to the 110 Freeway north. We rode with light conversation mostly around the aspect of the robbery; without her knowledge, I was being judgmental about her driving, looking for her weak and strong points, but I quickly drew the conclusion that her driving was up to part. If she could handle the Pasadena Freeway, we were well on our way to getting paid, and we'd still be on schedule. When we finally arrived at the critical section of the freeway, she was calm I noticed, she held the speed in check, and most importantly to me, she used precaution around every bend in the road.

She was the one, and we were three hours away from our planned over running of the credit union. She drove the length of the freeway until its road expired. We jumped back on the 110 heading southbound and double-timed to save every possible valuable minute. We made it back to the safe house with a little over two hours to spare. The crew was already up, and I could tell they were empted. I consciously declined a marijuana stick that was passed to me; I wanted a clear mind, free from anything that could cloud my judgment. I also issued a stern warning that no more marijuana was to be smoked by anyone after 8:00 a.m. I went about to double check all the weapons, the brownies, the pillowcases that were designed to be moneybags, and the low-rider that was especially selected to be the car at the second location awaiting the ice chest that would be full of money. I didn't want no surprises or anything else that would delay or impede the robbery.

I knew from experience that the low-rider with a lone driver wouldn't attract any attention from the authority; the police cruisers that would be responding to the credit union robbery would be looking for a blue colored Cadillac, which belonged to one of my homeboys who had reported it stolen days prior to the robbery. This way he would be cleared of all charges that involved the robbery, when they finally located the car at the drop point abandoned. My homegirl Mooky was to drive the 211 crew out of the area in a moderate speed, using my car. Everything was in place, and time was ticking. I ventured back to the house, told the crew to get ready to roll out; and thirty minutes later, we were on the highway some odd minutes away from the credit union. Upon arrival, the low-rider and Mooky were placed into position at the drop point, and the 211 crew inside the Cadillac was placed just blocks away awaiting the order to move. My homeboy Termite and I rode in a different car and stationed ourselves in front of the intended target. Everybody was in place, one last double check, and the orders were given to take the bank down.

One by one, the crew entered into the building; I jumped back over the walkie-talkie and told the drop point crew to prepare for the homies' arrival. I watched the front door intently daring not to blink for fear of missing something. As quickly as they entered the building, they were now bee-lining back out the doors, jumping into the Cadillac's back interior, and were off and moving. Everything was going smoothly. They were in and out in no less than a minute and a half; it was like snatching a purse. We headed westbound following the 211 crew, but we kept a safe and secure distance, all the time keeping a watchful eye out for any signs of police cruisers that were sure to be in the area within the next couple of seconds.

We made a left, then another left; the crew bounced out of the police reported stolen car and placed the water filled ice chest into the passenger seat of the low-rider. Without wasting another second, they bounced into my car with Mooky at the wheel. When they were all safely inside, Mooky barked: "Everybody lay deep down in your seat with no heads showing". The crew responded, and seconds later, we were all on our way out of the immediate area. Just like clockwork, everything went according to plan. Mooky held her composure as I watched from the distance monitoring her driving speed. Once on the freeway she was told to make double time to get the crew out of the vicinity.

An hour later, we were at the safe house celebrating and loud talking each other about our success. My celebration was cut short, as I wanted to be alone. I went outside with a personal sack of marijuana to give myself a private party. I wanted to think and reflect on the success: We were presently winning our wars with all enemies, we raided one of the many credit unions on our list of takedowns, and the hood was unified as one and ready to deal with any problems that were neighborhood related.

After our celebration I was back to business as usual, meaning driving through the city, price shopping for the best deal on a half kilo of cocaine. My homeboy Delroy sold me eighteen ounces of crack for six thousand and eight hundred dollars, and at that price, I was winning by two thousand and two hundred dollars, as I would normally pay nine thousand for such an amount of crack. I sacked most of the dope into quarter ounces, half ounces, and zones (one ounce of crack priced at five hundred dollars) and took the other half to chop it down to the lowest price possible. I issued out retail sacks to any homeboy or homegirl who wanted to make some money, took a portion of the profits, and sent it to the numerous fallen soldiers who had become victims to life sentences. Every morning when I woke up, I'd write at least two homeboys a short letter with an enclosed money order and some recent photos.

With the neighborhood's noticeable progress, the local police began their increasing activities to shut me down. At every opportunity, they descended on me with their threats and harassments. But I had all my homeboys, homegirls, and crack smokers as my eyes and ears. Every trap the police laid for me, I avoided it completely. Every move they made, I counter moved. Every piece of information they found out about me, I countered by doing something different. The same informants they tried to use against me, I in turn used them against them. I paid well for accurate and reliable information, which always kept me a step or two ahead of my predators.

But the local police wasn't the only one who had been watching me; the Harpys were also interested in all the activities, and in the people coming and going from my apartment. The Cholo gangs throughout the L.A. County have this philosophy about it being imperative to make people pay them rent, if they're pushing or selling anything in their hood. Asians with local stores were their most prized victims, but they were trying to even make the black gangs pay in their own black neighborhoods. They might share the area with a black gang, but they felt their hood took precedent over the Blacks, which inevitably led to wars with many casualties. All throughout L.A. Mexican and black gangs, who had traditionally shared the same boundaries, were now at each other's throat battling and drawing up new borders.

That was about to be our problem one late night, as a couple Harpy Cholos decided they had seen enough activities around my apartment. It was probably two o'clock in the morning when they came to our door. I usually slept hard throughout the night as my daily activities took their toll on me; Sheila had had enough of the banging on the door and decided to answer it. Initially she tried to ignore it, but the knocking became unbearable. When she peeked through the peephole, she tried to make sense of what some Cholos were doing at the front door so early in the morning. She thought they wanted some dope, and since we didn't sell any drugs at the apartment where we rested, she opened the wooden door and inquired about their needs. One of them demanded to speak to the man of the house. Sheila, still thinking they wanted drugs, told them she was the man of the house, and again asked them what they wanted. She got the same answer. Immediately she knew that something was wrong with them.

The Rollin 20's had never had any problems with the Harpys before, but the younger ones, who weren't familiar with the friendly past between our neighborhoods, were well on their way to ruining any ties. Sheila shook me hard, and it took her awhile to bring me out from my dream world. "Baby, Baby, get up." It was the urgency in her voice that grabbed my attention. She quickly and thoroughly explained the Cholos' presence at the house. I exited from the bed and made a straight beeline toward the front door looking to see a familiar face, but I didn't know any of them.

"What's up?" I asked them, all the time looking for bulges in their waistlines. I didn't sense any tension, so I figured their visit was friendly in nature. "Can we talk to you", the leader of the two asked, but his voice sounded strained, and that's what alerted me; I decided to play it cool. He was giving me some history on the area on Adams, between Vermont and Hoover, and he claimed it was Harpys territory. He further explained to me they had been watching my homeboys and me, and they knew for a fact I was pushing crack from my apartment, and that I was in violation of their turf rules of not paying rent to them in order to continue my enterprise. He then went on to explain about some old Harpy graffiti that was in front of the apartment driveway, thus confirming his claim of the area being his turf.

After I had listened patiently to his Cholo bullshit, the first question I asked him was about his age. He was twenty-nine. "I'm the same age you are", I told him, "and I grew up around these same streets you claim as your turf. I'm from 29th Street and if you were to walk around the corner on Vermont and 29th Street, and look on the ground you will see my neighborhood engraved in the sidewalk." I was mad at myself. I should have never dropped my guard. But more than ever, I was mad at the Cholo who had indirectly downplayed my neighborhood as lesser to his.

I checked myself, and calmly explained to them that I had become cold, and that I was about to put some pants on. I walked back to the apartment and, not until I had closed the wooden door behind me, did I allow my facial strain to show. I was furious. I went into the second bedroom and woke up Baby Insane and B-Brazy, who always accompanied me. I briefed them about of what had just occurred, and what my plans were at that moment in dealing with them. In seconds, we were all in killing mode.

I grabbed my 9-millimeter off the dresser drawer and checked the brand new infrared that I had just purchased from the Hawthorne swap meet, before I gave it to Baby Insane who wasn't heated. Both got the firm order not to shoot, but to put the red light specials on the Cholos as soon as we walked back outside. I just wanted to show them they had fucked up. After I gave myself the once over, we bee lined out the front door down the driveway. The Cholos automatically tensed up and the second I opened my mouth, the red beams dotted their shirts.

"Let me explain something to ya'll. My name is Gangsta Loko and I'm an O.G. from the West Side 20's, and ya'll got me fucked up and my hood. I would have ya'll capped right here on the spot, but I'm gonna keep it gangster. I'm gonna gather all my homeboys from my hood and ya'll do the same, and we can meet up at Hoover Park." I pointed to the one who had done most of the talking, and told him to meet at 3:00 p.m. Saturday evening.

After my speech Sheila lost her cool, she bounced in the Cholos faces with threats of harm for them coming to our apartment. "Motha fucka we got kids in there." She followed them up the block lashing out her anger and venom. The Cholos were now weary desired to get away from the woman who they had enraged with their bullshit. Later that morning sleep was far and evasive; I was restless, so I kept one ear to the air listening for any signs or sounds of enemy movement in my driveway, before I finally fall asleep sometime in the early morning.

When I woke up somewhere around nine o'clock, I bounced out of bed without delay, as I knew I had to rally the troopers for the date with the Cholos. With B-Brazy and Baby Insane, I was sliding up Adams looking for any other early birds. As soon as we reached LaSalle, we ran into a cadre of morning workers. They knew from my expression and the way we exited the car that something was amiss. With all the acting of my theatrics, I detailed the events that happened. Soon word had spread throughout the republic, and members from all the clicks showed up, they were ready to rally around the war cry. At 2:30 p.m., we were more than deep enough to take up battle lines.

When we arrived at the park some twenty minutes early, we positioned ourselves and waited. Three o'clock arrived, and passed; four o'clock arrived, and passed. Maybe they realized they were wrong and decided to leave things alone. When five o'clock arrived, and passed, we decided to visit the Cholo who did the main talking. We headed toward our destination traveling at high and dangerous speeds. When the numerous cars pulled in front of the apartment complex, the people out-front began to hurry along for fear of what the black gangsters were about to do. We bee lined up the driveway and some of the Hispanic residents began closing their doors out of fear.

The apartment I was looking for was in the back to the right. As I neared the front door, I noticed that it was slightly ajar. I looked inside and after seeing no one in particular, I banged on it. A Hispanic lady materialized out from one of the rear rooms with a surprised look on her face speaking her silent fear. Without delay, and to relieve the poor lady of our presence, I asked for her son. "Manual not here," she responded. "Do you know where he's at?" She quickly replied with a stern "No". "When you see him, tell him Loko came by".

I thought maybe that would be the last of our run-in's with the Harpys, but a week later another incident of serious nature occurred that quickly took our misunderstandings with each other to the level of a possible war. The 39th Street Harpys had crossed some of our graffiti out on a wall located on Adams Boulevard. To the average citizen spray painting the walls may be nothing more than a menace to the city's appearance; but to all gangs in L.A. it was just as imperative and natural as a lion, or a dog marking its territory with its scent and for somebody to venture into that claimed area was nothing short of war.

When I finally drove past the location of where the wall banging had occurred, I was beyond myself. I was the kind of person who took anything that anyone did against my neighborhood serious; they unknowingly committed one of the gravest crimes, which was equal to the death of one of my fallen comrades. They disrespected me, they disrespected my dead homies, and they disrespected our entire history as a neighborhood serious; it's almost like a flag burning of a country's national symbol.

I took a cadre of troopers in my car with Sheila, and drove to the liquor store on 23rd and Hoover, I knew the Harpys claimed that area as theirs undisputedly, and I intended to take my plan of disrespect to the heart of their turf. After Sheila dropped us off at the store, I bought spray cans of paint and each trooper his own 40oz bottle of Ole' English 800. Within thirty minutes, everybody was buzzing off their consumption of the highly intoxicating liquor. The troopers who had the heats were given orders to take them off safety as violence could arise sooner than later, before Lil Bear and Big Tippy-C.K. who were some of our best wall bangers made a statement to the Harpys on the back streets of their turf where their graffiti was mostly visible. After we had finished, a wall banging war erupted between our neighborhoods on a scale that was unprecedented.

Since things became more serious after each event, my O.G. homeboy Strawberry and I decided that we should put one last effort to avert a war with the Harpys. A meeting was called, and we agreed to migrate in vast numbers to Hoover Park, only this time with an offer of peace. When we arrived at the park, there were only two Harpys present. Strawberry and I advised the troopers to post up while we went and tried to broker a last minute peace treaty. Minutes into our conversation with the Cholos, I knew we were going to have some problems. The shorter of the two repeatedly ignored our offer, and consistently threw his neighborhood gang sign into our faces with the intention of showing his contempt and regards toward us. The other Cholo was giving us some light conversation about some things that were irrelevant. I had lost my patience with both, and so did Strawberry.

Before the shorter Cholo had the chance to withdraw his hands, Strawberry slugged him with an overhand right. The punch was so powerful and accurate that his eye split wide open. Whereas the other one wasn't even left the opportunity to react fully to what had happened because I was on him like some flies on some shit, hitting him with so many well connected blows that I hadn't realize the damage I'd done until his body lay next to his fallen comrade. Strawberry was furious, and as we walked away from the beaten up Mexicans, he screamed out our official declaration of war, "Now we at war, motha fucka's!" Without any delay, carloads of 20's covered our entire republic with the news. Everywhere throughout the turf, soldiers were placed on the highest alert status. We figured the Harpys would retaliate for the beat downs, but when and where was the mystery.

THE BEEF
(1997-1998)

That night the Harpys put all our contemplations to rest when they launched a military attack against B-Brazy's and Termite's shared apartment on 23rd Street by blasting multiple holes through the front door and windows, lucky no one was home. But retaliation on our part was mandatory, so we counter-attacked the next night by hitting them on 29th and Budlong. Big Snipe and Lil Snipe ambushed a cadre of them, who had been hanging out in front of the apartment complex on the north corner, and instead of waiting for a reply that was sure to come, we decided to strike at them again. As the bullets intensified the battlefront on Adams and Normandie, we knew we were well on our way to drawing some new borderlines conceding everything east of Vermont to the Harpys, and everything west of Vermont to us.

The next night the Harpys struck back at one of our strong holds on 29th and Van-Buren, but we were prepared. Baby Boo, Yogi, G-Boy, and Solo were posted and waiting, and in return to the heavy fire they received, they responded by serving the Harpys with their 45 and 9-millimeter automatics. The war was progressing, and the gunplay went back and forth with neither side gaining no real victories. I was prepared to lead my neighborhood with the manpower of all our clicks into an all out blood bath against the Harpys. I had even worked out an agreement with G-Shitty from the Black P. Stone Bloods about him and his click (the City Stones) participating, if things went from bad to worse. The City Stones were one of our closest allies, and we were already waging wars together against many other neighborhoods: the 18th Street, the Barrio Saint Andrews, the Mid City Stoners, and the West Boulevard Crips, and if the Harpys wanted to join this list then we had no problem of bringing them their hats.

Before the war really escalated out of control to levels that were considerate irreparable, I received a page from my homeboy Rocky. When I finally called him about ten minutes later, I couldn't believe the things I was hearing. He was telling me that a delegate of Harpys was at his house at that very moment, and they wanted to draw up some agreements with me based around peace. 'Ain't that about a bitch', I thought to myself. I felt really good about the peace offering, no, I'm not saying that I wanted to stop the war, or continue it either; but I felt good because they had come to us, and not the other way around. As silly as it may have sounded, but I took their offer as a victory for myself, and our neighborhood.

When I headed toward Rocky's house, I was all the time thinking about what issues I wanted to push on their delegation. As soon as I made my left turn onto 22nd Street, I touched the 9-millimeter in my waistband and made my beeline toward the delegation, which was three deep, as well as ours. Strawberry sat on the porch looking in my direction with this big ass cool-aid smile, and I knew without a doubt, he felt the way I felt. The Harpys wanted peace before anybody was to be murdered. They wanted to take our understandings back to the way it was prior to the war. The speaker went on about families being in the area, and that peace would be best for both sides.

After he finished, I asked him his name: "I'm Oso, and I'm from the 39th Street click of the Harpys", he replied. I informed him who I was, and explained to him that, since his homeboys were the main factors in our escalation of disrespect, my neighborhood would only agree to terms of peace through a final showdown between his and my wall banging homies at Hoover Park to let the youngsters rip into each other. I waited for his reply, but in my mind, I knew my offer of one last battle would be outright declined. I figured they were only offering peace to us because we had an advantage over them and their military personnel. By no means are the Harpys a small gang, they have clicks all the way in the Valley, not to mention their clicks that share a lot of the same areas as we do, but I'm assuming they would be spreading their forces too thin if they took us on.

When Oso finally agreed to the terms that we were to meet the next day to have the wall bangers from both sides to get down, and regardless of the wins and losses that nobody was allowed to get angry, I nearly gave away my pleasure by smiling. We shook hands and they departed. I shared a few more words of excitement with Rocky and Strawberry, before I went to prepare the republic's frontline soldiers for a last and final pitched battle against the Harpys. It was reassuring that our allies, the Black P. Stones assisted us greatly, as G-Shitty and a cadre of his finest troopers gave allegiance and support, they would be at Hoover Park with the biggest weapons in their arsenal.

When I finally walked through the door that night, Sheila was sitting on the coach with worries written all over her face. I plopped next to her and ran my tongue along her neck. From years of being together, I knew every one of her weaknesses, and I knew my warm tongue caressing her neck would sooner or later bring her sexual arousal to a level uncontrollable. My intention was to make love to her thus wiping away her worries of my activities of late. Some hours later Sheila was sleeping peacefully, but it was a problem of mine. I sat in bed thinking about all the possible outcomes in our scheduled battle session. After I went over a mental list of guns that were to be available with the result that our firepower was overwhelming, I got finally some sleep.

The next day I felt like I'd taken a whole bottle of Viagra, as I was hard up for any confrontation. It was 9:30 a.m. I woke Sheila from her somber sleep, and we headed to the local swap meet on 10th Avenue and Washington to buy ourselves some clothes for the event. After our shopping, we ate some chili cheese fries for breakfast and played a couple video games, before we headed toward our shared park with the City Stones. As we pulled up, I noticed only fragments of troopers scattered throughout the park already drinking some hard liquor that was considered their breakfast.

I kicked my day off with spray-painting the nearby park walls with my neighborhood multiple clicks, then I turned the can over to a Y.G. who ventured across the street and began striking on a freshly painted wall, making somebody's effort to keep it clean worthless. After I had enough of watching the youngster, I reached into my '93 sky-blue Thunderbird and blasted the tunes of D.J. Quik *Safe and Sound*. By eleven o'clock cadres of 20's were arriving and reporting their call to duty; by noon we were super deep, and before long the park was filled with hardcore gangsters. It was time for me to make sure everybody brought the guns and put them in the trunk of my car. Sheila was going to take the freeway thus avoiding the police cruisers whereas the republic's army and I caravanned with approximately fifteen to twenty cars deep straight up Adams Boulevard to our destination, Hoover Park. If the police C.R.A.S.H. units had been out in the area, for sure they would have had a ball in picking and choosing which car to pull over. Maybe they were keeping a safe distance probably with the hopes that we would annihilate each other; during our confrontation with the Harpys, the police hadn't made any arrests or any serious enquiries about any of the multiple gun battles that we had been waging against each other.

Our caravan arrived at Hoover Park unmolested, and as soon as I pulled up on one of the side streets by the park, I noticed something that disturbed me: The Cholos were totally and completely outnumbered by our forces. I kept thinking to myself they were probably keeping their troopers hidden to distort their real strength at hand, but as each car emptied its contents of our hard-core members, I stopped worrying about it.

I soon took pleasure in the sight of seeing the worries on their faces as their eyes took in the full account of the wrath we came to bring at my command. After inspecting the perimeter, I trotted into the park, scouting for any signs of the police. I began my command of the situation by addressing Oso and asked him the whereabouts of his homies who had crossed my hood out. He turned and called out some names, and within seconds, they had marched out from their rank and file to the front. I was satisfied that they were there as I had ever intention to pick some of our best fighters. This is no bullshit, but when I turned around to pick them, my homeboys were acting like school kids with their hands raised begging to be the one to fight for our turf. As I chose the best we had, some of the Cholos even had the look on their faces of "I can't wait to get this shit over with".

In the meantime, more Cholos had arrived. Some came by bicycles, others were walking up, and some even pulled up in low riders with the Mexican national flag painted on the hood of their cars. It wasn't too much to worry about, as we still had them greatly outnumbered. The troopers from both camps walked over to the selected area that was to be the combatant's arena. They squared off and the battles began, the combatants were locking hard giving their best efforts. I watched on with the skillful and trained eyes of a general who was already assessing the wins and losses. Without any doubt, we were on our way to a land sliding victory.

I wanted our troopers to prepare for the emotional outburst from the Cholos' side of the camp at the loss they were about to endure, and I told Sheila and the other few homegirls to leave the park for fear of a possible gun battle. True to human nature, as soon as the fights ended with us having a complete victory, one of the Cholos pulled some type of gun out from the shelter of his violin case he had been holding. He cocked it and began screaming aloud: "Fuck that! Fuck that shit! Fuck that shit!"

Every single homeboy of mine who had a heat in their waistband drew it, and just that fast we were inches away from a total blood bath. Oso, fearing for the worst-case scenario, jumped into his homeboy's face and told him it was over, and that was it. The unknown Cholo was steaming, but Oso held his grounds until he was certain his homeboy would back down from the imminent devastation they would endure, if they collided with us. Just when the Cholo had calmed himself and regained his composure, the entire park erupted with my homeboys screaming out our republic's chant call, "West Side, West Side Neighborhood, West Side Neighborhood!" That day we ended our beef with the Harpys on our terms; we played the game of challenges all the way to its end, and we won.

But 1998 wasn't all success and valor for me and the republic. Cadres of troopers were arrested on various charges, and we were feeling the impact; the local police department had labeled me their public enemy No. 1, as they tried everything from endless harassments, to paying people to accuse me of serious crimes in nature. They even spread rumors throughout the republic that I'd raped a teenage girl, something they knew would be unpopular in the gang world; they also arrested me for the murder of a Rollin 60's, but it was rejected in the courts, as there wasn't any evidence against me. They plotted on me at every chanced opportunity, and they unsuccessfully sweated and harassed my parole officer to violate me on some charges that were totally ungrounded. Every amateur attempt they launched against me to have me locked away, only made me more determined. Their actions didn't hamper my spirit; actually, it made me wiser to the vices and schemes that they used against people who they didn't like.

Soon I was so paranoid with precautions; I took into account every detail I needed to do to guarantee that everything would go smoothly. I was literally playing a cat and mouse game with them, and I had the advantage. I had the entire republic on my side. When they sweated me for driving around without a license, I countered by hiring a smoker chauffeur who I paid with crack cocaine. When they started making it difficult for me to move my dope to the selling location, I countered by hiring two human mules who would transport them for me for a small payment of cocaine. When they started taking all my homeboys and homegirls off the streets, making it hard for me to push my crack, thus breaking up my infrastructure, I counter moved by hiring myself ten dedicated workers who themselves were crack smokers, and who were paid with half the dope they were issued. When they started going after Sheila giving unnecessary tickets, threatening her life with violence, I countered by using their own against them. I stayed on the phone day and night with the internal affairs office, complaining about the southwest police corruptness; it wasn't all in vein either as I had three of the C.R.A.S.H. officers suspended for their over zealous attacks against us.

Soon I was under investigation for any and everything that occurred within the Rollin 20's territory. I was hot, and I had to try something different. I enrolled myself into school again; I went back to Trade Tech City College taking up construction, hoping to give myself a break from the streets, and to evade the all-seeing eyes of the police officers who had it out for me. I attended the college for approximately three weeks before they were finally successful in getting me a parole violation for a charge of hit and run against a sergeant police officer. My parole officer eventually gave in to their constant harassment just to get them off her back. Although they had succeeded in getting me off the streets temporarily, they unknowingly had created a monster that was now more possessed on out doing and out smarting them at every possible chance. In my one-year confinement in prison, I was gearing myself mentally and physically to win the war against them and the Harlems, and to win by all means necessary, I was going to succeed.

A Time of Reflection
(1998-1999)

There I sat in the grassiest area on the baseball field doing what I always did, I was taking my one year parole violation serious and as a time of reflecting and fore sighting on my impending parole date. Day and night, I sought out my seclusion, looking to take advantage of every opportunity that allowed me to travel in my mental depth: visualizing, acting, re-playing, and repeating out the reality that would be re-lived at the first chance given. Most of the thoughts were thoughts of my impending criminal activities, which were never changed, as I already knew with certainty what I wanted to do upon release.

Hours and hours of work were spent in my dream world living out the life as a jacker. I thought about tactics, emergency plans, and entrapment schemes that would ensnare potential victims. My mind took me to places I never visited before, and it rewarded me with money amounts that I never knew was possible. Upon my release, I wanted to make a statement to any and everybody who had counted me out as targeted and marked for failure. I wanted to be the boxer who took a beaten from my opponent all through the fight, but when it was time for me to knock him out, I would serve him with my vicious and well calculated maneuvers. On a daily basis, I sought out information from other gangsters who had lived the life of a jacker, or more importantly, who were still into jacking. I was gearing myself to be the ultimate jacker.

When I wasn't in my mental solitude, I was kicking it with my homeboy Big Mark in the kitchen at work. From the moment I arrived at Chino West (a parole violators housing location) Big Mark pulled some strings for me, and immediately thereafter, I was pulled in for work. We worked the morning shift that started at three o'clock. I was assigned to cleaning pots, pans, and dinner plates. Whereas to most inmates this was a job totally disliked, to me it was challenging in a deeper sense. I'm an optimist and I look for the good and benefits in everything. I worked with such vigor that most of the times I would be so caught up in my mind challenging obstacles that the day would soon be over. Immediately after work, I would be back at the task of trying to master the science of jacking.

My stay at Chino West would last indefinitely up until I was seen by my counselor, who was to make the recommendation on where I should be sent to finish up my parole violation. It was all a hurry up and wait game. Most of the counselors were lazy thus adding and making the stay at a particular location that much longer. Three months had passed since I had arrived, and I was growing tired of being there. I tried writing to the counselor to hurry up the process, I tried switching counselors to one who had a reputation for doing speedy processing; I even tried complaining to the counselor's supervisor about my lengthy stay. All around me, men were leaving to their next destinations, heading to where they were to finish the remainder of their time in a more pleasant environment.

I kept to myself after awhile, as everyone who I had a slight relationship with was gone. Big Mark paroled about a month after I had arrived; Slick from 6-Duse-Brim Bloods had left already, and my homeboy Tiny Loko was up to transfer as he had packed his property leaving on the first bus smoking Monday morning. Some two weeks after his departure, I finally received a ducat, which notified me that I had a scheduled appointment with my counselor. I was in high spirits, as I was happy and more then ready to get the process out the way. But the moment I walked through the door, and laid eyes on her, we gave each other a real chemical reaction. Right away, I knew she didn't like me: Her facial expression, her body posture, and the way she eye fucked me, told me that she was anything but friendly.

"Have a seat, Mr. Wright." She even spoke my name with a dryness that made it sound like a profanity word. Immediately she started complaining about my prison record, and that she felt I should be in solitary confinement due to my violent past. Here was a lady chastising me about something that wasn't even close to the truth. I knew she was basing her opinion around my past mistreatments of being housed in the segregated units, and I also knew her opinion lacked in substance. Out of the four years of my coming back and forth to the prison, I only had three write-ups for disruptive behavior and of those three only one was serious. Seven years had passed since I received my last write-up, and it was for a minor infraction of disobeying an order.

"What do you mean I need to be placed in solitary confinement?" I was in a mood for a mental challenge, and she was the perfect person with her dogmatic thoughts against me. "I believe you need to be placed back in the hole based on your disruptive past", she replied. "What disruptive past?" I bellowed with authority. "Show me in my prison file where you're basing your accusation of me being a dangerous and violent inmate." She took the challenge right away and began flipping through my file looking for evidence to validate her claim against me. I waited and looked upon her with contempt and a lack of respect. I've never been one to judge a book by its cover, but this lady deserved every bit of humiliation I was about to dish out to her.

She flipped through my file one last time, and looked up suddenly, "I'm not going to process your paperwork, as a matter of fact I'm sending this over to my supervisor for evaluation." She was steaming, and I knew I had defeated her; but I wasn't about to let her off the hook that easy, as I wanted to rub it in. "What's your reason for not wanting to process my paperwork?" I spoke with a tone of delight, and she knew I was rubbing it in her face. "Mr. Wright, you can leave now, your business is finished here!" She was angry, and her face turned stark red with hate toward a person who she knew little about. I stood slowly, drawing out my departure knowing my mere presence alone was irritating her in ways worse than a physical assault would. I gave her one final smile and bee lined out the front door with the soothing thought of climbing into my bed to meditate the day away. I was never again summoned by her.

Another month passed, and finally I was issued my transpacking ducat to prepare myself for my transfer to an unknown location. I examined the ducat pass, as if it was a piece of paper worth a million dollars; it didn't give me any indication of where I was heading, it was strictly notifying me to pack all my belongings as my number to leave had finally been called. The very next morning I hustled out the dorm quarters to turn my property in at R&R with another dozen inmates heading to Avenal State Prison, as I soon found out, a minimum level II institution that had a terrible reputation of being the home of snitches. Avenal wasn't referred by its name when spoken of, as inmates called it 'tell it all'. The day before my leaving Chino West, I was bombarded by a host of do's and don'ts. Most of the information and precautions were already known facts to me. I literally practiced an old prison adage: "Walk slowly and drink plenty of water". In translation it was telling me, if I walked slowly I would avoid a lot of bullshit, and if I drunk plenty of water I wouldn't be putting myself into a lot of bullshit.

My prison points had totaled to twenty-six. Initially I couldn't believe that I was a level II (due to my point range), as I had spent so many of my years in level III's and IV's. And I didn't know for certain, if I was cut out to be in a level II; a place undoubtedly petty, a place that harbored snitches by the busload, and a place where correctional officers probably disrespected the inmates at random and daily. The next day inside R&R, we were hurried through the mandatory strip search routine: crack your ass, bend over, and cough. We were all issued a yellow paper made jumpsuit that fit more like a bodysuit, and one after another, our names were called off in alphabetic order: "Thomas, last two numbers?" – "Valasques, last two numbers?" Each inmate gave their last two numbers on their prison numbers, which identified us instead of our real names. "Wright, last two numbers?" – "6-0", I responded dashing toward the comfort of the bus. It was three o'clock in the morning, and the wind chill was anything but friendly. I entered the bus and bee lined toward the back portion to the only seat that was left vacant. Some twenty odd minutes later, we were coast bound heading to Avenal.

Once arriving I gave myself some stern rules on my behavior conduct. Avenal was a penitentiary nothing like I've ever experienced. It was wide open and loose, literally. In all the level III's and IV's I've visited, the environment was totally strict and laced with multi-tiered of rules and regulations of what a convict should and shouldn't do. But in Avenal things like rules and regulations were of foreign origins and nearly non-existent. I knew it was going to take a conscious effort to keep my past military training and discipline in effect, as this environment made it easy for anybody to drop their guards. After the typical orientation process, I was shipped off to yard 2, known as the gang bangers yard, and where the fuck-ups were sent. This was somewhat reassuring to me, as I didn't want to end up on some soft yard which reputation preceded it. It was already bad enough that Avenal had a larger than life stigma, not to mention some of its soft yards.

I was housed in building No. 230, and my homeboy Shorty Kapone was already awaiting me. The prison grapevine traveled fast, and before you realized it, everybody knew about your arrival, and was expecting you. It had been two years since me and Shorty Kapone had kicked it. The last I'd heard about him was he had been sentenced to fifteen years with eighty percent for a drive-by that I had orchestrated. After about an hour of conversating, I realized that he had changed from the little boy image I last recalled. He had evolved while traveling down the same road that so many men had traveled on their journeys in the many California prisons.

The first sure signs of his changing ways were his overwhelming aggression toward the K-9's who he referred to as 'The Beast'. Another evolving phase was his reference to black women as 'sisters', and not as 'bitches'. But the one thing that broke the camel's back was his deep desire to change the entire neighborhood from its self-destructive course once he was released. I was lost for words most of the times, when he went on one of his heart convincing speeches; I knew what he was going through, as I had traveled the same exact road. It's something like what each president of the United States goes through upon entering the White House. They become lost in the theoretical notion that they are the chosen one who will be successful in wiping away the country's poverty, alleviating the high crime rates, and building an America where everyone can receive a piece of the American pie. Bullshit! But it wasn't for me to pour water on Shorty's endeavor, as I knew sooner or later the realm of reality would slap the common sense back into him demonstrating that he would be fighting an up-hill and losing battle with no for sure victories in sight.

Shortly after my arrival, he was rolled up and sent to the hole for being too over zealous toward a sergeant who he felt was a racist. That was the last time I had seen my little homey, as rumors had it that he had been shipped off to a level III institution. After his departure, I was gearing myself to become a jacker. I was self-possessed on my hang-up of going home and jacking ballers for all their hard-earned cash and drugs. There was only one for sure and quick way to join the status, and that was to take what the ballers had. With my mental comfort zone and my gangster mentality, it would be like taking candy from a baby; and there was nothing that could change my mind on my near future quest.

Some two months after being in Avenal, I was assigned a job in the kitchen as a line server. The kitchen's free cook supervisor was a black lady named Ms. Vee; and she was one of those black women who would recite a biblical verse and curse you out all in the same breath. If she wasn't cursing out one of the kitchen workers, more than likely she could be found in one of the inmate's ears complaining about her cheating and no good husband. Ms. Vee was somewhere in her late fifties, and she was like the hyper grandma who lived her life through all the kitchen workers. But when it came to her relationship with the correctional officers, she had this pet peeve about them venturing into the kitchen and taking our food. She strongly pushed the rule of the food being for us and not for the C/O's; and she had no problem telling them to bring their own food to work, as they made enough money.

It was around this same time when Sheila and I began having our misunderstanding with each other. I would send her letter after letter with no reply in return; unknowingly to me she had abandoned ship on me and found love elsewhere. I tried to take it all in stride, and shrug it off as a passing moment in my life, but as the months came and went, I learned hard that the stalk reality of her leaving me for dead was as real as it could ever be. I set myself into a rigorous program that helped block out any unnecessary thoughts of her and my crumbling life. Day and night until bedtime, I occupied myself with things to do not giving myself a second of thought of anything that could wreck havoc on my state of mind. Most of my avoidance of the outside world came from being at work. The kitchen was my stress releaser, my heaven. Ms. Vee had promoted me to a cook position, and from that day all hell was about to break loose.

Immediately I began my monopolizing of the black market and lucrative food trade that the kitchen provided and made possible. Every taken food item was traded and converted over into the highly desirable payment of regular food from the prison commissary. A piece of chicken at the prison's expense was equaled to trade of two commissary noodles; a rack of cookies or a glove full of sugar was equaled to five commissary noodles; and prison sweets were equaled in value to their demands on the black market. Literally, everything in the kitchen that wasn't tacked down had a value on it and was a part of my vast empire. All the players prior to me, who had their hands in the trade, were outmaneuvered and placed on a lower level of the totem pole that I'd created with the utmost vigor. Most of the weaklings, who lacked in real skills, were weeded out and dropped by the wayside due to my aggressive nature of overtaking the trade. With each passing day of my hustling, my prison locker was soon unable to maintain the constant flow of goods.

I was pushing over two hundred pieces of chicken, boxes and boxes of cookies of all assortments, cans of jelly and peanut butter, and soon enough everyone in the kitchen was working for me. They stole anything they could find and sold it to me with the promise that I'll pay them as soon as work was over. From anything I purchased from someone in the kitchen, I was sure to know that I'd make my money back, plus profits and extras. The main important reason most of the kitchen workers sold me items at discount prices was that I was the only one who had the means of moving so much stuff out under the nose of so many correctional officers who tried in vain to stop the vast booming black market.

Every single day the prison office clerks came to the kitchen to get ice for the staff in their large orange colored ice chests; and every single day before they arrived at the expected time, I would already have all my goodies pre-wrapped and ready for shipment. Therefore, when they entered the kitchen, all my merchandise would be stuffed into the bottom. A large plastic bag was then placed atop, and then filled to capacity with ice. I was the big business on the block, and I had the means, resources and goods monopolized completely.

When Ms. Vee caught wind of my enterprise and its multi level of players, she tried in vain to intervene, but it was too late. With over fifteen kitchen workers stealing any and everything possible, it made her task of watching everyone at best impossible. I reigned supreme over everything in the kitchen; nothing moved out unless it went through me for my expected cut. Once Ms. Vee found out the intricate infrastructure I had established, she immediately threw it into the faces of the other workers that I was the smart one and they were all being pimped by me. But regardless of all her rant and raving, the operation went on unabated. The kitchen proceeds carried me all the way until my parole date, and it provided me with the things I needed after Sheila had abandoned me.

The weekend nights at Avenal were the most memorable for me because the gamblers of the building would find a space in one of the corners in the dorm, and the monopoly-stolen dice would role thus setting off a long night of betting. It's very few things that send black men into an adrenalin rush, but without a doubt, shooting dice is one of them. Besides me, Big Spung from the Harlem Crips was one of the biggest gamblers who actively participated, and we soon established a friendship. He was a frontline soldier, a five star general, and most who knew him respected him.

Then there was Little A.C. from the 39th Street Harlems. He was a happy person who reminded me of the Pills Bury Dough Boy, and he had a habit of playing games all the time. At every possible chance, he would drill me for hours to talk gang talk with him. He loved being in my presence, and actually I enjoyed his company. We passed a lot of time together, and one of his favorite games was our challenging tactics of playing Stratego. I grew up playing that game and once I taught A.C. how to play it, it soon became a daily ritual of military skills being put to the test. In hindsight it was kind of weird, he was a Harlem 30 and I was a Neighborhood 20, we were sworn enemies to each others republic, and there we were playing a military game where there could only be one winner and a for sure loser. I guess that was one of life's little curve balls that weren't meant to be understood.

My time in Avenal was coming to an end, as I was preparing for my departure back into the world. I was placed on S-status, which means I was thirty days or less to paroling. Thereafter, every morning I would faithfully hit the monkey and dip bars working on building my muscles and strength. My workout partner was E-Mac from the Marvin Gangster Crips whose turf is in the deep west side of Los Angeles. Every morning we pushed each other to the brink of collapsing. By now I had given up on Sheila coming back into my life, actually I was content with her maneuver of ditching me. I was coming home a free man, womanless and unlike 1993 when I was frighten to that aspect, I was eagerly looking forward to going after all the girls that Sheila knew wanted me. I was going to have a ball, and I was fifteen short days away from setting all my plans into motion.

When the morning of October 23, 1999 rolled around, I had to do all I could from preventing myself from running to R&R. I was ready to go, as I was empted up on the mental high I had been feeding myself. My family had sent me my dress outs (parole clothes). When I rode the Greyhound bus in deep thought, I relived all my mental endeavors, and visualized all the activities that I had dreamed about for so many days. I was ready and focused. Whenever the bus made its scheduled pit stops at designated locations in route, I dropped coins into the nearest phone dialing Sheila's number looking to talk to her, so I could lash out for my months of her cruel treatment. She was playing a game with me, as every time I called, my homegirl Samantha answered the phone denying any knowledge of Sheila's whereabouts. For every time I called and received some bullshit reply from her, I was becoming more bent on revenge and retaliatory acts against Sheila and anyone else who had betrayed me and counted me out as through.

MOSES
(1999-2000)

When I arrived at the L.A. bus terminal sometime in the evening, I had plenty of time to go somewhere, find a female friend and blow a sack of weed. I decided to ride the city's transportation to my destination thus saving myself some money. Two hours later, I was dropped off at Adams and Normandie. It felt good to be back in the grips of my neighborhood. I walked the short distance to the local gas station, bought some chocolate blunts and headed south up Normandie toward 27th Street to Mignon's house. Mignon was my homey, lover, and friend, and I knew all the stress that was boiling within me would be cleansed from my being after spending some quality time with her.

Later that same night I contemplated my list of things to do: I had to report to my parole officer within forty-eight hours; I had to make contacts with the people who were relevant to my endeavors; and I had to go and visit my mother. Mignon shuffled in my arms thus breaking my train of thought. In seconds we tore back into each other for our own personal reasons, she, maybe because she had really missed my loving and my person, but I for the reason for wanting to wash myself clean of anything based around Sheila. Mignon was helping me to drive away all my insecurities, to sooth my bruised ego, to alleviate my mental dependency upon Sheila, and to satisfy many months of longing to be with a woman in every possible way.

When I was for certain that she was fast asleep, I quietly got dressed and made a Houdini exit out of the front door vanishing into the night. I had too much on my mind to sleep, so I figured I'd go out and see who I might happen upon in the vast republic. The moment I began on my expedition, an unnerving fright overtook my mental comfort. It was as if shadowy figures of times past began an all out attack on my imagination; the neighborhood that gave me a sense of wholesomeness now seemed different in the cold of darkness that blanketed the entire night. Before I realized it, I was in a full-scale run bee lining up 27th toward Raymond. Being paranoid has always been one of my survival skills that I used faithfully; it made me continuously think of all the 'what if's' out there, but I was beyond myself as the cloak of darkness somehow irritated me.

As I rounded the corner of Raymond, I halted my run and fell in a fast pace walk.

Maybe I was being over reactive I rationalized; maybe it was the marijuana I had smoked earlier, as some marijuana did make me paranoid. Whatever the hell it was, it was convincing me to run again and before long, I was back into a full gallop bee lining up Raymond. In fact, I was so into my run this time I sprinted right passed some of my homeboys and homegirls who were standing on the sidewalk. I couldn't help but think how badly they were slipping. I could have been an enemy trooper sent on a seek-and-destroy mission, and if I were, I would have scored multiple enemy deaths as all of them had their guards down. I locked eyes with more than one of them, and they looked upon me as if they had seen a ghost. By the time, my facial recognition kicked in, and they realized it was me; I was already completely out of earshot.

I ended up at my mother's house later that night, and it was from there my entire life and death plot and planning would be blue printed. Terrey and Shavon woke me the next morning with their loud laughter and playing, as they both were all over me. It was evident they had missed their father, and the moment they realized I was awake, they climbed into bed with me. We snuggled for most of the morning, and after the large breakfast my mother had cooked up, I remained on the phone for the better part of the day, reconnecting myself with the right people who were going to help me reach the immediate goals I had set out for myself. Sheila had dropped off some of my clothing at my mother's house, and from what I had to work with I wasn't too impressed. I was going to need another wardrobe, but more important to get my own apartment. In days passed I was successful in reconnecting myself with the appropriate people as I was now sitting on a hundred-forty grams of crack cocaine, a pound of marijuana and a thirteen shot 9-millimeter Beretta. The only obstacle I had was on a location where I could push it from.

I was back in the neighborhood and dealing with all the vices and treachery, it had in store for me. After the tedious work of sacking all the dope and marijuana into their individually wrapped packages, I went to seek out a goldmine location that was already established and run over with a vast clientele. It didn't take me long to find what I was looking for as I soon located the biggest goldmine in the republic. I have always held the stern philosophy that if you are not a dedicated Rollin 20, or a firm supporter or sympathizer, you would not be allowed to push any narcotics within the boundaries as long as my presence was around. I felt since I was a dedicated trooper, a defender of the republic, and a provider to soldiers inside and outside of jail, I shouldn't have to compete with any non-combatants, especially not with civilians who were taking all the proceeds that we established.

The goldmine, I stumbled on, was being run by one of those non-combatant civilians. His name was Moses. From the preliminary reports, I received I learned he was a Belizean who had no ties or understanding with the Belizean soldiers of the republic. That was strike one against him, as the Belizeans made up more than half of the active troopers, and if they didn't know or respect him I definitely wasn't about to extend him that courtesy. I also learned that he was chased out of the area of 23rd and Hoover by the Harpys; and up until that point, I was informed that he paid them rent just to continue his enterprise in their area. That was strike two against him, as I didn't have no respect for a man who bowed down or showed a lack of courage to another man who breathe the same exact air as he did. Strike three was easily justified as he was pushing dope on 27th and St. Andrews within the republic's territory without permission and without the green light say so of any republic's personnel, who may have favored him. Moses was about to feel the wrath of a calculated well thorough gangster.

Besides him, I had another problem to deal with. Next to his apartment was a cadre of Belizean weed sellers who had failed repeatedly to close shop or suffer the consequences. Day and night, they pushed non-stop with little or no regards to my ultimatum. Due to their non-compliance, the time was at hand to serve them a military blow that would leave little doubt in their minds that they were dealing with a force bigger than themselves. Since they were more numerous in numbers compare to Mose's solo enterprise, it was prioritized by me that they should be dealt with first and foremost. I held a military briefing in the St. Andrews apartment with two cadres of Rollin 20's troopers to inform them in detail about the importance of the establishing goldmine and the financial benefits, if our mission was a success.

Every evening I staked out the popping weed spot looking for the perfect opportunity to launch the pre-emptive raid. "Tonight would be the night," I thought. I stood motionless in the shadow gripping the handle of my thirteen shot automatic, and watching for the moment to spring my trap on the unsuspecting Belizean weed pushers. Every republic personnel knew their roles on the mission. The pushers were busying themselves with fixing one of their cars that had stalled and wouldn't start. They never knew what hit them, as our superior numbers and pre-orchestrated roles descended on them with multiple shot automatics pointed at their beings.

My target was the occupant sitting behind the wheel of the car. The moment he looked up, he was faced with the barrel of a gun pointed at his dome. All around me, hard-core troopers took down their intended targets and within seconds, we had overwhelmed and overran the weed pusher's perimeter. I barked on the occupant to exit the car immediately with his hands stretched skyward. He was their leader, and I merciless pistol-whipped him in front of everybody. I was releasing my built-in anger on him for shunning my demands; and with every slap from the barrel of my black Beretta across his head and face, I felt better and somewhat appeased. We pushed and shoved our victims into the apartment's interior. Once inside I slammed my opponent onto the floor and lost all control as I repeatedly bashed the skull of him. "Rollin 20's say close this spot! Rollin 20's say close this spot!" I had lost all grips on my normal calculated self.

While I busied myself on driving my message home in a for sure way, the troopers were stuffing their pockets full of the three pounds of marijuana that sat atop a T.V. I pummeled my victim for a few more minutes and gave him a life or death order to turn over the keys to me at noon the following day. If he failed to do so, I was going to send him home to his maker. After our destruction raid, we all headed in different directions. I left the crowd feeling elated about our success; I was back to my old self, and I was doing what I did best, plot and planning, seek and destroying, and uniting the republic's army under the banner of the Rollin 20's sovereignty.

The following day everything went according to plan, the keys were turned over and I replaced the previous pushers with troopers who were eager to have a hustle that placed money in their pockets. Our next move was against Moses, which was proving to be more of a challenge. He was never at the rock house, as he had himself a faithful and dedicated rock smoker worker named Ms. Tee who always met him outside the jurisdiction of our turf to handle his business. He never showed his face, thus preventing me the opportunity to inform him he had to close shop. Moses didn't know me personally, and he didn't know how relentless I could be or was when it came to anything that was neighborhood related.

At the first sign of nightfall, a cadre of troopers and I were going to shortstop every sell that had the intention of going to him as a sale. Ms. Tee knew me personally and I tried in vain to sway her dedication to Moses by convincing her to go to work for me with a promise of a bigger sack and protection, but she wasn't budging as she was already sold and bought by Moses completely. They both had left me no other choice but to hit them where I knew it would hurt them the most, their pockets. Of the hundred-forty grams of crack I had, I issued Tiny Loko and Skeme each twenty-eight grams expecting five hundred dollars in return. I had fifty-six grams on me and a couple advantages over Moses: All the smokers in the area knew me and they wouldn't put up any resistance to buy my dope; and unlike Moses' dope, which was chipped off due to Ms. Tee's continuous smoking habit, I was selling full-scaled bigger grams.

Everything was going smoothly, just like clockwork, and within two hours of short stopping, I had sold each and every gram of crack. I walked up the street double counting my net total of fourteen hundred dollars, unable to believe the money amount that flew around 27th and St. Andrews. But I knew one thing for sure, this person they called Moses was about to walk on water and anchor himself somewhere else as I wasn't about to give up the goldmine that he had been milking for God knows how long.

While my homeboy Skeme still pushed his dope, Tiny Loko and me sat in the shadows blowing some weed with Sheila who had recently pulled up to check on me. She was trying to befriend me again, and I was playing hard to get; actually, I was enjoying my liberty on being a free agent and assigning myself to any woman who I desired to be with, thus making her attempt to win back my heart a futile move at best. Another reason why she came by to visit me that night was her attempt to force a combined enterprise with me, something I was rejecting at that moment due to her leaving me financially dependant on the state to provide for me while in Avenal Prison. But there was no harm in our smoking weed together as I held no ill or hard feelings toward her. The way I looked at it, it was her loss to lose me as I was always down taking care of my woman and it was obvious she wasn't doing too well at that moment. It was my gain by her leaving me, as I didn't have to report to no one but myself.

After the marijuana smoke had cleared, I was feeling its effect on my mental. Sheila had blazed some chronic which is ten times more potent than the regular weed I was used to smoking. Just as I was falling deeper into the depths of the chronic effects, a commotion in the distance drew my attention. From where I sat, it looked like my homeboy Skeme was squabbling with somebody, somebody that wasn't a friend to the republic. In my cloudy state of mind, I figured I'd just go over there and test out my knockout punch. I began an instant beeline toward the unknown enemy, but as I neared, I noticed that Skeme wasn't fighting back; he was being pistol whipped by the unknown who now had the drop on me.

Although the chronic had initially fogged my mind, obscured and clouded my judgment, I instantly sobered up at the frightening reality that death lurked no more than two seconds away. I was counting down on me being wiped away from this earth by the impact from a bullet in its chamber, waiting to do its duty. Without any hesitation, I lurched my entire body leftward in a desperate attempt to avoid the hot slug. "Boom", the sound echoed through space and based on my split second reaction, I began a hastily zigzag run down St. Andrews with every inch of my body screaming survival. "Boom, boom, boom, boom, boom," a bullet had slammed into a street light pole that I had just passed. My defensive tactic was working, as each bullet he spent in his attempt on my demise was a guarantee to me that he would be out if we kept up the pace we were into.

As I rounded the corner of 28th heading westbound, I became consciously aware of the fact that my predator had stopped his shooting. That didn't stop or impede my run as I was looking to live another day. I lay in the cut some distance away after hopping a multitude of gates watching my would-be assassin jump into his parked car and drive away. Ironically, I wasn't scared at the experience I had just endured; in fact, I was so hard driven for my urge to seek revenge that any thought of being petrified was wiped away. I waited in my hiding place for a minute or so to calm myself and to clear my thoughts, when Sheila, Tiny Loko, and my homey Skeme bent the corner prepared for action. They were a little too late.

Before I departed with Sheila that night, Skeme debriefed his accounts on the enemy, who was none other than Moses. I gave stern orders to Tiny Loko and Skeme to meet me the following day at the complex at two o'clock sharp for my plans of bringing the wrath of my anger down on Ms. Tee and her boss. By the following morning, the news of Moses' attempted murder against me had spread throughout the republic. Sheila's phone rang repeatedly with concerned troopers vehemently expressing their anger and telling me at my orders Moses would be as good as dead before sunset.

Sheila and I headed to St. Andrews and 27th where I was to meet two of the republic's highly skilled killers. When I arrived on the scene, troopers were already in gathering looking to be led into a relentless assault on Ms. Tee and Moses' dope house with only one winner in mind. Sheila pulled up to the back gate of the complex, I exited the car quickly with a 9-millimeter Beretta in my waistline, and made my way safely out of the vast gated parking lot to our new headquarter, the St. Andrews apartment. Baby B-Rock and Baby One-Punch pulled up some minutes later. I knew from years prior of dealing with them that they were some of the best and ruthless killers of all the Y.G.'s throughout the republic. They were cocky, confident, and neither could keep their hands away from their waistlines.

As we descended on the perimeter of Ms. Tee's apartment, Baby One Punch banged on the door with the butt of his pistol. Ms. Tee poked her head through the window curtains where she was met by a host of automatics. She retreated as fast as she had appeared. "Ms. Tee, Ms. Tee, come to the window." – "Please don't shoot me", she gave a reply by the demand made by One-Punch, but it was obvious that she was far away from the window. She was petrified and she knew she deserved nothing short of death as she was the one who had made the phone call to Moses, reporting to him of our short stopping activities which almost led to my death. When she was rest-assured that no harm would come to her, she reappeared once again in the window clearly shaken. "Call Moses right now, and tell him Baby One-Punch said for him to come over here so I can speak to him."

It didn't take a rocket scientist to figure out that Moses wasn't going to come, and sure to my mental contemplation he sent a Blood member from the Fruit Town Brims as a negotiator to seek peace from me. He swore through him that he didn't try to kill me last night, and that he didn't know it was me he was shooting at. I was infuriated once again and vowed from that day forward that I was going to wreck havoc and economical disaster on Moses' spot. After the Fruit Town Brim had spoken, I blasted him verbally for his intervening in Rollin 20's business on dealing with non-combatants, especially those who sucked money out of the republic. Moses failed to show up, and I began my immediate plot and planning of reigning total disruption on his goldmine that was destined to become mine.

With some of the money I had accumulated, I rented out a one-bedroom apartment for six hundred dollars in the Wilshire area on 9th and Fedora. I chose that area for security reasons. I wanted an apartment on the outskirts of our republic, a place where Crips wouldn't be a bother, a place where the local police wouldn't be able to spy on me, and a place where I knew once I entered through its domain I wouldn't have to worry about all the ills that I faced every day in the hood.

I took a few days off, borrowed a van from a smoker named Black, and began settling in my apartment that was to become my new headquarters for many planned missions on my jacking sprees. In two days I had it furnished to my satisfaction; on the third day I drove around shopping all over the city for miscellaneous items like toilet paper, drinking glasses, shower curtains, food, et cetera, finally ending at the local market on 8th and Normandie.

From the moment I entered through the door, my breath was instantly swept away at the most beautiful and loveliest sight of a woman who by far surpassed the elegance and sexiness of any woman I had ever been with in my life, including Sheila. I had frozen in my steps and stood there gazing at her loveliness as she spoke to the store clerk about a T.V. that was on display. The more I digested her with my eyes, the more it dawned on me that I knew her, as her face looked overly familiar. I could have sexed her right then and there on the spot in front of everybody, as she looked that delicious in every possible way.

Once regaining my composure and shaking off my initial shock, I bee lined to the counter to get a better look at her. As I approached her from her right side, she twisted her neck upwards to get a look at the person who now stood over her shoulder. "Hello." I addressed her in my best voice possible. "How are you doing?" – "Me doing okay." When she responded in her Belizean accent, I was losing control of myself. One part of my mind told me to leave, before I made an ass of myself, and the other part told me to charm my way into her heart. I chose the latter as it made more sense and beside I couldn't let something so beautiful and perfectly created to slip pass me at least without an attempt at her digits.

"Don't I know you?" trying to sound sexy, romantic and like a gentleman all in the same breath. When she looked upon me to respond, it dawned on me on how short she was; something I could get use to. "Me don't know, maybe, maybe not." Her thick accent was driving me crazy and sending chills from my toes to the top of my head. She was a 'dime piece' as we would say in the hood, and she had all the credential to break me for every penny in my pocket. "Do you know somebody who lives on Adams?" The statement must have hit a chord within her as her head shot upwards with the inquisitive look in her eyes of 'how you know that'. "Yes", she hesitantly replied. I pushed on since I knew I had her attention. "You don't remember seeing me on Adams in that sky blue Thunderbird with the loud music?" – "Oh, that be you who be driving that car with the dark tinted window?" I didn't waste a second in confirming her identity of the car that me and Sheila had shared together.

She had dropped her guards and soon we were chit chatting about people, places, and areas that we both shared a common interest in. Upon realizing that she was walking, I offered her a ride home, especially since she was carrying her freshly purchased television. She lived on 7th and Vermont. There's one thing I give myself credit on being good at, and that's being a great conversationalist with a sense of humor. Before I reached the parking space in front of her apartment, I had already gotten more than enough laughs out of her. Surprisingly to me we ended up exchanging numbers, and as I departed, I found myself hoping I had left a lasting first impression. I was hoping like I've never hoped before.

Some time later, I was back on the block with a cadre of troopers in the shadows of the St. Andrews tree line, which formed a complete square around the vast parking lot. I was drilling them on their assigned roles that each was to carry out precisely once briefing was adjourned. At 9:00 p.m., everybody headed to take up their battle positions. I stood in the cut waiting for the perfect moment that would give the raiding party an advantage of over running the apartment without much difficulty. All the troopers held their positions as I gave the first signal for them to prepare for their pre-emptive raid onto Moses' dope spot; a smoker had walked up to the front door and as was expected, Ms. Tee opened to receive him.

At that moment, I gave the signal to move. The squad leaped from their hiding spot of the bushes and before Ms. Tee could react or comprehend what was transgressing before her eyes, it was already well too late, as she was overpowered in seconds. "Help! Help! Help!" She was screaming at the top of her lungs, as she was picked up and carried back into the apartment's interior. The would-be crack buyer bee lined away from the area for fear of being attacked by the masked men. I stood across the street watching the front door and wondered was my tactic of intimidation going to be suitable enough to discourage Ms. Tee. Seconds later the dope spot's front door blew open with a force of a charging bull and the crew bee lined rapidly out. They had robbed her of all the dope and money, and had ram shook the apartment's inside. After my post-raid briefing, everybody was told to get off the streets for that night and to meet me the following night at the same exact time.

    I hurried home to my new apartment with two things in mind: paging the Belizean girl Sofia, and rolling myself a big size philly blunt full marijuana. Some ten minutes after I had paged her, Sofia called back, and I was like a little kid with a lollipop at the sound of hearing her sweet voice. We held a brief and light conversation and set a date for the following day around noon. We met each other at the local market to buy some blunts for the marijuana I had brought along. Without a shadow of a doubt, I was completely attracted to her, and being so, I was waging a psychological, mind altering, and telepathic war to win her over.

    We walked our way southbound down the back streets heading to Olympic, where she was to board the bus that was going to drop her off at her work. As we were walking, I couldn't help but notice her intentional act of lagging behind me; she was worse than me on my checking out her assets, as she was doing some serious scoping of my body parts. I knew my body was desirable as I always kept myself in excellent shape, and since I knew this one for sure fact, I also knew I had one for sure victory in my goal of winning Sofia over.

SOFIA
(1999-2000)

I headed toward the neighborhood to blow yet another sack of weed with my homegirl Tama, thus burning some more daylight hours which I avoided intentionally. In the daytime I made it a habit to be seen as less as possible, and all my moves if I did travel were preplanned and calculated thus keeping myself clear of many problems. I was on a mission to firmly establish myself, and I knew it was going to take time, patience, hard work, and dedication. Tama and I always enjoyed each other's company as we had a lot in common: We both loved marijuana, we both had a history in the neighborhood, we both were great conversationalists and we both were great listeners to each other's concerns and problems. She was my partner on a platonic level, and I was hers; and it was on this level that we fed and nourished each other's thirst. Spending time with her always seemed to make time fly by, and before long the darkness of night told me it was time to head to the headquarter of the St. Andrews apartment.

I bee lined up 29th walking fast, checking all movement in front and behind me against my over sensitive radar of deciding whether it was friend or foe. I walked down the back street completely aware of all the dangers that could arise at any given moment while keeping my hand on the 9-millimeter just in case somebody had to meet thirteen challenging replies. When I reached the apartment, troopers were already waiting. Without any delays, I began my briefing and reassessment of the situation. After finishing my speech, I was told that Ms. Tee had voice fully exclaimed that her presence wouldn't be intimidated by our pre-emptive attack from last night which meant I was going to have to play some hard ball with no intention of striking out. I knew I was about to raise the ante, as the stakes in the game of control had just went up a notch.

Thirty minutes later, everything was in place for the mission. My plan wasn't to bring actual harm on Ms. Tee; it was designed to pump fear in her heart, thus swaying her judgment that it would probably be a brilliant idea if she left well enough alone while she still had the chance. Everybody was ready to go. The only thing that delayed my go-ahead signal was the apartment building owner's presence. He was on the scene doing odd jobs on his run down building, so we waited.

After an hour of time had passed, I was losing my patience, it was nearly 10:30 p.m., and I had to make a decision. I held a last minute session. After everybody was back in place, I waited again for the perfect moment. Lil Quick had stern orders not to shoot Ms. Tee, but to bring the bullets as close as possible to her to give her the impression that the unknown gunman had tried to take her life. The owner stood no more than ten feet away from Quick fixing on one of the tenants front door, and he was oblivious of the danger that lurked around him. The moment I had been waiting on happened as a smoker walked up to Ms. Tee's apartment to purchase some crack. I gave the signal for everyone to prepare.

When Ms. Tee opened her door, I gave the go-ahead order. Lil Quick became a robot of war as we stepped from the shadows blazing with the big 44 Python with bullets meant to spook Ms. Tee into submission: "Boom, boom, boom, boom, boom, boom." Immediately after expending his last shell, he bee lined across 27th Street to the St. Andrews parking lot. The owner ran into the apartment which door he had been fixing on minutes prior. The troopers performed their assigned roles precisely and within seconds after the attack, we had blended away into the night like the passing wind.

I decided to lay low for a couple days to see which way the wind would blow and how the local police department would react. I concluded after my bus ride home that I needed some wheels, and I needed them bad. I had been home more than a month and a half, and I was tired of buses and cabs. I decided to call up one of my smoker clientele who I knew had a credit card. We negotiated that I pay him a sizeable amount of rock cocaine for renting me a green 1999 Buick Regal. After the deal, I went back to my apartment to see if I could arrange a date with Sofia. Some twenty minutes later, I had worked out a time to pick her up. Really, it was just enough time to take a quick shower, to change into some fresh gear, and to eat some breakfast food for dinner.

Thirty minutes later, I pulled upfront of her apartment, slapped my hazard lights on and dialed her number from my freshly purchased cell phone. "Hello", she answered. Every time I heard her accent, it thrilled me, literally; I always found myself taken aback by its melody-tuned sound: "I'm parked out front." I swerved the Regal around preparing for an immediate departure. Some five minutes later she strode up to the passenger side and slid in. "Hello", I said trying to sound like a well-spoken diplomat. "Good evening", she replied in that voice that was going to be the cause of me falling in love with her prematurely. As I pulled away slowly driving toward Vermont, I handed the pack of philly blunts and a half ounce of marijuana to her. She knew what to do, as she went to work immediately. I drove with the flow of traffic keeping my speed in check thus avoiding the attention of the black and white police cruisers who loved pulling black men over, especially those who fitted the profile of a gangster.

By the time I reached the area around Adams and Normandie, we were well into a full-scale marijuana session. I pulled the Regal into the Shell gas station at the sight of numerous homeboys who were piled out front, in what looked to be a gang meeting. When I asked what they were in gathering for, Baby Boo informed me of events that were unknown and new to me. The 51st Trouble Gangster Crips, located on Normandie and 51st had recently wall banged against our hood by crossing us out which had erupted into a full scale wall banging war and my homies were on their way with a couple of 9-millimeter automatics to ante up the pace with the Trouble Crips.

I spoke a few selected words to the troopers and everybody headed to their respective vehicles. The moment I slid back behind the wheel, Sofia was on me as she had sensed something amiss. "Whata going on?" She was buzzed off the marijuana that made her accent sound thick and uncut. On my reply, I knew I had to choose my words carefully as I didn't want to spook her too soon with the revelation of what my homeboys had just relayed to me. I dragged each word out: "What you are about to witness only happens in the movies." She looked upon me with a true bewildered expression that spoke her confusion. Not being content with my answer, she drilled me again for information: "Whata goin on wit yo friends?" In response I gave her the same dragged-out reply as the first time, at that she left it alone.

I followed close behind the caravan of speeding cars that slid up Normandie heading to the liquor store on 51st, which was a known hangout for the 51st TGC's. Our caravan slowed to a moderate speed after we had reached the Trouble area, but we were slightly disappointed at not finding anyone to mow down. We circled around the block, and as the element of danger swerved its head in all directions, it became clear to Sofia that something was wrong. Just then, two carloads of TGC's pulled up on Normandie looking to make a left turn onto 52nd. The lead car turned in our direction, and as if they had a premonition, they suddenly swerved their vehicle in a wide right turn back into traffic. "Bust, bust, bust, bust!" At the sound of my stern command, the soldiers began an ear deafen noise of hot bullets slamming and piercing into the two cars.

When I looked to my right to check on my date I thought she had jumped out the car, as she wasn't sitting in her seat. As soon as all the gunplay started, Sofia slid her entire body to the floor of the car. I knew I was wrong for bringing her on a date that turned into her witnessing a drive-by, but I knew if she was going to accept me, she was going to have to accept the gangster's side of me, which was an intricate part of my life. As I drove up Normandie trying to figure out what to say next to my frightened date, the two carloads of 20's smashed by at a high-speed heading back to the republic.

Finally, I found the courage to speak. "Are you alright?" Sofia was mad at me and she had every reason to be. When she responded to my question the anger was evident in her voice: "I thought you didn't gang bang!" Her statement was raw, and it had caught me by surprise, as I didn't recall telling her nothing of the sort. "I don't gang bang," I retorted off handed. "I just wanted to show you the life I used to live." I allowed my words to sink in, but somewhere in the quietness I picked up the message that this would be my last date with her, probably forever. After blowing the remaining marijuana, I promptly dropped her off at her grandmother's house over in the jungles. I drove away feeling empty and not sure what to think. I had ruined my opportunity to charm my way into the Belizean woman's heart. But before I let the love bug overwhelm my mind, I shrugged it away, as I had more important things to attend to, than to worry about the thoughts of a woman I hardly knew.

I drove through the night with my mind drifting about all the built-up desires of me becoming a jacker of the highest degree. There was one person in the republic whose reputation preceded him as a calculated jacker always on the prowl, and it was time to click back up to put our hood on the map. I'm talking about my old roll dog, friend, homey, and comrade Mr. Tray-K. I parked my car in his family's driveway and made my way to the front door where he greeted me with his unusual sense of humor: "Yes, may I help you?" Instantly I broke into a smile at the sound of his high-pitched tone voice. I decided to play along with the game he'd started: "I'm looking for a Mr. Tray-K, would he happen to be around?"

Tray-K had lost his composure and broke out into an uncontrollable laugh. "What's up Blood?" I asked, changing our humor into the serious nature at hand. "What's up Loko?" he cracked the door and stepped out onto the porch. I didn't waste any time to speak about the topic of jacking, as I wanted to get going as soon as possible. "What's up with a lick?" At the request of my words, Tray-K lit up and turned to face me. When he responded, he spoke with pure excitement, as jacking was something that he had a knack for. "On Bloods, I got a lick. Meet me here tomorrow night at 9:00 p.m." That night I slept well while I had two dreams that fought for control of my subconscious state, the aspect of jacking for large proceeds, and the Belizean girl named Sofia.

The following afternoon I awoke with vigor. I was empted about the idea of going on my first jacking mission, and I knew I was ready for it, as I had prepared myself long ago for this occurrence. I had plenty of hours to burn, so I decided to pick up Lakeisha, one of my little honeys and blow some weed. We took a ride out to Compton under her condition to spend the entire day together; that was cool with me for a couple reasons: I was looking to burn time in company of a female friend, and the other reason was that Lakeisha didn't smoke marijuana, which meant more smoke for me. When I picked her up, she appeared in a body dress that hugged every crack, curve, and crevice. She was blessed, and she flaunted it at every opportunity.

As she bounced toward the car I couldn't contain my eyes from sucking in her well shaped image, the moment she slid in, she began her role acting of proper talking: "How you doing, Honey?" – "Hi Keisha", I responded high as hell. "Could we get something to eat Terrell? I'm starving." I don't know what irritated me the most, her fake proper English or the fact that she hadn't grabbed a bite before I arrived. The only thing that soothed my mind of my irritating thoughts was the fact that I was sitting next to a woman whose body held all the secrets to my many weaknesses. I lit up another marijuana stick and smashed out toward the 110 Freeway heading southbound. It took me all and nothing short of an hour to reach the east side of Compton. When I pulled upfront my Aunt Mae's house, my cousin Cardett had been standing out-front watering the front grass. As he registered me, he dropped the water hose and obliged me by opening the gate. I rolled yet another blunt for him and me. From the moment Lakeisha stepped from the car, his eyes locked and loaded on her well-shaped ass, we both gave a little chuckle at what I was working with. It always makes a man feel good when another man views his woman.

A few seconds later, I bee lined into the house to give my aunt a warm hug and kiss. From the moment I laid eyes on her, I knew something was wrong, she was sick. My heart leaped in my chest, as I had never seen her like that before. She was sitting in her kitchen chair now smiling at the familiar sight of me, but she looked aged. She knew without doubt I loved her and cared very much about her. I guess she felt self-conscious about her appearance, as she immediately began telling me how sorry she was about her health. I pretended not to hear her statement; instead, I bent down and gave her a warm kiss and a hug that spoke a thousand words. "Hi Ainny!" I stated, trying to hold my emotions in check. But the more she talked about her health, the more my emotions were inching closer and closer to overflowing my heart. My visit in Compton was to be cut short, as I couldn't accept the deteriorating health condition of a woman who was equaled to a mother to me.

When we drove back to South Central, we didn't talk. After dropping Lakeisha off, I decided to take a nap thus allowing my mind to relax from the reality of my aunt's condition. The continuous vibration of my pager some hours later had jarred me from my somber sleep. Instantly I jumped out of bed. The pager displayed Tray-K's number repeatedly, as he had been trying to contact me for the last thirty minutes. I checked my watch; it was a quarter to nine, I was fucking up as I had nearly overslept. I grabbed my 9-millimeter and my cell phone, and headed toward Tray-K's family home.

When I finally arrived, he was accompanied by his relative Doc, who had put the lick together, and milked it up perfectly to the present moment. The intended victims were some outer Towner who had ventured to California to price shop around for a half kilo of cocaine. Doc accidentally bumped heads with them at a barbershop, and it was from there that the ball first started to roll, thus involving Tray-K and finally me. The vics were estimated to have at least ten thousand dollars on them, which we were to equally split. When we arrived on the scene on Cypress and LaBrea, the outer Towner were already awaiting us, something I didn't like. From years of reading Sun-Tzu, *The Art of War*, I knew that it was an advantage for the ones who reached the location first. As we pulled up, we had to be alerted in any way. I scanned every shadow in the darkness looking for potential jackers who were to do what we'd come to do. So far, I'd counted only two heads, and if there were more in the area, they were hiding themselves well.

As we exited the car, I realized at how calculated my train of thought was; I had rehearsed for hours and hours in my mental world, gearing myself for such a moment that was presently at hand. My mind was working overtime, and it impressed me with its comfort of keeping cool under such a nerve-wrecking situation. I was going about the lick like I'd done countless ones before, and like it was just a routine to perform the way I did. I even forgot that Doc was with me all the time. I greeted the two vics with a handshake, and we were ready to get down to business. After one of them had finished counting out the ten thousand dollars they were expected to have, I whipped my heat out, "click clank!" The noise of a round being chambered, ready for delivery sent one of the outer Towner bee lining down the street. He had moved so fast that he had caught me off guard. I held the Nina steady at the other vic, the one with the money. "Get your mother fucken ass down, before I bust a cap in your ass!" The vic responded promptly and lay face down in the dirt without delay. I snatched the money from his left hand and pulled another thousand from his pockets. As I prepared to depart, I gave him stern orders not to look up, and if he did so, he would be forfeiting his existence. We jumped into the car where Tray-K had waited all the time, and smashed back to the turf eleven thousand dollars richer. Later I took my share of the cut and headed home feeling exhilarating about my first successful and easy lick. Another lick two weeks later brought me in possession of an easy eleven thousand dollars retail price worthy chronic portion.

Everything was going smoothly as everything I wanted to achieve I had, two apartments, tens of thousands of dollars, and a flock of females to select from. I had barely been home two months, and I already accomplished what it would have taken most men years. Christmas came and passed with calm, as everybody who was important to me received either money or a X-mas gift; and with X-mas out the way, I prepared for the coming of the new year of 2000. I already knew in advance that I wasn't going to be doing too much movement once the new year rolled in as I believed in the fear of the killer bullets that came back to earth with velocity. I guess you could call me scary, but I believed in being precautious, and most of my precaution bordered on being scary which have saved my life on numerous occasions.

On New Year's Eve, some two hours before midnight, I was already celebrating with a sack of my stolen chronic and a glass of Hennessey. I decided I would post up with some crack at my St. Andrews apartment and bring my new year in with a cash flow from the goldmine that I had overtaken from Moses and Ms. Tee. After pumping overwhelming fear into Ms. Tee, I rented out an apartment in the same unit, but some four doors away from hers. The risk I undertook in stripping Moses and the Belizean weed pushers was paying off every night. The massive money they were originally receiving was now redirected to me; on a slow night, I made an easy two thousand dollars, and on a good night, I racked in three thousand and five hundred. Regardless of the amount of cocaine I brought at any given night it would all be sold within the twelve hour time period from once I opened up at 6:00 p.m.

I was celebrating all my successes. After all the crack was gone, I sat in the apartment alone deep in thoughts about the fears that the bullets were descending back to earth and striking me, and that everything was going to shut down due to the computers not being prepared or up to part. Around one o'clock in the morning I was still sitting in the darkness drinking myself into a stupor when my pager was signaling that somebody was hitting me up. I couldn't help but wonder who it could be. I didn't recognize the number, but the code was familiar. It was the code of the Belizean girl, but it couldn't be, or was it?

I rushed to the kitchen to get my cell phone, dialed the number back, and sure enough it was her with that voice that always sent my blood rushing through my body at high speed. It had been a month since she last contacted me, thanks to that drive-by date. I wondered what she'd paged me for so early in the morning. In her phone background, I could tell they were partying wherever she was. "Hello" – "Did somebody page me?" I was pretending as if I hadn't recognized her code, "Yes it's me Sofia." – "Oh, what's up?" trying my best to sound surprised, "How you been doing since last we'd talked?" She responded that everything was okay with her, and went on to explain that she'd been real busy lately with work. After conversing for some odd ten minutes, she'd asked me to come and get her and her girlfriend Tasha at her aunt's home on 46th Street and Normandie. That location spelled 4-6 Neighborhood Crips to me, and that meant I had to take precautions going into the area. I cleaned up the apartment making sure that everything was tidied up for the company I was about to go and retrieve.

Traffic was surprisingly heavy to me. Maybe everybody was heading somewhere to get themselves some more to drink. When I reached the house of Sofia's aunt, I was blasted by some lady in the living room with a mike in her hand singing some Mexican song. I figured somewhere in the Belizean girl's family tree there must be some Mexican blood. Later I found out the Spanish singer was her mother Brenda which I would have one of those I-love-to-hate-you relationships because she concluded I was too thuggish for her daughter, which was true, but that didn't stop Sofia as she had a hidden infatuation for me.

When she finally walked onto the front porch, I couldn't help but notice the effect her beauty immediately held over me. I thought I convinced myself after Sheila that I wouldn't be duped into the emotional realm again, but all those restrictions flew out the window at the sight of Sofia. "Happy New Year's" she spoke with her sweet and lovely voice. "Happy New Year's to you", I responded, feeling the effect of the Hennessey I'd been drinking some minutes prior. After a quick and formal introduction to her girlfriend Tasha, we were on our way back in traffic to my dope spot apartment. In route, I blazed a fat chronic blunt, which took its effect on everyone, as soon we were all coughing uncontrollably. When we finally pulled up at 27th and St. Andrews, Tiny Loko and Killa Jess were out-front waiting for my arrival. The second Sofia stepped from the car; Tiny Loko broke into a wide cool-aid grin at my latest conquest. Sofia was definitely beautiful as she had all the qualities that most men look for in a woman.

As soon as we were inside, we went immediately into a full-scale session of drinking and smoking. Blunts were being passed all around me, and since I wasn't much of a drinker the potent Hennessey was having its effects on me. Everybody was soon buzzed and the chronic smoke was thick in the air as we kept a fresh blunt going as soon as one was finished off. Some two hours later the thought of going to sleep had crossed everybody's mind at least once. It was four o'clock in the morning, when I invited all of my guests to my apartment in the Wilshire area to get some rest. I couldn't help but think of the beautiful woman sitting next to me, as it had been nearly three months since I first met her, and here she was accompanying me home. I was going to be a gentleman I convinced myself.

Once inside the apartment I pulled out all my sleeping material: blankets, sheets, t-shirts for the girls, and mattresses. After everybody was settled in the living room, I took Sofia by the hand and led her into my bedroom where I had every intention of making sure she got a good night's rest. I locked the door, put some tunes on, rolled up another blunt of chronic, and poured us each another glass of Hennessey. After tucking her into bed with only a t-shirt on, I went about romancing her and stripping myself clean of all my clothing except for my men's brief. I couldn't help but notice her eyes roaming my well-proportioned body. I slid in bed and began doing what she had already been doing, sipping on some more Hennessey.

After the final blunt was finished off, I knew she was relaxed and comfortable around me, as she was laughing at my corny jokes I'd been telling; and then out of the clear blue, I dropped a lug by asking her could I have one of her legs. "You want my leg?" She replied looking up at me being positioned on my elbows. "Yea, I want one of your legs." – "Yea, you can have my leg." With her permission I began massaging her left leg with my left hand in a circular motion making my hand travel up, and the further I got, the more intense it became for the both of us: We were losing control. By then I was completely aroused, as my hand had found its resting place on her wet womanhood. With each intense massage of my fingers, she slid away more into ecstasy enjoying the beautiful feeling of passion. The more contact my fingers made with her loveliness, the more I was becoming oblivious to my heavy breathing. Before long, we were kissing each other passionately, tasting each other's lips, and savoring in each other's twirling and hungry tongues.

She was beyond arousal as her spread legs declared her state of mind, and my fingers were more than damp as her love juices flowed out of control. Before I realized what I was doing, I was pulling her atop me and releasing her breasts free of their captivity. I was beyond myself now as the desire of love making throbbed in every part of my body. I attacked her breasts with a hot and eager tongue, and our bodies responded to each other through one rhythm. For every move I made she counter moved taking us that further into ecstasy. I wanted her more than I had ever wanted any woman in my life. It was time to up the ante, and I pulled my manhood free of its confinement nearly releasing my load just from the sudden change. I had never felt as alive as I was at that moment; she was a very sexual charged woman, and she was driving me nuts as each level of ecstasy I put forward, she met me accepting the challenge. Soon I was grinding upwards with my manhood, rhythmically massaging her wetness.

I knew it wouldn't be long before I probably lost control over myself, but the effort of holding back was well worth the try, as I didn't want the passion I was enjoying to end. Somewhere in the mix of kissing, touching, massaging, and suckling, her damped panties were pushed to the side, and now my manhood glided back and forth across her entire wet length. With each motion accomplished, our blood levels raised to heights of bursting over. I realized she was in full stride of satisfying her sexual build up; and then suddenly and unexpectedly on her last sexual motion, I slid inside her thus giving me my first taste of what it meant to be pussy whipped. Our sexual encounter was still in motion, and I was already whipped at the warmth of her womanhood I was feeling. I was in heaven and she must have been there, too as her face was contoured with pleasure. She held her grinding motion as long as she could, and then she lost it: "Uh! Uh!, Uh!" With each moan she released she pushed herself downwards with greater and greater force, thus putting us into the act that we both wanted and desired.

On her fourth or fifth downward thrust, I turned into the two-minute man, and it was all over for me. She was in total disbelief that I had ejaculated on her just as she was heading into first gear. "Did you come?" I knew I was in trouble. It was like if you answer yes, I'm going to kill you, so I decided to lie: "No!" I tried my best to keep a straight face but she wasn't convinced. "You did come in me you bonehead." Either I was tripping, or she had just called me a bonehead, in both cases I became angry and it was time to defend my actions before she had. "It was all that damn teasing you did before allowing me to penetrate you." I guess my reply wasn't too convincing as she burst out crying still sitting atop of me. Now I was really confused. I don't know if she was crying because I had screamed at her, or because she didn't get off as I had. She plopped off me looking like her favorite pet fish had just died.

Some times later, after we had taken our showers I lay in bed next to her holding her in my arms listening to her rhythmic breathing as she slept peacefully. I felt connected to her in a way that was beyond our sexual experience. She made me feel alive, and I noticed the few short times I was around her I felt some tugging in my heart for her. I didn't believe in love at first sight, but if it were true just by a slight chance, I wondered then was I its latest victim. I was awake for quite some time drifting over my endless thoughts, and right before sleep swept over me the last thought I remember thinking was the scary fact that I knew I was in love with the woman now lying next to me.

G-Kev
(2000)

Some two weeks had passed since I'd last talked to Sofia, as she was still upset at me from my premature New Year's explosion. Every day that came and went, I fought the relentless urge to call her up with the promises that I'll satisfy her next time around. But I couldn't do it as she was holding to her guns, which made me determined to do the same. Besides that I had a rule that I believed in 'never jock a female', and if I were to call her first, it would be an early admittance of my jocking her, so I held out.

Around that time, I received an unexpected call from my roll dog Big G-Kev. He wanted me to pick him up at Centinela State Prison the day of his release, which was some odd two weeks away. Now it was really going to be on as he and I spelled trouble with a capital "T". A day before I was going to pick him up, I received a bizarre and barely understandable message from Sofia on my voice mail: "Fuck you, you bonehead, me da gonna teke care of this pickny by myself, uhh!" I replayed the message over and over again trying to make sense of it, and realizing I couldn't. I finally had to find a translator who would interpret the Creole language. I was in shock; Sofia was claiming that she was pregnant by me. I was elated by the news, as it was music to my ears. The good fortune of winning her heart was now accomplished, or maybe I cheated just a little, but now I set out to put the icing on the cake.

I ran out the front door with Tiny Loko heading to pick up my now baby mama. I guess my holding out had paid off as everything I wanted was coming to past, but the pregnancy was a bonus. I smashed through traffic in the recently acquired Cadillac truck to Sofia's grandmother's house over in the jungles where her girlfriend Tasha opened the door. Sofia didn't know I was coming as I wanted to surprise her, and when I turned the corner of the bedroom, her face lit up. She tried to contain her pleasure and happiness but the smirk on her face was giving her away; it finally ended up in a full-scale grin.

I sat down next to her on the bed, and before I really had any thought in what I was about to do, I leant forward and placed a warm and affectionate kiss on her lips. Her eyes told it all as they shined with pure joy brimming over their edges. "Pack your stuff up you're going home with me." My stern and unexpected statement took her aback, as she looked up at me as if I'd just asked for her hand in marriage. Once again, she fought to control her happiness, and when she replied she had stripped all the emotions from her voice, "okay." Most women probably would have taken hours and hours of packing their clothes and other girlie items, but Sofia broke the record when she laid out a bed sheet onto the middle of the floor and placed all her belongings into it. Some thirty minutes later Tiny Loko, Tasha, Sofia and I were all in traffic heading southbound. After Tasha was dropped off, it was time to celebrate the news of the pregnancy. I couldn't be happier than I was with the fact of being with Sofia and the expectation of having another baby.

The following morning I jumped on the freeway to pick up G-Kev with an ounce of the boom bonic chronic, and a bottle of Hennessey for his splurging, something I knew he would like. Some five hours later, I had arrived at a small town Greyhound station sitting around with many other families waiting to pick up their love ones. After spending the remainder of the morning being bored, some odd minutes before noon the prison van pulled up and discarded itself of its contents. One by one the inmates were filing off the bus, until I finally caught a glimpse of the familiar face I had been looking for, and some minutes later we were heading back to the terror dome of South Sintral Los Angeles.

It seemed the more marijuana we blew, the more hyper and disrespectful G-Kev became on my cell phone dissing all the girls who had performed badly, or had failed to live up to his expectations of taking care of the business that he felt was important to him: "Fuck you bitch! Yea, I'm with Loko, and I ain't coming home to your rat ass!" He was speaking to Denisha also known as Dee-Dee. She was just one of the many victims who endured his tongue-lashing of insults. Since he was free out no more than a few hours, Kev had called it quits on the marijuana, whereas I was still pulling, as I was a true weed head. Kev dosed off as the chronic took its toll on him, and I allowed him to sleep, as I knew he was going to need all his energy and awareness when coming home. One slip could cost you your life, and we were veterans of the streets, so we knew of the importance of paranoia being a survival skill.

When we were back in the turf, I shook Kev from his sleep, and he bounced from the car feeling alive and happy. The second we stepped in the door of my apartment, he wanted to have a session. This time I declined, as I was hungry from all the weed I'd already consumed. I passed the rest off to him and ordered me a pork chop dinner at the nearest Mississippi restaurant on 28th and Western. I also dialed up Sofia to see what she was doing. On the third ring, her sweet voice sung its musical tune in my ear: "Hi Baby!" Just as quickly as she had greeted me, she demanded of what I was doing, already she was displaying early on traces of jealousy. After a light chitchat, I was given firm orders to come and pick her up after I'd gotten my pork chop dinner.

Kev didn't waste no time, he was blown all over again. In route to pick up Sofia at her granny's house, he drove as I took down the dinner that had the whole car smelling. I knew it was just a matter of minutes before he stuck his paw out for some of my food. The second he inquired about it, I doubled over laughing as it tickled me that he had held out that long; I promised him I'd save him some. On reaching the jungles, I passed the remainder of my food to Kev, and bee lined to get my girl.

After watching Sofia and me cuddle and kiss away at every opportunity, Kev had seen enough and was eager more than ever to go and swoop up Mishalay Sanders, also known as C.K. Shay. Shay was Kev's boo, and if there was one woman who had left their impression on his psychic, then without doubt she would take the cake. I threw Kev the keys, slid a couple hundred to him and continued on my mission to please my sweet tasting woman.

In the days following his release, I couldn't help but notice G-Kev's relaxed and changed priority on security measures. Normally he would be as committed as I am about issues that are relevant to our well-being, but somewhere on his latest journey to jail, he had lost his military edge on being keenly aware of his surroundings. The first signs of change came slow, but with each day's arrival, it became clear to me that my roll dog was a safety hazard to himself and to me: At any given time inside my dope spot, I always kept the lights turned off, but Kev left it on, advertising to the world that we were there. Since I always had a gun and large amounts of dope in the spot, I also kept the front door secured; but with Kev's arrival, it stayed open more than it needed to be.

The one thing that weighed heavy on my mind was he had developed a drinking habit. Every morning he would start his day with a bottle of Hennessey, something that the old G-Kev would never do. Day and night, I drilled him about his changing ways, and that he should do some self-reflecting. He knew I loved him, so when I went on one of my chastisement speeches he couldn't do anything but smile at me, indicating he knew I was right. But as the days turned into a month, his behavior went from bad to worse; he deteriorated to the brink of where he just didn't give a fuck. Making money wasn't a priority for the new Kev; keeping an automatic pistol around wasn't a priority for the new Kev; and more importantly, the neighborhood's continual conflict with our rivals wasn't a priority for the new Kev; but to the old G-Kev, these issues and more would be at the center of his life.

Around this same period of his new revelations, he went and did something that was totally out of his character: He jacked our homeboy Lil E-Kapone at gunpoint. The atrocity act of putting a gun in E-

Kapone's mouth, taking a quarter kilo of cocaine and an undisclosed amount of jewelry from him, weren't the overwhelming factors. Krazy-K and I considered E-Kapone to be a buster, and Kev's taking of his belongings was his problem to get back. But the one concern that we held firmly, was to not allow anarchy to reign without being checked by our leadership. We knew that if it weren't checked in its stride, we would have our hands full all throughout the neighborhood to prevent what Kev had just committed.

Krazy-K rode around with me trying to locate Kev. I called his cell phone repeatedly, and then finally a break through. "What's up Loko?" He began his little boy laughter, muffled somewhat due to his thumb in his mouth, as if it were a habit he had no desire to break. "You mad at me, Big Homey?" He knew that he was working on my soft spot I had for him: "Kev, just meet me on 23rd and Congress, so we can talk to you." I fired up a sack of the cough medicine, and we waited on the arrival of my ace koon boon, Mr. G-Kev. Some time later D-Hogg pulled up with Kev in the passenger seat looking like he was innocent of all the pending charges. While Krazy-K chatted with Kev, D-Hogg pulled me to the side as he had a concern of his own since Kev was his blood relative. "What's up Loko? What do ya'll tend to do with him?" Sensing the worries in his question, I reassured him that Kev would be dealt with respectfully for the impending neighborhood charges against him. After a lengthily conversation of the wrongs that he had caused, we also discovered that he had two Y.G's with him that night. Baby Krazy-B and Tiny Jimbo, both were highly respected foot soldiers skilled at their trades.

Krazy-K and I decreed that Kev and the two Y.G.'s were to be issued a discipline of having to fight other homies at our park. Reluctantly G-Kev agreed, and after tracking down Tiny Jimbo and Baby Krazy-B, we bee lined to our republic's capital, the Loren Miller Park. Kev was assigned to fight his victim E-Kapone, thus giving him the chance to exert his anger against Kev. But true to the cowardice that flowed through his blood, he was pure frighten. More or less it was a one sided fight with Kev serving E-Kapone at his every whim. Upon seeing that Kev wasn't about to receive the justified discipline, Lil B-Rock was assigned to the job.

He hunched up and didn't waste a second on his mission, connecting a well-placed punch that drove Kev to the pavement. One of the many things that I loved about Kev was his determination to never give in to the odds. He was a squabbler, a true soldier, and a gangster highly respected to the utmost degree in my book; and as I expected him to do, he recovered from the slamming punch, bounced back up, and zeroed in to get some get back. I watched in amazement as he exerted all his remaining energy into Lil B-Rock, and before long my dog was completely out of fuel. B-Rock tried to take advantage of it and slid in to finish him off. All the love in my heart that I had for him screamed at B-Rock to back off as his fight was officially over. But he was adamant. I finally jumped in between them both to put it to an end.

After a short pep talk about our do's and don'ts within the republic, I had one final problem to deal with. Not only had Kev taken E-Kapone's dope, gun, and jewelry, he had also taken the keys to his one bedroom apartment, and had subsequently kicked him out. In front of everybody, I ordered Kev to give him back his house keys. Suddenly E-Kapone, never seizing to amaze me, spoke up and clarified that he wanted neither the keys nor the apartment. I buried my hard stare into him and I knew that moment without a doubt, I could have bust a cap in his ass and not felt any regrets or remorse about his demise.

There was one thing that I couldn't stand in my presence or anywhere around me, and that was the life and limbs of a true fucken coward. To this day Lil E-Kapone didn't realize how close the fire came to burning him for being an outright punk. Without any delays and mostly from keeping me from popping him right then and there, he was dismissed from the park. Since I felt Kev didn't deserve the apartment to himself entirely, I decreed that it should have three owners, selected from our three biggest clicks: Kev from the 27th Street; Lil B-Rock from the 2nd Avenues; and making the ownership a whole, I elected myself as a member of the 29th Street click. After all the steam blew away, we bee lined to the new apartment for a full session of smoking, drinking, and gambling.

In time, everything was back to normal, but one thing had changed. Which disturbed me greatly was the sudden disappearance of Lil E-Kapone. I noted his absence, as I would normally see him in his little white Toyota pushing dope to the large clientele that we often competed over. All his actions of late, the relinquishing of his apartment, his lack of desire to fight, and his disappearance from the turf stuck deep in my psychic, and it would be something that would bother me always, as something was wrong with the picture. G-Kev was finally gaining his old-self back little by little, and soon we were out seeking a fourth apartment that we could turn into another crack spot for the large amount of dope that we were buying of late.

Around that same time, Kev met and fell in love with a Hispanic girl named Lorraine. In all my years being around him I had never witnessed him having his nose wide open for any woman as it was for Lorraine. Lorraine was straight: She had long pretty hair, a soft side that was adorable and an ass on her like a black woman. Whatever voodoo she worked on my boy, it worked perfectly as jealousy outbursts from him were becoming a daily habit. Lorraine had the problem that she was a little flirtatious and his outbursts were justified at times; but then, there were other times, he just went over the edge tripping on things I couldn't understand. I kept a conscious effort to stay away from Lorraine, as she had showed on more than one occasion an interest in me; she had even given me a nickname, 'Papa Chulo'.

Kev exploded on her one day as he had heard and seen enough of her flirtatious acts: "Bitch shut the fuck up! Don't ever talk to Loko like that again!" She would try in vain to put up a fight to justify she meant no harm, but Kev wasn't having none of it. After awhile he started keeping her away from us when we were out conducting business. But after a day or two, she would soften him up, and all over again she would be back at the spot under the watchful and jealous eyes of my dog who seemed to be at odds with himself on what decision to make on her faith.

Sofia was becoming intricately a part of my life as the days turned to months, and with each day's new dawn, we both knew in time that we were the victims of cupid arrow. But our love affair was something that didn't sit so well with Sheila who was still harboring emotional attachments for me. Since she was a part of my economical structure, her presence around me was more than Sofia would have liked. They were open enemies to each other's well being, and words of 'hello', 'hi', or 'what's up' were foreign in thoughts when they viewed each other. Their hatred for one another reached a boiling point one day when all hell broke lose.

We were riding in Kev's black Maximum four deep, with Sofia and me in the back seat, Kev driving and Sheila in the passenger seat, returning from purchasing a large amount of crack in which I was holding on me besides a pistol. When Kev pulled up in front of the St. Andrews apartment, I jumped out and made a straight beeline for the front door to put up the illegal contents. From the moment I entered into the apartment and Sofia didn't follow close behind I knew then I had made a grave mistake. Sofia's and Sheila's truce was only due and acknowledged to my presence, and we all knew that if they were alone together for too long, the fight bell would ring, and they would bore into each other like two old rivals.

After securing the dope, I noticed the car was gone, which made me look frantically up and down the block trying to locate them; just then, I spotted them flying around the corner at high speeds with two of the doors wide open. My heart jumped in my chest as something was wrong with the picture, I instantly thought of foul play. I bee lined back into the house, grabbed my Nina off the T.V., and in clear view of anybody who may have been looking, I chambered a round. I was under the impression that another car with enemy personnel in hot pursuit of G-Kev's Maximum would bend the corner any second, and I was going to be the welcoming party. But soon that notion was put to rest as Kev stopped out-front.

Sofia and Sheila couldn't wait to exit the car. They bee lined in on each other with destruction and annihilation as their imminent mission finally getting the chance they had been looking for, and as I watched from a distance realizing they weren't in danger of any enemy forces, they locked hard like two racing cars on a suicide mission. "Bitch," they were screaming at each other hollering profanity, and pulling on each other's hair. After watching for a few seconds, I had seen enough, and an overwhelming anger overtook me. They both were about to feel the verbal wrath I had in mind. I ran back inside, placed the gun on the T.V. and bee lined to intervene on the on-going fight. By the time I arrived, they held each other in grip locks with each having a handful of hair. I jumped behind Sofia and began prying her hands lose of Sheila's hair, and Kev did the same with Sheila. The moment they were pulled apart, I threw a full-scale nutty attack. Sofia had never seen me blow up before, and she didn't know how to respond to the venom that was pouring from my mouth, so she opted to be quiet.

After the fight, Sheila was subsequently cut from the team on our economical endeavors; and as a result, I severed all ties with her on my future projects. In Sheila's shortcomings of being laid off, I replaced her with my homegirl Tama, a student at Trade Tech City College. Sheila on the other hand immediately went behind the scenes to plot on my destruction; and anyone who wanted to be a part of her team and had an interest to lash out at me was taken aboard her bandwagon. For an entire month she staked me out looking for a break in my defenses, and in her being relentless, she had found it. Serena Moore was her avenue of getting closer to me, and helping her achieve the maximum damage that she wanted to severe against Sofia and me. Serena was a part of my economical circle that helped me to make some large sales of chronic to a clientele in the Hollywood area. But after the fight with Sheila, Sofia had me eliminate most of the female posse, one by one and somewhere in the rapture Serena, too was out. But she still had a key to my apartment on 9th and Fedora, and due to her and Sheila's common denominator of having ill feelings against me, they clicked up to rob me at every chanced opportunity.

The first sign was when items from Sofia's purse began mysteriously disappearing. The second sign was when I had left about three thousand dollars and my red pager on the living room floor that I couldn't find. I flipped the house upside down. Still my suspicious wasn't placed on its highest alert, as I convinced myself I had lost it in traffic. But the third and final incident did prompt me to take some new precautions. I had freshly purchased a half kilo of cocaine, and I knew with a hundred percent certainty that I hadn't touched the dope at all. When I arrived back home the next day, I noticed at least a quarter of my dope was completely missing. Then and there, I knew somebody had a key to my apartment, as there was never any sign of forced entree.

That same day I changed my locks on the door. I didn't find out until sometime later through confessions of a third party that Sheila and Serena had been robbing me blind to avenge their revenge against me for choosing Sofia over them. In time, the females that were once a part of my team were laid to the wayside. I burnt many bridges in the process of pleasing Sofia, but they compared to her style and charisma weren't even close to a match up; she had won decisively with hands down.

Shortly after, Tray-K had finally come through with another lick. He called and gave me some brief details about a chronic buy worth thirty-five thousand dollars, and that he was setting the lick up for me to be the supposed buyer. Another lick was just what I needed as I had run into a long line of bad luck. Besides Sheila tearing a mud hole into my pants pockets, I being absent-mindedly misplaced a quarter kilo of dope. Bad luck was waging a personal war against me, and presently I was losing it.

After everything was set up and the final touches were put into place with, the chronic deal was set to go down in a few nights, scheduled at a location somewhere in the republic of the Rollin 60's, and in fact some of them were expected to be involved in the transaction. Tray-K gave me stern advice not to proceed if it were more than two people inside the home. Arriving on the scene, we pulled along side a parked Yukon truck to check out its occupants, two baldhead Cholos, who were probably a part of the impending deal. We exited the red Durango S.U.V. driven by one of Tray's Hispanic females and bee lined to the shack size apartment of where the deal was supposed to go down. In route to the front door, I placed my trigger hand on the Beretta in my right pocket and reassured myself that if anything went wrong, I was able to put in some major work.

The lick went from bad to worse, as there weren't two people inside but four. Tray-K inquired about the Hispanics outside in the truck, and just that fast the perfect lick went down the drain, as they also were a part of the deal. That meant it was six to two with only one gun that I held and them having the odds in their favor. Pounds and pounds of chronic lay all over the living room floor in plain sight of my greed and thirst, which made the problem for me a catch 22. But deep in my heart, I knew if it's a will, it's surely a way, I just had to figure it out. One of the unknown Crips lit up a blunt to allow me the chance to sample the marijuana that I was expected to buy, he unknowingly bought me some more time to think about my problem at hand. I blew on the chronic keeping control of myself so I wouldn't cough from its effect, pretending that it wasn't any good. "Ah homey", I began "I can't buy no chronic that don't make me cough, you know". The Crip panicked and sensing that the deal was slipping through his hands, he began on his salesman pitch: "Maybe the blunt was rolled too tight, let me roll you another one."

Just then, Tray-K realized what I had done; he knew me well enough, and he knew without doubt that I had set into motion the take down of the spot. He stood right in my face and looked me right in my eyes, telling me through words unspoken that the deal shouldn't proceed. But it was too late. My focus and energy was tuned into the occupants in the house, and despite Tray-K's blurry vision in front of me, I was bent on taking the spot down single handedly. The Crip had finished rolling another blunt. I pulled on it hard and went into an uncontrollable cough. I pulled on it once more and passed it back to him. That was my cue. The moment he took it and turned in his chair, I chambered a hollow point round into my gun.

"This is a motha fucken jack, everybody down!" Since the apartment was no bigger than a regular size shack, it was easy for me to place control over all the occupants and to keep them all in view. I swerved the Nina back and forth across the air placing its deadly reality into the psychic of my robbery victims that this was as real as it gets. After control was established, I went about snatching up pound after pound of the weed that was scattered all across the floor. I caught a glimpse of a figure to my right that registered in my automatic mode as becoming threatening. The actions were those of a person who was about to make a move. I swerved the Beretta in his direction and barked my uncompromising command: "On Blood Gang, I'm inches away from busting a cap in your ass!" The would-be assassin slid back to the floor reluctantly and buried his face deep into the carpet.

After snatching the last bag of the cough medicine, I made a bank robbery exit from the residence with my pistol pointed downward. Tray-K and his lady-friend were in the truck waiting for my appearance. The second I slid into the back seat Tray-K's Latina lover slammed on the gas pedal and the truck lurched forward; I covered our exiting escape by hanging out the rear window with the Nina focused on the front door that had just paid us thirty-five thousand dollars in product. We drove back to the hood, split the dope up, and I immediately went in search of G-Kev to share the news. I located him and Baby G-Kev in the parking lot of the St. Andrews apartments. Kev knew I had scored again, as my smile stretched from ear to ear. "You hit, huh?" To answer his question I pulled out a bag full of the sticky icky chronic.

We ended up blowing blunt after blunt, and before long, the time had stretched into the morning hours the next day. Before I left, I proclaimed to them that I was going to buy a kilo of cocaine and that I was giving the St. Andrews apartment to them to push from. "You hear that Baby Kev? Yeah that's our spot now!" My boy was happy. We departed in different directions to get our rest for the day's activities, I would have never guessed it, but it would be the last time I would see my roll dog alive.

04 – 11 – 2000

Around noon of the same day I headed back to St. Andrews with my homey Poeboy to push the crack, when Lil B-Rock pulled up erratically crying and screaming that Kev was dead. The words that came from his mouth bounced off my ear, as I didn't want to believe what I was hearing. "Kev dead, Loko!" As he continued screaming at me, I felt myself zoning out and having an outer body experience; the news was too great for me to bear. It was beyond my train of thought. "Where at, B-Rock?" Poeboy was screaming at B-Rock, "Where he at, B-Rock!" Between sobs and choking back tears, he informed us that Kev was around the corner on 28th Street. The whole time I was running to the location, I was in denial of the reality that was to alter my life forever. The police had a roadblock set-up, which prevented me from getting a good look of the person who lay in the street with a white sheet covering only a portion of his body. I couldn't believe it as my heart told me it wasn't Kev, and that everything was going to be all right.

I bee lined back to the apartment to get a pair of binoculars. When I looked up the street at the body I was in denial about, I immediately had a faint spell pass over me, as I had instantly recognized the brown shoes that I just bought for Kev. It was he, and from that moment on my heart thumped a warrior's tune of revenge against everybody, who had something to do with his death. It didn't make a difference to me, as it could have been some government secret service men. All I knew was, the perpetrator, who had taken my friend away from me, was going to feel the boiling wrath that flowed through my body. It was on! I had seen enough at the crime scene to know that somebody was going to be as good as dead before the sunset.

I drove up Adams heading to the liquor store on Budlong where I bought myself drinks I had never drunk before. I was hoping the hard liquor would help me accomplish my painful mission. I don't recall much afterward, but one thing was for sure, an entire day had passed since Kev's demise. I was told I had drunk myself into a stupor swearing throughout the night to everybody that revenge was mine. Ignoring my hangover, I proceeded to kick my day off correctly with nothing short of taking some souls to help me relieve myself of the overwhelming pain I was feeling at the loss of Kev. The second I stepped on the scene, the republic troopers knew the task at hand was about to be a bloody campaign against all odds. We were about to commit ourselves into the whirlpool of violence spinning out of control on our quest to satisfy our appetite to make others feel what we were feeling.

I was being bombarded with information concerning everything from what people had seen to who was already claiming responsibility of killing my dog. But of all the info, only one could be dealt with right then and there which was the accusation against Baby Tray-K and G-Kev's girl Lorraine. They had allegedly cuddled up together in the hours proceeding G-Kev's death and worse they had spent the night together having sex. After hitting the St. Andrews complex where the perpetrators were, I dispatched a homey to go and notify Baby Tray-K that I wanted to speak to him.

As the seconds ticked into minutes, and the minutes into hours, the parking lot was filling to capacity with angry hard-core members waiting for the orders to launch some massive retaliatory attack against the foe that was to blame for a crime that shook the entire republic of the Rollin 20's. "What's up Loko?" Baby Tray-K walked in my direction, knowing all the time that he was walking a tight rope that could lead to our collision, if he answered wrong to any question I was about to ask him.

When he was within striking distance, my aggression against him poured from my entire demeanor: "Did you fuck Lorraine last night?" I screamed on him standing inches from his face, and his reply almost cost him a broken nose. "What do you mean, did I fuck her last night?" Either he was stupid as hell, or he was nervous. I slammed my car keys to the ground and demanded once more of the accusation of his acts of atrocity against my friend. "Naw I didn't fuck her Loko." – "Then we don't have no beef." I was steaming out of control, and all the troopers in my presence knew at the moment of watching me deal with Baby Tray-K a lot of heads were about to roll. I sent for Lorraine. I wanted to see, if she'd have a slip of the tongue about the accusations against her, but she hadn't.

With no more time to waste I orchestrated the republic's personnel into cadres of killing teams that were ready to take the revenge out on the 30 Harlem Crips who it had been confirmed and recently verified to be Kev's killer. In days following recon teams were issued walkie-talkies. I stood in the St. Andrews parking lot with my binoculars watching a liquor store on Jefferson which the 30's had been known to visit, looking for any signs of enemy movement.

My determination had just paid off as a big body black S.S. Impala drove past my field of view, but it was too fast for me to make a precise decision whether they were non-combatants or foe. "B-Rock, where you at?" – "I'm driving up Jefferson." – "Blood there's a big black S.S. Impala traveling westbound up Jefferson, tell me if you see it." I waited, hoping like hell that he would locate the car. Some few seconds had passed and B-Rock was speaking sweet tunes to my ear: "I got the car Blood, we traveling northbound up Arlington" – "Stay on him Blood, I want him." The troopers around me listened and waited with excitement as another chance to eliminate a Harlem had been stumbled upon.

Just as the silence became thick enough to cut it with a dull knife, B-Rock was back over the walkie-talkie telling me something that made my heart jump with pleasure: The damn car was heading up 27th Street directly at us. My mind began racing fast. I ordered three troopers with some heavy automatics to drive to Western and 28th to await further orders. Seconds later the enemy car drove past with a lone driver, undoubtedly on a recon mission. That was the moment to give out the republic's signature. Following my lead the Y.G's around me banged on the passing car. "B-Rock, get off the car, I repeat, get off the car!" I was back over the airwave informing the hit squad to prepare for their target. Just as I expected, the enemy recon car made a complete circle thus running right into the cadre of killers whose mission was to wipe another 30 away from existence, as a good 30 was a dead 30. "Loko we got him!"

"Wait for my order, and keep me updated." The recon car was driving back up Jefferson, heading back into my binocular view. I watched him, and hot on his tail the hit squad. "Loko he stopped to talk to some females, can we take him?" With no delay of letting the fish lose, I gave the executive order to peel his cap back. "Boom, boom, boom, boom, boom, boom," in rapid concession the hit squad automatics cracked the anger, releasing the feelings we felt against the Harlems as they were to lose countless dead homies at the expense of the gravest mistake in their history that would weigh heavy in my heart to times long past.

Up until G-Kev's funeral, we faithfully launched three to four preemptive attacks daily and sometimes around the clock, against our rivals' strong holds. Support for the war effort was pouring in from all reaches throughout the republic, guns of all magnitude and size, boxes and bags of bullets, and volunteers were readily lining up to help.

G-Kev's funeral day had arrived, and in days prior, I had purchased a 1984 Monte Carlo low-rider with ten switches on it. I wasn't too much into low-riders at that time, but I bought the car with the desire of placing G-Kev's face on the hood of it. With his sudden demise, I decided to patch up and reconcile an understanding with Sheila again, as I knew how much Kev's departure had disturbed her, whereas she performed yet another selfish act minutes into the funeral proceedings. Sofia and me bee lined to pick her up at the local hair salon on Crenshaw, when she promptly demanded that she should be allowed to drive the low-rider in the funeral caravan. That was too much; I made a clear quick decision to leave her ass right there on the spot pondering what she had done wrong to anger me. Then I drove northbound up Crenshaw heading to the Angeles Funeral Home on 39th and Crenshaw.

The place was packed when we arrived. Once inside I braced myself for the inevitable. The shock, the tears, the heart pain, and the deep love of wanting to exchange places with him so he could love and be happy again. The closer I got to his casket the more the tears swelled within my eyes soon over flowing uncontrollably. The pain and suffering I had been feeling since I lost him, swelled ten times as much as I looked down at him lying in a box that wasn't meant for him.

My friend was supposed to be happy and alive, living, caring, giving, and breathing, but instead he lay motionless in a fucken box that didn't sit well within my psychic. I bent over the casket, leaning toward him and placed a light kiss on his forehead whispering to him that I would revenge his death until my demise. At that moment, I lost all control of myself and fell against the wall wailing about the anger and loss I was experiencing.

G-Kev's departure would be my turning point of becoming careless and reckless; it would be the moment in my life where I didn't give a fuck. Sofia held me in her arms desperately trying to sooth the obvious pain I was enduring, but there was little that anybody could have done to erase the grief I felt. There was only one remedy that affected my grief, made me feel a tad bit better, and that was the seek-and-destroy missions into the 30's republic.

The funeral goers headed to their parked cars and prepared to leave for the Washington Cemetery. Sofia, Dee-Dee, and I headed to the lowrider. I handed Sofia a red and white 'T' hat, which symbolized our republic. Then I inserted the East Siders cassette tape, and positioned my car within the quarters of some other highly decorated troopers. The long funeral caravan packed with the republic troopers and G-Kev's large Belizean family began its snake like movement heading northbound up Crenshaw. All around me, gangsters from the republic wore their 'T' hats proclaiming to the gang world at large that we were from the West Side 20's Bloods.

The car pool made a right turn onto Exposition, taking us directly into our rival's playing grounds. The moment we reached the area of Exposition and Western, the black and white units of the local police department put themselves into plain view for us. We detoured up Normandie making a straight path to Washington Cemetery. Once we crossed over the demilitarized zone of Jefferson, we entered back into the territory that we all had placed a personal claim on. We were the Neighborhood Bloods and that day of April 11, 2000, we all shared in the same pain and loss of our friend and homey, Anthony 'G-Kev' Moguel. True to the old saying for every action, there's a reaction, and due to our massive barrage of gun playing against the 30's in the days following Kev's death, we finally received our response call from them on their now boiling anger of losing one too many homeboys.

A week after the loss of Kev, I received news from a dear and special friend by the name of Tana Vernon about the death of her brother M-Dog, a highly decorated soldier of the fields. His death could have been prevented entirely, if the people who were around him that day had used just a little common sense. The BZP (Belizean Posse) had a spot located on 30th Street and Halldale, and they had been doing a lot of drinking that day. Shortly after running out of beer, M-Dog volunteered for the mission of acquiring some more, but there were two factors that should have been considered before allowing him to leave. The first and most important one was the place of where they had their intention of getting the beer from, the Denker liquor store, which is a highly patrolled area for enemy personnel who frequent the store around the clock. And the other factor was the fact that M-Dog was already drunk and about to go on a suicide mission with only one outcome at best.

But it was presumed since he was packing some heat that he would be all right and able to take care of himself. That wasn't to be the case as the alcohol clouded his skillful military training, which would have dictated to him to take actions of life and death precautions. The moment he entered into the liquor store, he was confronted by cadres of 30's, who immediately hit him up on his color allegiance. Somewhere in the conversation, he had told them he didn't bang and that he was a Belizean. The rivals, who had already been taking a severe beaten from our endless stream of drive-by shootings, weren't convinced of M-Dog's story and responded to him by saying that all Belizeans were slobs.

I know without any doubt, were M-Dog sober upon hearing those words, he would have calculated his next move, and when the time permitted he would have placed well precise bullet holes into each and every enemy personnel who stood within his kill zone. But that's not how it all turned out. When he bee lined out the store, the 30's were in waiting to execute their ambush blasting him once in the stomach.

The moment the news was broadcasted, I received a phone call from Tana informing me of him being in surgery and in critical condition. Her words sent me into a state of mind that could best be described as being lifeless. I was being drained of all my energy at the loss of my friends falling one by one, and I knew in my heart that I wasn't ready for another funeral. Then I got the call that would drive me of breaking all my habits of taking precautions, and being calculated on my impending military mission. M-Dog was gone. At the first sign of nightfall, I prepared with a cadre of shooters for an imminent military and successful operation against the enemies.

I knew we were doing too much, and I also knew with the latest of shootings, we couldn't go back to the hood, as the one-time probably would be looking for us. We ended up in the jungles at the apartment of Sofia's grandmother where we smoked ourselves into oblivion trying to erase the pain through the only way we knew. Days later, we buried M-Dog in the same cemetery only inches away from Kev, and once again, the pain flowed all around.

I was suffering, and my change of actions was noticeable as the days drifted by. I lost my interest in hustling and jacking, and spent most of my days getting high and drifting away from reality. Sofia nourished me and brought the comfort, love, and sense of okayness back into my life that had abandoned me. We grew together in such a way that we soon began discussing marriage plans. I was ready for marriage as it would be just one of many antidotes on my return stages back to a normal and secure life. I loved Sofia so we proceeded at full speed ahead and set the arrangements for a marriage day. My sister Virgina and her husband Big Wimp from the East Side Mad Swan Bloods accompanied us to Las Vegas.

On May 13, 2000, some thirty-two days after Kev's absence from my life, I took my vows to love and cherish my new wife until death do us part, in my heart Kev was my best man. I was really eager to slow my life and turn over a new leaf. On my thirty-first birthday I gave a picnic retirement party to proclaim to my friends and family that I was giving up my ties to the gang world. I was tired of all the pain and suffering.

After I succeeded on my first two implementations of distancing myself from the only world and experience I knew, I ran into a problem. My money was low and since I was officially a family man, I decided I would need one more lick to set me on my way of totally severing my last ties to the 20's. During the retirement picnic, one of my homeboys gave me the chanced opportunity to participate in a large jewelry store robbery. He said, it would be my wedding-gift-lick that would give my departure from the turf a gangster's exit. For days, a cadre of Y.G's and I went over valuable information pertaining to the lick, and it was plenty to be digested. The jewelry store was located in Beverly Hills; it would be the lick of all licks and it would test my calculated jacking skills. The security measures of the store would prove the most difficult, as there were twenty-one cameras inside and two security guards in addition. We poured over all the details making sure we dotted every "i" and crossed every "t".

Some eight days after my retirement announcement the lick was set to go as planned. Sofia was nervous and somewhat reluctant to let me go. I don't know if you could have called it premonition, but she wasn't feeling this one lick. She held me tightly for fear it would probably be her last time holding me if things went array. I proceeded to do what I would normally do before any mission of such magnitude and measures. I gave a pep talk to the cadre and my wife, and more importantly to myself. During my speech I was convincing myself that everything was going to be okay; and that I was coming back home to my wife. In route to the jewelry location, Sofia's face continuously bounced in and out of my mind. I had to stay focused I knew, but thoughts of my wife clouded my mind, and I knew then I couldn't fail her by not returning home.

Arriving on the scene, I pulled the car in front of the targeted location, and like clockwork, I zoned out into my autopilot mode and set things into motion. My homeboy G-Boy and I exited the car first and made a straight beeline for the front door. Once inside we encountered the two security guards that we knew by name from our tedious homework and surveillance of the place. "What time do ya'll open up?" The black guard responded that they would be open in some twenty to thirty minutes. As my heart picked up its rhythmic pace, I knew the moment to set it off had arrived. My hands were already in my pockets, and as the sonic booms thundered in my head, I whipped the Nina out and swung it on both guards: "This is a robbery motha fuckers!" As I swung the Beretta to level on the white security guard to make sure he didn't touch any devices or buttons that would notify the police, the black guard made a beeline exit for the front door only to be met by G-Boy who held a 357um (Magnum) now pointed at his head.

After securing the lobby area and the amateur security guards, we rounded up all the employees who were upstairs unloading the four vaults of their jewelry contents. We entered into the elevator with the two bound and gagged guards who were pushed onto the ground directly in front of the open elevator doors. I made a hastily beeline for the first person in sight who was to be rounded up. After all the employees were huddled together, we took the twenty-one video tapes out of the VCR boxes, before we executed making us two million dollars richer in jewelry. I drove through a multitude of back streets through Beverly Hills and Culver City, finally making it to the jungles. News of the robbery aired for three days with rewards for our immediate arrest.

"Maybe they're the new narcotic division," I commented aloud to no one in particular. I had counted at least fifteen cars that continuously drove past my apartment, back and forth. Undoubtedly they were one-time, but who and of what division was unknown. "Pack up, everybody pack up, we outta here." I assumed a narcotic raid was only seconds away from occurring, and I didn't want to be trapped inside the apartment when it happened. I waited for what it seemed like an eternity for the cars to slow on their circling the block, but it turned into hours as they continued on their mission. Finally, during a break, we made a speedy exit, when I received the dreadful news that would soon set my life into a downward spiral, a life that I had never experienced before, a life on the run.

The multitude of cars belonged to the Beverly Hills Task Force, assigned to take us down for the robbery of the jewelry store called '14 Carats'. I jumped over the airwaves on my cell phone and made my reservations and plans for a Houdini disappearance. I hopped from one motel to the next, trying to figure out my next move. I kept my ear to the wind grabbing any information that would be important and helpful to make sure I was one step ahead of my new predators: the entire Los Angeles Police Department. I was a marked man feeling the grips of the law tighten around my neck daily, as I lost control of myself. Some two weeks had past since the robbery, and I was becoming restless and tired.

Being on the run wasn't something I was good at, as I couldn't make my mind up on what for sure actions I should take. The stress of always looking over my shoulders soon had its effect on my relationship with my wife. Initially she had tried to brave it out, but as I deteriorated to where nothing seemed to matter, she lashed out. We argued about everything that bothered us, and we fought each other for control as we lost control of our surroundings and movement. Our sex life had all but stopped and weighed heavy on our relationship.

As I spiraled out of control falling deeper into a pit that I was creating, my days on the street soon became numbered as I wasn't the same calculated person anymore. I tried to put myself back on track by doing what I did best: organizing and orchestrating. I bought a half kilo of crack and designated my homeboy Baby B-Rock to push it for me. I bought a new car that would be unknown to anybody, and I found an apartment so I could stop the entire motel hopping. When I sat in the car out front of the new apartment patiently waiting on my wife's return who was putting the final touches on the agreement with the landlord, a black and white squad car bent the corner. My heart thumped in my chest like never before. The occupants eye-fucked me, then they drove up the street, pulled into a driveway, and made an about face heading back my way. I pretended not to see them, as my patience screamed for Sofia's return. The car came up slowly, and for a split second I thought they were about to bounce out, forcing me into a run that would probably be my last run in the free world. But my hyper erratic thoughts gave way to calm as they drove by and bee lined around the corner.

Some minutes later, Sofia entered the car telling me the apartment was ours, and that we could move me in when we were ready. Those words were a blessing in disguise, as I was tired of running all around the city. Now I could relax and take a time out to reflect on everything that was moving so fast around me. I cautiously turned the same corner the K-9 had, all the time keeping an eye out for their presence. We drove up 9th Street heading west toward Western with the plan of returning to the Y-Tell Motel to get our few belongings. I was ecstatic. I desperately needed the time out and my marriage needed a time to heal and build. We were talking about our new prospect of taking hold of our lives, when the nightmare began.

The same police car that passed me earlier was about to pull me over and do what they did best to most inner city residents: harass and bother. I made a quick left turn and smashed on the gas pedal to give myself some distance just in case I had to flee on feet. In my rearview I saw the K-9 unit making a hastily u-turn, they were about to give chase. I waited a second at the corner. The squad car was making a beeline approach in my direction with the inevitable occurring faster than I could compute. I bended the corner toward Western, another right turn at the corner of Western, and gave the gas pedal a push to put some space between me and the pursuing car that I thought was closing in from behind. They had manipulated me into believing they were going to pursue me up the block, but they had double backed, and my plan of escape had exploded in my face, I had to face the fact that it was now over.

"Baby, I'm about to go to jail." The confession of my end in her life stunned Sofia so suddenly that she released a deep nightmare sob that filled the entire car. "No, Baby! Please, God no!" Sofia was beyond herself, and like my receiving of the news of Kev's demise, she went through the same mental phases: disbelief, denial, and the overwhelming shock. The black and white unit jumped behind me, and all in sequence, the stages of my removal from the street unfolded with a wave of sickness that was beyond a cure. The colorful lights on the squad car began spinning, signifying for me to pull over. I had to think, I had to come up with an immediate plan. A name, I needed a name that had no warrants or red flags on it. Yes, that would do, my brother name would do, it was gonna be all right now, if I could just remain calm. I pulled into a supermarket parking lot with the K-9 tailing me closely. I exited my car having an overwhelming urge to say to hell with it, and to make a straight beeline run looking for the first gate to hop.

Instead and soon regrettably, I chose the formal option and decided to play it cool, as things weren't probably as bad as I had convinced myself. The clean cut one-time approached me cautiously, and immediately began asking me a series of questions: "Are you on probation? Are you on parole? Do you have any warrants?" I responded "no" to all his questions, but somehow I felt I wasn't too convincing; and again I battled with myself about running. "What's your name Mister?" Finally, the moment of truth was at hand, and the nerve-racking that was traumatizing me took my whole train of thought. Before I could stop myself, I blurted out "Charles Wright". It was the gravest mistake I had made while I was on the run. I'd given my brother's first name, but added on my last name. I wanted to stop the officer as he headed back to the car, and I wanted to tell him, "Look Sir, I made a mistake, really, my name is Charles Casey, not Charles Wright. The police officer typed the name I gave him into the computer, and again the battle waged in my head about running or staying. Before a decision could be reached on what I should do, the officer was returning with my faith hanging on the tip of his tongue. I looked over at my wife who was showing all the signs of a young widow.

Run! Run! Run! The K-9 reached for me with handcuffs in his hand. I dashed hard to the left literally, avoiding the long arm of the law. "Freeze! Freeze!" The voice of the officer bounced in and out of my head, like a radio station that wouldn't come all the way in. I ran faster and faster, thinking I'd be able to out run the two over weight K-9's. I felt my cell phone slipping off my hip, and in the heat of running, it never crossed my mind that the police would mistake its black exterior for a gun. "Look out Baby! Nooooo," unknowingly to me, but the two K-9's went down on one knee, aimed their automatics at me and contemplated whether I was about to become a threat to their well beings. I spun my entire body around, held the cell phone in the air and began screaming aloud: "No, no, no, no, no!" By the time the phone had reached the pavement cracking into many pieces, I was already back into my full stride of trying to get away. I zoomed pass a group of construction workers, who all could have been on the payroll of the L.A.P.D., as they took up the chase helping the police out who had by now been out-runned.

The bright light of escaping was soon darkened with the aspect of so many new people, giving chase to the now exhausted and winded me. With every step I took in my ever-slowing run, the freedom I once knew was slipping away. I made one last effort to shake my pursuers by running up some stairs, which mistakenly led into a dead end. It was over, finally, the running, the sleepless nights, the indecisiveness, and the fear of being out of control. They didn't have to tell me to lie down, as I had already spread eagle. I closed my eyes and began viewing the images of the life that I once lived.

COUNTY JAIL BLUES
(2000)

Sofia and I were both hauled off to the Rampart substation; from there I was picked up by some Beverly Hills detectives who transported me over to their substation. I was rebooked over again and placed into a holding cell by myself. After spending a few days in Beverly Hills, I was once again moved. The transportation bus traveled through the multitude of streets bee lining toward the courthouse where I was to be arraigned on more counts than I cared to count. I sat in my seat day dreaming and looking at the people we passed on the street thinking of how lucky they were to have what I was about to be denied of for a long time to come.

I was back on my way to the County Jail. Going through the process of being processed, they bombarded me with the reality of where I was at every twist and turn. "How many strikes do you have?" Man either I was high of some drugs I didn't recall taking or the person who put the lady up to asking me that question had to be the most stupid mother fucker on earth. For God sakes, we are criminals, and to ask us to tell them something so sensitive that could affect our freedom entirely was beyond me completely. "I don't have no strikes that I remember!" She looked at me, eyeballed my old tattoos and the word she didn't speak came traveling across to me. I knew she wasn't convinced of my answer, but it wasn't a substance of truth in me, especially with all the pending charges, I was facing. I would be the laughing stock of all who knew that I fucked myself by telling her I had strikes. I walked away from that window with the world on my shoulder, and God it was heavy.

After the interview that left me with a slight headache, I made a straight beeline to get next on one of the multitude of phones. It had been three days since I've last seen my wife, and I was starving to talk to her; but I had to wait, as there were plenty of men in front of me. My mad dog attitude and stare was locked and loaded on anyone who wanted the challenge that I was offering. Everything about my demeanor radiated a person who was on a suicide mission, and who didn't give a fuck at all.

I dialed the only number I knew, and I was hoping she would be there to answer. On the first ring, she picked up and the smile that had been suppressed for days slid across my face. The happiness I was feeling at the sound of her voice was like the joy of a father who was holding his first child. It was beyond words. "Hi Baby!" My wife was as excited as I was. "What's up Baby?" I asked her trying to control the tremor in my voice, "how long you been out?" I knew they were gonna release her as they didn't have anything to charge her with. But although they took her to the substation with me, with the hopes to squeeze her for information about the robbery and the whereabouts of the jewelry, she didn't bite on their tactics of threats, as she voice fully told them to go and fuck themselves. After they had drilled her for a while, they soon realized they were dealing with a solid and unshakeable woman.

It felt really good to know she held my best interest at heart, and it was reassuring to know they had released her unabated. We chatted up until it was time for me to head on to the next phase of the process. It took every ounce of strength in my hand, and all the will power I could muster up to hang the phone up on her. It was time to go, and ironically, I didn't want to leave. "I got to go Baby, before I get into trouble. I promise to call you as soon as I get to my next location, okay?" My wife wasn't budging. "Baby, look I got to go before I get into trouble!" Reluctantly she allowed me to go, but only with the promise, I would call her with the first chance I'd get.

The next phase of the process was something I had been looking forward to, eating. Normally I wouldn't have an appetite for sandwiches that were dry and tasteless, but the draining experience of returning to jail had depleted me, and gave me an overwhelming hunger. I ate the two plain sandwiches with such vigor that it took a second for me to realize that I had nothing else to eat. I was still hungry so I traded my hot fruit drink and hard cookies to somebody who didn't have the stomach to eat the sandwiches. I was trying to get full, as I knew from experiences that it would be a long time in coming until my next meal.

The check-in into the County Jail was truly a classic hurry up and wait episode. We would be rushed into one process, then forced into one of the many holding cells, and then to wait for a long time. After hours and hours, we were finally led through a long hallway, heading into a different realm. The County brakes off into two main sections. On the one side which is separated by hallways and elevators is the second floor which is referred to as the 2000 floor; above it is the third floor which is referred to as the 3000 floor; and above there is the roof for recreation. On the other side are the 4000 to the 9000 floor, and its recreation roof.

Once inside the belly of the jail, it really didn't make a difference where they placed me. In so many ways, it was like any battlefield environment: It was important to know what members from what particular neighborhood were monopolizing the floor, as a person's life could be forfeited, if they were your immediate rivals from the streets. The

County was a place where the weak suffered all the losses and vices humanly possible at the hands of men who were nothing short of being brutes. I was led to the 2000 floor and placed in module 2200/2400, inside a four-men-cell, along with two Mexicans and another black inmate. My military mind frame wasn't completely on point, as I desperately needed a good night's rest, before I could fully comprehend the danger and threat of my new housing.

"Chow time, Homeboy!" I was hearing voices, but in my relax state of mind I was too out of it to recognize that I was being told about breakfast's arrival. The tranquility of peace and sleep was shattered at the sudden realization that I was in jail. The pale walls blanketed with graffiti of various gangs from all over the city jumped out at me, the noise, the smell, the voice of the inmate who had screamed at me, shaking my mind to the reality of my new life. "Here's your tray Homey." Abruptly I sat up in bed and took the plate that had clumps of cold food, which looked to have been slapped onto it with little regards. Signs of nausea swept over me as I inhaled its unbearable smell. Unlike the cold sandwiches of last night, the cooked food was uneatable. I gave the tray away and made a straight beeline to the phone located in the back of the cell.

I had to call my wife as I was gonna need some money on my books to purchase some commissary. I wasn't into junk food that much, but with the prospect of choosing between the County slop and the junk food, hands down the latter would win every time. My wife had been waiting on my call all night long, and she expressed it promptly: "Why you just now calling me Bonehead?" I learned any time she called me a bonehead; she was angry or upset at me about something. I would soon be a lot of boneheads, as I didn't have any control over the phone periods.

My stay in the Men's Central Jail lasted some two or three days, and once again I was being moved to the Wayside Honor Ranch: the terror dome of riots. Wayside was prone to violent riots between the Blacks and the Hispanics, and everything inside was divided along the color bars including the bed areas, the shower area, and the phones. At all times the environments remained thick with aggression in the air always ready for an outlet, the reason why the precaution of divisions was strictly largely adhered.

The black gangsters in Wayside had two imminent problems to face and to content with. The first problem was the highly organized violent Cholos, who were strictly unified along a new obligation once entering into any jail facility; and the second problem was the drama caused by the Crips. With no delays I set about to unify the various Blood groups to at least give ourselves a fighting chance, before I established a diplomatic military agreement with the opposing army of the Crips. It would be beneficial to us to display a unified front against a group who had no problem kicking off a racial war based on a whim.

Not soon after, I was summoned to the gang unit office, O.S.J. (operation safe jail). The only thing I could think about was they were about to justify their actions of placing me back into high power, a place I had no desire to go. On my way in route to their office, I was accommodated by other Bloods who also dreaded the reason of our summons. We were told to have a seat until our names were called. I was nervous to be there, as it was never a good sign to be called by O.S.J. Nevertheless, I waited patiently to see what faith held for the first person, as it may be an indication of my outcome. After a lengthily interview and photo taking for the O.S.J. updating system, he returned with the grim news that we were all being sent back to the Blood gang module of the County Jail.

Usually there are a few reasons why a gang member would be placed there: One is because a homeboy already in the module requests another person to accompany him. Another reason is due to a person's highly published case, and the charges surrounding it; and the last reason would be due to a person's high-ranking status in the echelon of the gang world. I soon discovered I was being sent there due to all three reasons. The gang module was another world in its entirety, as it fostered unbelievable stress, anger and violent outbursts, which even pitched Bloods against Bloods. The environment was purely depressive and a moral breaker. Countless numbers of the otherwise strong relationships crumbled and fell apart due to the hardship and experiences from the module. It was a challenge that only the strong would survive and overcome.

True to their words, we were on the first bus smoking south on the Interstate 5 back to the Men's Central Jail. On arrival, we had one final step to complete before we were to be housed with an approximate one hundred and fifty hard-core gang members that came from all reaches of the city. We had to be interviewed once again, but this time by a different set of O.S.J. deputies. Each Blood was sent through the tedious routine of questions and answers, then the snapping again for another Kodak moment. "Wright, your turn," I walked up the flight of stairs through the entrance into the interior of the office and sat in the chair facing Deputy Williams. He sat at his desk going through a book with photos of Bloods, looking for the familiar face of mine. I glanced around the room, and everywhere I looked, there was something reflecting the aspect of their jobs. Gang photos of Bloods splattered one section of a wall; Asian gangsters from various areas and gangs splattered another section, and in the distance, another wall displayed photos of Mexican Mafia victims who were murdered for one reason or another. The entire O.S.J. office symbolized the gang world in almost every form.

"What's up Loko?" Williams was the only black O.S.J. deputy, and from my past dealings with him, he was considered an all right person, especially when compared to the other over zealous deputies who were always looking to kick some ass. In his presence I always felt relaxed without the typical barrier that I normally held in a presence of a deputy. He inquired about the case in a subtle way. I gave only light conversation around it, as it was still in its beginning phases, and I didn't want to say anything that would damage me, or my crime partners. After receiving our clothes, changing into the blue and white jumpsuits which symbolized the gang module, we were marched a short distance down the hallway to the module 3200 where the Bloods were kept and locked away almost twenty-four hours a day.

Each cell was designated to individual neighborhoods. Down stairs on Baker Row, there were the Nickerson Garden Bounty Hunter Bloods (cell No. 2 and No. 12), the Miller Gangster Bloods and the Athen Park Bloods (cell No. 3), the Black P. Stone Bloods (cell No. 4), the Mad Swan Bloods and the Neighborhood Family Bloods (cell No. 5 and No. 6), the Pueblo Bishop Bloods and the Blood Stone Villians, before they went to war with each other (cell No. 7), the East Side Outlaw Bloods and the East Side 30 Bloods (cell No. 8), the Brim Bloods, the Six Duse Brims, and the Fruit Town Brims (cell No. 9), the West Side 20's Neighborhood Bloods (cell No. 10 and No. 11), the A.F.C.B. (All For Crime Bloods; cell No. 13), shared by some other Blood fragments. Upstairs on Denver Row there was also a multitude of Blood gangs such as the Crenshaw Mafias, Inglewood Familys, Neighborhood Pirus, Compton Pirus, Pasadena and L.A. Denver Lanes, Carson Bloods, and Bloods from other far to reach places. It was just one big house full of Bloods.

I bee lined up the row looking into each occupied cell searching out familiar faces: "Loko, what's up Loko Blood?" A face appeared from one of the cells to acknowledge me; it was Big Bang from the Be-Bop Watts Bloods. The moment my name was yelled out, I was acknowledged from all around. After I entered into cell number ten where my homeboys eagerly awaited on my arrival, Lil B-Rock, Chucky, Lil Quick, and Poeboy greeted me with nothing short of courtesy and respect. They informed me that I had just missed a war between the Black P. Stones and the L.A. Brims, which was carried out mostly through chunkums. I was briefed in great detail who had started the beef, who struck first, and who had won in their opinion.

Since the module was an unpredictable place, where the wind blew calm and peace in one minute, and in the next, it blew chaos and war, I set about the task of creating an alliance with other Blood neighborhoods that have always held peaceful relationships with our republic. I'm talking about Big Fish and his few troopers from the East Side Outlawz 20's, Big Lep from the Swan Bloods, and the Brims. Of all the alliances, the latter agreed to share information as well as weapons, and that if one was attacked; it was an attack on the others as well. Our weapon stock was weak, and in my opinion ineffective, and I was determined to bring it up to part. I was completely military minded and highly thorough in anything I ventured out to accomplish.

As the first day of my arrival rolled to a climax, I decided to call my wife to arraign for a visit for the following day. The anger in her voice about me not calling her in hours past was vehemently expressed. "Baby look", I tried to remain calm, with the hopes of calming her. "I been really, really busy around here, trying to get myself together." But she wasn't trying to hear nothing but the argument that was pouring from her lips about my lack of concern for her; and the stronger accusation that I probably was on the phone with another woman. It took a couple hours to bring her back to her normal state of mind. Soon we were sharing in sweet laughter chasing away the inevitable pain that always reared its ugly head. We were giving each other our endless love and support to say that everything was going to be okay. The strength and mental resistance I used to fight off the dreadful reality of my new environment was going to have to be filtered or transferred to my wife somehow, as I don't think she was completely prepared for the hardship and toughness of the task at hand.

The long list of names of inmates who were getting visits the next morning, were read off one at a time. I braised myself hoping that my wife had made it in with the first stream of visitors who stood outside for endless hours battling the long slow moving lines and the ruthless elements. "Wright, 80, Baker 10, you have a visit!" I jumped out of bed immediately bee lining around the cell like a mad man gearing myself for the visit. One by one, we were released from our particular cells and handcuffed with long waist chains that bounded our arm movement to almost nil. Nearly twenty Bloods from various neighborhoods snaked up the hallway under escort by a multitude of deputies who were our transport officers. Our caravan was viewed with the stop and stare look from the general population inmates who were free of being cuffed up.

After taking our seats in the visiting blocks, we patiently waited for the arrival of the mothers, sisters, wives or girlfriends who would be streaming in to spend time with their visitors for the period of fifteen minutes. It was a sad case of arrangement if you asked me, three to five hours of endless waiting in line to get through the building's entrance, then another hour just to turn the visiting pass in; and all for the reward of a flat fifteen minutes visit, conducted over the phone and through a thick depressive Plexiglas window, placed in an isle with at least forty other visitors beside and behind, communicating in an ever rising volume. It was all anti climactic in a way, but desired and longed for in a greater way.

I sat in my seat restlessly trying to hold my anxiety level in check, as I waited to see the lovely face of my Belizean wife. The moment she bent the corner, one of the first things I noticed about her was the dress she was wearing. She was lovely as ever as I viewed her body curves through the material that hid little to the imagination. Her full sized breasts swayed back and forth on her chest, and were one of her greatest assets. Our eyes locked with an intensity that could have melted the glas away if it were humanly possible, and the silent love affair continued until the visiting phones were cut on. "Hello? Baby pick up the phone", I was signalizing her with my hands. "Hi Baby, I love you" Sofia exclaimed excitedly, "I love you, too Mama." – "I miss you, Terrell and I want you to come home to me!" The stark reality of her desire was beyond my control, and in essence deep wishful thinking, something I wasn't into. My thinking was dictated by reality, and the reality of my dire situation was I wasn't going anywhere anytime soon, and for a long time to come.

Up and down the gloomy visiting row, the same game was evolving and playing itself out: The women were looking for words of encouragement, something from their spouses that signified that things would be okay, something that would give them a sign of hope to hold on to. I stirred my conversation around the mind-boggling aspect of going home, focusing Sofia's energy on the importance of procuring some money. "Baby look, when you get back to the spot, we have to talk about some very important things." The sadness she had been feeling suddenly sprung from her eyes as the flood gates holding her fear, anxiety, and loneliness over flowed pouring out her heart due to the separation the Plexiglas enforced and compounded. "I love-" the phone cut my sentence in mid stride; the tears flowed harder as the pain in her heart became unbearable. That was the worst part of jail for any man of being capable to maneuver and stir away from the endless bullshit that aroused at every corner along the way.

The deputy entourage arrived immediately there after and without delay, we were re-cuffed and re-secured to be led away, as the thousand mile stares of our women looked on telling the story of our lives. Anger swelled in my chest as the desire to hold my wife again boiled from deep within, leaving me feeling incompetent and worthless. Our entourage snaked its way heading back to the gloom and grey atmosphere of the infamous Blood module.

For a while, I lay in bed drifting over thoughts and ideas, all the time still waiting on my turn to use the phone. Since it was five of us inside the cell with only one phone, we had to rotate its access every so many hours, and my turn was next. I glanced around the cell looking for my other homeboys. My little homey Chucky was at the front bars playing a challenging game of chess with Twin, and somewhere in between the next move, an argument erupted that quickly led to words of war. I don't exactly know what kicked the disagreement off between them, but I knew it was in the best interest to intervene and quite the dispute. "Chucky, Blood, let that go!" Chucky was reluctant at first as he was the kind of Y.G. who had grown up in the company of men who taught him how to be aggressive in anything he did. His up bringing poured from his mouth unedited, and unknowingly at the time, he was setting off a chain of events that would inevitably lead to me being stabbed numerous times.

Twin walked away from the cell irritated by Chucky's bad mouth, and instead of me giving the situation its due analysis, I chalked it up as something that would blow away in the wind. I instead placed the energy in my phone conversation with my wife, something I would come to regret. After lunch the next visiting line was marched out, same procedure, same drill. Chucky was with that chain, and what happened when it returned was beyond my train of thought and totally unsuspected. The Black P. Stones had made pre-emptive plans against us with a scheduled assault targeting Lil Chucky.

I was still into my deep sex conversation with Sofia when I heard a scream of fright hollering out my name to help. Danger! Danger! Danger! With little regards for my wife, I instantly dropped the phone and made a hastily beeline toward the cell's front portion. Chucky was running up the tier screaming that he'd been assaulted by the Black P. Stones. All the troopers in the two cells that we manned voiced our reaction and distaste at the pre-emptive attack that we felt wasn't justified. The cell gate opened, and before Chucky had the chance to enter, we massed out in numbers heading to cell No. 4, the home of the Black P. Stones. We wanted to know why they'd attacked him. Before I could take control of the entire situation, the Y.G. troopers were vehemently expressing themselves with words nothing short of an imminent war. Fuck it I thought, why not let them voice their contempt. After a couple days of hard negotiation and promises of respect for each other, we ironed out our differences and smooved things back to normal, at least for the time being.

DO OR DIE
(2000 – 2001)

A short time later Chucky was released after serving his one year County Jail lid. As soon as he arrived home, the chain reaction began: His girlfriend Diamond was a Black P. Stone Bloodlette to her heart, as well as her father T-Roger, one of their founding originators. But that wasn't the problem, the problem aroused when the P. Stones in the Blood module began calling collect to Diamond's apartment. Every time Chucky promptly hung up on them, leaving them hot tempered and angry.

Soon the collect calling became annoying altogether, and Chucky asked me to intervene from inside the County by reminding the P. Stones of the peace agreement that Twin had originally broker with me. I wrote a brief kite to Lil Ase, who had been the main person calling, and waited on a response that never arrived. In fact, the calling got worse thus setting off another round of events that were unknowingly to us brewing in the distance.

The following day my wife came early to see me. What I didn't know was Diamond had pulled out her homeboy Lil Ase, to talk about the calling issue with him in person. On the way to visiting I noticed two developments that caught my attention: Lil Ase had been drinking some prison made wine known as "pruno", and the other thing was he hadn't shared any words of acknowledgement with me about the kite I had sent him. Both of which weighed on my mind, but not alerting me to the danger I was about to face. The pruno had taken its full effect on Ase by now, as his face was contorted into the mad dog stare. When the visiting process began, I couldn't help but notice the person who had pulled him out, as she kept staring at me. After a five minutes conversation with Ase, the unknown female made a beeline toward my window to acknowledge me.

It was Chucky's girl. She briefly spoke to my wife, seeking approval to inform me about her business at the County. Sofia gave into the request, but the jealousy streak covered her entire face as she stood eye fucking me. Diamond sat and immediately jumped into a friendly conversation with me, all the time smiling a woman's seductive smile that spoke a million flirtatious words while Lil Ase was left alone at his window feeling neglected and mistreated.

He was deep in thought, probably drawing up his battle plans to do a pre-emptive attack against me first chance given. After my wife and Diamond departed, I took a couple glances in his direction, trying to read into his body language and facial expression that would give anything away as a sign of aggression: There was none that I noticed, at least not then and there; but something was amiss, and I continued my surveillance on him.

The first sign of aggression occurred the moment we arrived back in the module. Of all the inmates in our caravan, he was more than eager to have the deputy take his restraints off him, something that stuck out as peculiar. Every sonic boom and alert system in my life saving defenses told me that something was about to occur. Ase's irregular actions sent me into overdrive with thoughts preventing anything that could be hazardous to my health. Big Fish from the East Side 20's was up the tier playing chess with one of my homeboys through the bars; I bee lined up to him with not a second to waste: "Ah Fish, check this out Blood!" He looked up abruptly sensing the tension in my voice. "What's up Loko?" – "I need you to watch my back! I think that fool Lil Ase from P. Stones is tripping on some bullshit."

At that moment, the deputy was taking the restraints off Ase. With Fish in tow, I made a beeline back up the tier asking the other Bloods to have my handcuffs removed for fear of some kind of pre-emptive attack by Ase. I knew I wasn't thinking irrational, as I was for certain, I read him correctly. I walked up to the gate just as he was walking away from it. The intensity of the tension I felt sent my mind racing with unfounded frightful thoughts of imminent violence. My heart thumped in my chest as he spun on me drawing a prison made knife from his pocket with his radar locked and loaded on me. Just as his courage level rose to the launching point, an image weighing at least three hundred pounds slid into his path and grabbed both his wrists.

Big Fish was six feet and three inches, and all of three hundred pounds. Ase was furious and he expressed it: "On Black P. Stones Fish let me go!" I stood there in silence knowing my faith of not being stabbed rested solely in Fish's hands. "I can't let you stab Loko". With that response, I immediately sought out the deputy to have my restraints removed. Fish was buying me the valuable seconds I was gonna need in my defense. Even with the knife in his hand, I had little doubt on my capability of defeating Ase decisively, if I could only get the cuffs off. Just as I was about to get them removed by a deputy who later reported he didn't notice nothing amiss, Ase snatched his arms free and buried the knife deep into the backside of my neck.

Initially I thought I was punched, as my mind hadn't registered the fact that I had been stabbed. The force of the assault drove my head forward, slamming my forehead unrestrained into the iron bars with enough force to send my head spinning in all direction. Ase drew the shank back and buried it in the backside of my head sending me once again in a forward motion. The deputy who had been attempting to remove my restraints, made a straight beeline exit. He had panicked and was leaving me for dead. By the third strike, the blood was flowing from me pouring into my sight, blinding my view, clouding my judgment, and draining me of my lifeline. It had landed onto the top of my head. My mind was flipping over the assault trying to adjust the bombardment I was now enduring.

Fish who had been asked to protect me, instead took refuge against the far wall with no desire to stop or impede my attacker. I was doomed as the attack continued on with my mind believing that I would be murdered right there on the tier. As Ase was sliding in for another strike, my homeboy Lil Insane somehow had relieved himself of the long waist chains, and was bee lining in on his target with the intent to give me a breather, and to wreck some havoc on the enemy who was already feeling triumphant. Ase never knew what hit him as he was focused on his annihilation of me, scoring valuable points. "Boom," the waist chain was wrapped around his head, and the initial shock from the slapping sent an immediate wave of confusion across his face. His mind raced to understand the pain he was receiving, "Boom!" Lil Insane was dropping the heavy chain perfectly at his target.

For a split second, I thought Ase would fall out as he stood there stunned and motionless. I took advantage of his dizziness and bee lined passed him as Lil Insane slid in for a third assault on him. In our haste, we collided in our paths thus sending Insane to the pavement. Fortunate for us Ase was still dazed and motionless, as I found some relatively safety in the back of the module. As a cloud of indecisiveness set on Ase and my homey Insane, a train line of deputies descended onto the tier with their batons twisting and twirling looking for a chance at some action. "Get down! Get down! Everybody get down!" The deputies fanned out bunny hopping up the tier, taking inmates down as they proceeded. They rushed me away making speedy travel through the hallway to the ill-equipped medical area with me leaving a bloody trail in my wake. Inmates all along the way stared at the mess.

"What's up Loko Blood?" My homeboy Bolasko was sitting on a bench in the medical area. My mouth opened to speak and acknowledge him, but my transmitter wasn't working as my hollow words were barely below a whisper. The pathetic medical assistants were getting more blood on themselves than I had on myself. They didn't know what to do as they zoomed around me aimlessly and trying to look more important than they really were. Bandages were poorly placed over my injuries, and after the bureaucracy bullshit was worked out, I was immediately transported to L.C.M.C. medical facility, where I could receive some more appropriate attention.

Revenge against the Black P. Stone Bloods was a priority of the highest decree, and dominated ninety-nine percent of my thinking with the remaining one percent dwelling on my deep tissue flesh wounds. Once arriving at L.C.M.C., I was taken through a serious of doors to an area where a multitude of nurses and doctors were busy at work tending to the sick and wounded, it looked like a war zone. The hospital atmosphere made my head hurt. Minutes later an Asian woman walked in my direction.

"Hello!" She spoke with a slight traceable accent of her original tongue. "How are you?" – "Oh, I'm alright, just sore from my few bumps and bruises." My comment drew a bright smile from her. After checking my body temperaments, she dashed away blending back into the crowd of doctors and nurses who were coming and going. The stab wounds began throbbing by this time, and my head began to show signs of swelling. Unknowingly to me then, my wounds were also swelling from the inside, treating my central nerve system. After a lengthily wait the Asian nurse reappeared and bee lined on me with packages of large needles, guards, sponges, and an assortment of other things for the task at hand.

She was inquiring about my state of mind again, but I believe the only reason why she did that was that she knew she was about to bust on me with those lengthily thick needles she had. "I'm okay, just a little tired." I was lying like a mutha fucka, I was petrified of the needles that lay only inches away on a tray. "Okay, Mr. Wright, this won't hurt at all, it's medication to clean the germs around the wound." She dabbed the wounds clear of all the dried up blood, before she proceeded to prepare the needles to numb the areas for the staples I was about to receive.

"Uh", I began not certain how to state my thoughts, "I don't want the medicine in the needles." She eyed me and thought I was probably just trying to be a macho, but little did she know I was truly petrified of those crazy looking needles, and since I had an option, I declined their assistance. She then opened a package that contained a device which I eyeballed curiously, not for sure what to make of it, until it dawned on me, it was a damn staple gun. I broke out in instant chills that traveled up and down my body. In my mind I rationalized that I'd be hit with the gun maybe two or three times, so I geared myself for the pain that was about to occur.

"Okay, Mr. Wright, lean forward." I felt the gun being positioned against my head, and the moment she stabilized it, my eyes teared up right away, as the staple gripped my skin tighter than I thought was humanly possible. "Pop!" I clenched my fist to somehow absorb the pain. "Pop!" The third staple made me contemplate the idea of stopping her and asking for the medication in the needle. "Pop!" Shit, I had had enough, and it was time to call a timeout. "Can we stop for a minute please?" My voice was cracked with the strain of a man who was going through a difficult time in his life. She now looked at me like 'See I told your ass, but naw you wanted to be tough'. She was ready to go at me again, and at that moment, I started to dislike the lady with the staple gun who was eager to pop another round in me. After regaining my composure, I gave the crazy nurse the okay to proceed.

With no problem of continuing, she busted on me again, "Pop!" I almost jumped out my skin, "Pop! Pop! Pop!" I was braising myself for the next staple, and then I realized she was stopping altogether. "You finished with me?" I asked the question after I'd been hit with a solid dozen, hoping to God she was. "You have to take some tests for the wounds behind your neck, so we can analyze the extension of your swelling." Some time after she had departed, I flipped over her words again and again, trying to estimate the extent of my damages. To me she seemed evasive about her statement, leaving the explanation in details to the doctor.

Finally I was heading to my next location where I was to receive some cat scan x-rays. After a couple roll-ins and outs, I waited for the results. They weren't too promising. The doc informed me, if the swelling in the neck continued, they would be forced to stop it. My neck seemed normal to me; I wasn't in any kind of pain; it wasn't overwhelmingly sore, but the x-rays obviously told a different story. That night I was hooked up to some computer which monitored my status for improvement, while my thoughts were spinning around my new obligation to declare an unconditional war against the P. Stones until a peace treaty was begged for on hands and knees. I dozed off, thinking of my knife being buried deep within Ase's chest, literally draining all the life out of him. The next morning I awoke to be greeted by an armed female guard who had stood watch over me the entire night. "Good morning". I figured to make some light conversation with her since she was relatively good looking. "Good morning Mr. Wright. Did you sleep well?" At least she wasn't snotty, as I had first thought she would be. We conversed up until the doctor came in to check on me, then finally telling me the good news that I would be okay. The same nurse came in sometime later with another staple gun to finish where she had left off.

After spending a couple more days in the hospital, I was taken back to the gang module. I returned feeling like General Mc Arthur who had promised the Philippines that he'd be back to rescue them. As I bee lined up the same row where the assault was launched, I couldn't help but look around to see if any of my blood was splattered on any of the nearby walls. When I walked in my cell, I was greeted by a host of out pouring love, respect, and most importantly revenge. The troopers were ready for war and the energy of violence flowed from each and everyone. But we had a problem: All the Black P. Stones were gone, except for one. They were all taken to the hole immediately after the incident; the only one who remained was Crook. Crook was Mexican, and since his allegiance was to the Black P. Stones, he was going to be a dead Mexican first chance given.

Some five hours after I'd been back, Crook dashed my military hopes. He rolled it up for fear of his life being forfeited, and the O.S.J. escorted him off the row never to be seen again until months later. The program was back to normal as the atmosphere was clear of any impending violence, until the rumors started. It was said that the P. Stones were coming back to the gang module soon. That prospect excited me as my mind was racing a thousand miles per hour. All I could think about was revenge. For days, I stayed on the phone to find out who from the turf was in the County Jail; and before long, I had a list of names of troopers who were all in the mainline. Without any delay, I shot the urgency call over the wire for all of them to have the O.S.J. unit transfer them to the gang module, and very soon after, soldiers from all rank and files poured into our two cells, maxing out their occupancy.

Days later, the Black P. Stone Bloods rolled in. One by one, they made their presence known. Most of them I didn't know by face, and I was slightly familiar with their names, but in time all that would change. Later that night, I drew up immediate battle plans and prepared our troopers for our first of many pre-emptive attacks. In my military mind frame, there was only one outcome: Every Black P. Stone in that cell had to be knocked down with a knife. But we had yet another problem that was to delay the war for a minute. The deputies, assigned to work in the Blood module, had stern order not to open cell number four with cell number ten and eleven at no given time period. But in life as most people know, mistakes are bound to happen.

The first mistake occurred when we had least expected it. Bolasko was on the module row passing out the evening lunches to each cell, something he did every day. Some seconds later, the deputy announced over the P.A. system for inmate Matthews (a.k.a. Lil Ase) in cell number four to get ready for an attorney visit. Immediately I jumped out of bed and ran toward the front bars, and Bolasko, already knowing what I was thinking, ran back to the cell to get the knife I had prepared to hand off. "Put holes in him Blood." The knife was approximately nine inches long, and it had all the elements of danger within every inch of its shape. Lil Ase bounced out of cell number four and placed his back against the opposite wall. Just as Bolasko was given the okay to become a flight risk against his well-being, the second mistake occurred when Big Herk returned from court coming through the front gate.

It was one of the most exciting moments in my life, as I watched the drama unfold. Lil Ase was feeling the pressure now as he stood in the middle of two dedicated and hard-core members of the state. His head twisted back and forth. Herk was free of his cuffs and now proceeded up the tier, and just as Ase reared his head to watch him, Bolasko launched his attack like a wild cheetah on the chase of some scared antelopes that were inches away from being taken down. By the time, Ase was returning his head to check on him, it was already too late. All he has seen was a dark figure overshadow his presence. Bolasko drew the knife in Ase; making him feel the pain, confusion, and helplessness, I felt when he assaulted me.

The whole module was up on the bars watching Ase take a multitude of hard blows from Herk who looked like he was trying to break his rib cage. Bolasko continued his shank assault, as I watched Ase struggle to run and seek for help. "Stop, stop," the deputies were scared to enter the row and opted to spray their maze on the combatants who ignored their orders to heed. They descended on the roll in numbers, and only then did the combatants depart with the victim running through the front gate, seeking the help that was a little too late. Bolasko bounced up the tier as the hyper deputies scrambled to establish some sort of authority. The knife was passed back through the bars and immediately disposed of. Needless to say, Herk and Bolasko were marched off to the hole and Ase to the hospital.

Later that evening we received reports from other Bloods, who had went to court that morning, about a one sided chunkum between Big Herk and G-Nut from the Black P. Stones. Eyewitnesses reported that Herk had literally slung and punished G-Nut. That was only the beginning of the conflict, as the war was to pick up in momentum and intensity in the days following. Ase was brought back days later, and I plot and planned for another pre-emptive attack.

I sought out all the real names of the opponents, and after making many phone calls contacting many people, I soon knew the details I desired. The next part of my operation was to find out each individual's court date, and then compare them to any dates of troopers from the republic: We had some solid matches. Sad Dog now had the task of assaulting and dealing with two enemy personnel. He and Ase along with Ase's homeboy C.K. Bone had an up coming court date in a few days. To ensure that my trooper had the advantage despite the odds, I crafted a weapon that had the lethalness to keep three to four enemies at bay at the same time. The morning of the court date, I was up early, giving Sad Dog stern instructions on what to do and not to do. He was on his way to the holding cell downstairs, where they placed all the Bloods at going to court. I gave him orders to launch his attack the moment they freed them from their restraints. Then I waited on the news, while my anxiety level was rising high.

Finally, some five hours later Sad Dog returned with enemy blood all over his County Jail jumpsuit. He paraded on the tier proudly and boldly proclaiming his victorious and successful assault against Ase and C.K. Bone; to add insult to injury of his success, he stopped in front of cell number four telling them: "Fuck your neighborhood, and take a look at your homeboys' blood!" He paraded up the row like the triumphant American's return after their war against Hitler and his regime. Once inside the cell I had Sad Dog debrief every intricate detail on the assault. He reported that he was attacked the moment he stepped into the holding cell. They knocked him to the pavement. Once on his back, he immediately drew the weapon and began swinging it aimlessly and blindly. In the final aftermath, Ase received a total of twenty-nine staples to his face and neck area, and C.K. Bone received an unknown amount of stitches in his right arm. He had more sense than Ase, as he had backed away from the weapon that was wrecking havoc on them. Sad Dog walked away unscratched completely.

As a result of our second successful attack on Ase in a one-week span, he was subsequently placed in P.C. (protective custody) in High Power at the fear that we were trying to kill him. We now had four successful attacks under our belt, and we bathed in our victories, especially me. Soon after I set about to work out a peace treaty with the P. Stones, but my offer was flat out denied. With no other option, I continued on my plot to destroy them. Our new target was Big Fish from the East Side 20's who was added to my list of enemies, as he had left me for dead when he allowed Ase to break free of his grip, and assault me completely unabated. From the day of my stabbing we had broke off all alliance and cut all diplomacy ties with him and the East Side 20's inside the module.

I quickly devised up a plan. Every Y.G. trooper was told to implement a friendly relationship with Fish, to give him the impression that all was good between them and us. Out of respect for the East Side 20's, I established political agreements with certain East Siders and asked for approval from inside and outside the module to launch my assault against Fish. A great percentage of the Bloods in the gang module held more than enough respect for me and surprisingly the request was given.

For days, I failed in my repeated attempts to get two dedicated hitters on the tier at the same exact time with Fish; so I settled for a planned hit through the cell bars. I knew Fish liked to gamble; therefore, I devised up plans using his own weakness against him. Sad Dog was selected to assault him with firm orders to make it count. The day of the hit, the module was eerie quit. Fish was the only person who was denied the knowledge of knowing his faith. The arrangement continued as scheduled. I watched Fish from the back of the cell as he began his first of many chess games against Sad Dog. Sad Dog knew he was to lose the games intentionally, but not at a rate that would draw his opponent's attention.

For two games straight, he suffered defeats from Fish, who thought he had a victim who he was going to be robbed of all his food. A couple noodles were put up for wager on each game, and Fish was now hooked on his victories. He took the bait just as I figured he would, and he played right into my trap due to his greed level. He sat on the outside of the cell on a crate, while Sad Dog sat on the inside. The chess game and the bars were the only things that separated them. I watched from a distance as the element of danger began to swerve its head. The knife lay some inches away from Sad Dog's right foot. It was in plain view of us inside the cell, but out of complete sight of the intended victim. Sad Dog knew he had one shot, and he knew he would have one complete motion in his attempt to succeed or fail. Every time Fish prepared to make his next move, with the hopes of winning some more noodles, he dropped his head forward, blinding himself to the danger that swirled its reaches in his direction.

I slid out of bed with the intention of brushing my teeth, and just then, Sad Dog made his move placing himself on a pedestal. All in one motion his hand dipped downwards, gripped the perfectly wrapped knife, and before Fish had the opportunity to react, Sad Dog was already extending his hand through the bars and lurching forward with such quickness and momentum that it literally bent the knife upon contact with his opponent's head. The shock of being shanked sent Fish into a desperate backward attempt to out run his assailant arm. It was too late as the left side of his head was bleeding profusely from the deep penetrated wound. His body fell off the crate and slammed against the wall thus adding some minor injuries to his serious ones. Instantly he jumped up and bee lined up the tier to spread the news to his homies. He soon discovered and found out the hard way that everybody already knew about his preplanned date.

The news spread quickly, and in no friendly way. I started hearing in the wind about people wanting to seek revenge against me for all the stabbing we had been doing. Word in the air was I was sending Y.G. troopers on suicide assaults against people whom I didn't like, which led to two war fronts: the one inside the County, and the one on the streets in which Big Jimbo was heading. He was a five star general, who influenced me over the years, and without doubt, I held faith in him on leading the troopers into unprecedented victories. With me, Big Tray-K, and Big Jimbo there was no way we were gonna lose in our on going battles.

After assaulting Crook, the only Mexican P. Stone inside the Blood module, two of my homeys were charged with attempted murder. We had won the war officially with the plea request from the P. Stones for one last head up squabble with our highly decorated foot soldier Sad Dog. I agreed to the fight that was to symbolize our truce, and I wanted to give them the chance and outlet to save face. The fight was arraigned with no dominating combatant, and then and there, our war ended inside the County as well as on the streets. We were still keepn' it gangster.

KEEPN' IT GANGSTER
(2001)

After our bloody and overwhelming victory against the P. Stone Bloods, the gang module erupted into a spontaneous full scale riot against the deputies. We were protesting the inhumane treatment we were receiving on a day-in and day-out routine. Refusal to lock up in our cells, brandishing weapons of all sizes, and tying down of our cell bars were just a few means we used to express ourselves. We were fully aware of the County Jail's reputation, and we knew it was just a matter of time, before they responded with an endless bombardment of tasers, smoke grenades, and the cutting off our lifelines.

As expected, they didn't waste no time. First, the water was shut off; the phones were next, and then mysteriously the lights. Before long, we were under a full-scale assault. Explosions and sonic booms echoed off every wall in the module. All around me, men were feeling the affect of the gas that was now wrecking havoc on our body systems. The smoke choked us merciless; it blinded our eyes completely, and suffocated us to degrees almost unbearable. Soon confusion was reigning supreme as men all around were screaming for help and begging for the bombardment to stop. Keeping with the military procedures the deputies performed their next move to complete the mop-up program with vicious beatings and stompings of those Bloods who put up none or light resistance.

The sporadic fightings continued throughout the night with us awaking the next day to be greeted with the victors moving their P.O.W.'s out of the module altogether. Due to the hazardous contaminated air, which was laced with smoke, many men were becoming ill and sick. Cell by cell they emptied the module, thus ending it officially. We were shipped to the regular general population, something we were all grateful for because it meant no more restraints during movements, no twenty-four hours strict confinement to our cells, and more importantly, we went from two to four visiting days. Fifty Bloods, including myself, were rehoused in the general population, called the mainline.

From the moment our entourage entered through the doors of our new home, the Crip majority population was up in arms and asking for head-up chunkums from the Bloods just to hold up the rivalry from the streets. Some arrangements were made to accommodate their desire, but I announced to the entire new module that no Rollin 20's were to be molested or harassed in no kind of way, and if were, it would be nothing short of a full scale war with us launching our pre-emptive attacks against all Crips with the exception of the Rollin 60's. The fights went ahead as scheduled. C.K. Bone from the Black P. Stones and No-Name from the Swan Bloods gave us an overwhelming victory, but we soon lost a couple chunkums to the Rollin 60's with the defeats of Smoky and Baby G. Brown, who were from the largest Brim Blood gang in the County, the Six Duse. After the fights went back and forth, we soon squashed the beefs altogether, and I immediately set about the task of unifying all the Bloods under one umbrella.

One of the first priorities was to secure a trustee broom pushing position, which was an easy task. The lead trustee had already packed all his belongings and was scheduled to depart the following morning to the Delano Reception Center for Men. He had selected me to take his place. It was too good to be true as the wind of good luck and blessings had blown my way. After developing a respectful rapport with the deputies of the new building, I soon established a vast arsenal of weapons for the entire Blood population, which wasn't a difficult mission to accomplish, as raw metal stock was visible all around.

Eventually we had more weapons than troop personnel did; but I still pushed on the assembly line of knife sharpeners to continue to produce them. The way I looked at it was you could never have enough weapons, as you could never tell, what type of wars lay ahead, especially with the reality of being on the mainline with two essential groups, who always poised an imminent threat of war. First the Cholos, controlled by the Mexican Mafia, who were solid soldiers always putting up a credible and relentless fight; and second the Crips who usually weren't as effective as they could be due to their continuous ongoing internal tribal conflicts which I set about to capitalize on.

My crime partner Ken-Dog was the unelected prime minister of the Rollin 60's, one of the main factions, who have participated in Crip on Crip violence as far back as 1979; therefore it wasn't much of a problem for me to establish military ties with them by assisting them on their endeavors to rid the 2000 floor of all their Crip enemies. On the other hand, we were the Bloods and we stood as a collective entity across all our boundaries and divisions. Our differences of opinions and philosophies didn't matter when it came to us being a unified front. We even set aside our war differences with the Black P. Stones, so we could be seen as one for all and all for one.

After our military objectives were firmly established, I put my hands in the lucrative, but prohibited tobacco trade that reigned supreme and unabated through every section in the module 2600/2800. The Cholos and the Asian gangsters had the tobacco trade locked down completely, and I knew it was going to be a long uphill struggle for me to put my hands firmly into it without drawing too much attention, which could possibly lead to war. When I approached the heads of the two groups, respect and courtesy was extended. The Asian leader, named Rusty, was short and weighed not more than a hundred pounds; but on the Asian row, he was highly respected and feared. In their world, he was the man, and I planned to offer him a blue print economical plan that would make the both of us into County Jail ballers. It was a widely known fact that he received large amounts of tobacco from a particular deputy that we'll call The Mayor, who sold him packs at a hundred dollars wholesale price; and Rusty in return resold them to the vast inmate population for a hundred and seventy-five dollars a pack.

The black market was blooming out of control, and Deputy Mayor was just one of the many deputies who had their hands buried in the brown money. I worked out an economical adventure with Rusty. For every tobacco pack I bought at the prize of a hundred and seventy-five dollars, he would front me one on consignment. I then created a unique system not seen before in the County, at least not on the scale I operated. I took each pack, sacked up fourteen small size tobacco balls, and priced each one at twenty-five dollars. In the end, I pulled my hundred and seventy-five dollars re-up money and additionally raked in another hundred and seventy-five dollars profit. With a clientele as large as approximately seventy-five percent of seven hundred inmates, I soon had all my niches and loose ends ironed out, and was grossing thousands of dollars monthly.

Since the 2600/2800 module was a transfer module, and men were always coming and going, thus the evolving problem of some gang tension was rolling in: A Mexican Mafia Cholo, who supposedly had come from the Cholo gang module, had sent for the two representatives of the Bloods and the Crips. I assigned myself to converse with this Cholo, who I was hearing, was a true warmonger looking to justify his launching of a pre-emptive attack against the Blacks first chance given. Big Head, Lil Ken-Dog's younger brother was the spokesman for the Rollin 60's, and since they were the deepest Crips on the floor, he was unofficially the spokesman for all the Crips.

We bee lined to the cell on Able Row 2600 side to see what type of agenda the new Mexican shot caller had in mind. The Cholo's politics swayed with the changing of the evening breeze. The moment he acknowledged our presence, he bee lined to the front bars. "What's up Homey, my name is Loko from the 20's Bloods, and this is Head from the 60's Crips." – "Well, I'm Bandit from the Latin Kings, and this is my house now." He was referring to the 2600/2800 module being under his political control. "I was sent here to take this house, and I'm letting you two know right now I have the keys to this place."

Seconds into the conversation, I knew we had a problem on our hands, as Bandit truly was a warmonger, and a young one at that, which usually meant bad business. "I don't like the way this place is being ran, and I plan to clean this shit up!" He was ravaging on and on about his likes and dislikes. Then he caught my attention with words that I knew were words declaring war. "If your people disrespect my people, and I don't feel you'll discipline your people appropriately, we go rock this motha fucka! If your people talk too loud after the lights are out, and disturb my people who are sleeping with court the next day, we go rock this motha fucka! If your people touch my people regardless of the situation, we go rock this motha fucka!" Bandit went on and on, and he did little to hide his contempt for the black race.

After a lengthy conversation, we wrapped up our session. As Head and I bee lined off the row, I looked over at him and told him something I don't think he had even contemplated: "You know we at war already?" The question drew a curious and blank stare from him as he eyed me trying to figure out, what I meant exactly. "Head, we at war with the Mexicans, and I'm about to put the fifty plus Bloods on war status." Head was a warrior in every aspect of the word, and I wanted him to also prepare the two dozen 60's members.

I informed with my County Jail roll dog No-Name the Blood army of a possible war with the Cholos, depending on which way the wind blew. We passed out an assortment of knives ranging in all sizes, lengths and widths. After making sure the Bloods were armed to the teeth, I called an immediate counsel meeting with the Blood trustees. Somewhere in our setting one of the troopers suggested that I used my influence with the deputy to have the shot caller's cell integrated, as it contained all Mexican Cholos.

The more I twirled that idea in my head, the more I liked it. It had its advantages in every aspect: First, I would be breaking up the shot caller's strong hold; second, he may be reluctant to start a war, if he had Blacks in his cell thus putting himself in harms way. The idea was accepted, and would be implemented with the strict and stern orders to butcher him, if he kicked-off the war during shower time. My only obligation and objective to the Bloods and in a bigger sense to the Blacks was to make sure the motha fucka, who started the war, would be punished to the fine threads of death. After placing knives on both sides of his cell, I went in search of Deputy Andrade. Andrade was a young and cocky deputy who held a lot of respect for me and my command over the Bloods in the module. He was the kind of deputy where he'd give respect, and he demanded it uncut. He was also one of those deputies who would turn a blind eye to the drama inside the module, as long as it was controlled violence.

"Andrade", I began, "I need a favor". His given nickname to me was *Old Man*, as I was the oldest of all the Bloods in the module. "What you want Old Man?" Andrade always spoke with a trace of excitement and challenge in his voice. "I don't need you to ask me no questions; I just need it to be done!" I knew I had his attention, and when I told him I needed a cell integrated, initially, he was hesitant, but after finding out it was an all-Mexican cell, he quickly obliged, as he hated Mexican Cholos. Some twenty minutes later, he announced over the P.A. system for three of the six Cholos to roll up their belongings for immediate cell moves.

After the cell swap of Mexicans for Blacks, the drama unfolded with a burst of intensity. The Cholo shot caller was complaining and making threats of harm against the three Blacks, who had become his new cellmates. "Ah Loko, your people have to leave this fucken cell right now." He was hot, and I honestly believe his anti-black mindset had clouded his assessment and miscalculation of what type of person I really was. He was so caught in his ideology of Blacks being inferior to the Mexicans that he wasn't able to see that I was more than a formidable foe to be taken serious, dead serious. "What the fuck you mean my people gots to move from the cell?" – "They got to leave, this is a South Side Mexican cell, and your people go leave one way or another!" I had him, as I wanted him, not thinking. "Look Bandit, you got me fucked up, and you got my people fucked up, and they not going anywhere." His face turned red as he blew the loose fuse I knew he would.

There was a Cholo on the tier with us, who had been standing in our midst. Bandit spoke rapid words of Spanish to him, and whatever he conveyed, it sent the Cholo running up the tier soon returning with an envelope which he slid through the bars where Bandit withdrew a large knife that we call 'bone crusher'. He took the envelope, wrapped it around the end part of the knife, and created what was supposed to be a handle. "Oh they go leave this motha fucka one way or the other; if they got to squeeze through the bars, then that's what they got to do, but they leaving this South Side cell!"

He had crossed the final line, and more than ever, he had fucked up. The Mexicans had a policy in the jails: If you draw a knife, you have to use it. It was time to show Bandit he had been out maneuvered by a black gangster, who was dedicated to his trade, but more importantly, he had been out maneuvered by a Blood. It was time to play my cards. Instantly I and the other Blood troopers, who had been standing in front of the cell, slid three bone crushers through the bars so the three black inmates could quickly take up battle ready attacks. Just that fast the scale of balance was tipped in our favor as the other two Cholos inside the cell were unarmed; and with the prospect of a blood bath Bandit was ready to tone it down a bit. But it was too late as I was ready for drama, and the outcome was now in my hands.

"Now motha fucka get busy you tough ass gang banger, get cracking!" I was burning with rage, whereas he tried at a failed attempt to slow the drama. "We can do this different, Loko. We don't have to go down this route." I couldn't believe what I was hearing coming out his mouth. This was the same hard-core shot caller who just seconds ago was telling me my people had to leave his fucken cell one way or another. He was accepting his defeat too easy, and I hated a coward, as that's what he became to me in those few seconds. "Get this gate popped Blood, I want this motha fucka myself." I blew my fuse right then and there. While drawing my knife out of the pocket I repeated: "G-Sta, tell the police to crack this gate!" Bandit was silent and looked astonished at the sight of the Blood troopers who all stood outside his cell with bone crushers in their hands poised to attack him the moment G-Sta from the Pueblo Bishop Bloods got the gate popped open. Everything in the module came to a stand still, as everybody watched through their cell bars. Other Cholos, who I had rapport with, were screaming over the tier to let it go. It was too late as I wanted to fight, and Bandit was my intended target.

In the heat of the moment I almost didn't hear the Blood catcall which signified that the K-9's were coming. We reacted swiftly, recovered all the knives from the three Blacks, made a hastily beeline up the tier, and gave our arsenal to Dusty from the Black P. Stones to hold. Some seconds later, the deputy entourage arrived for action and ordered us off the tier. They went straight for cell No. 5, where we had been, and ordered everybody out with their hands on their heads. In all the confusion, Bandit was caught off guard. He was caught dead bang with his bone crusher and hauled off to the hole where he had more than enough time to lick his wounds of being humiliated. Immediately after the incident I was approached by some other Cholo shot callers who told me they were going to right the wrongs that Bandit had committed. One of them even shared with me by swearing on his neighborhood that Bandit was going to be blasted (shanked) the first chance given. They apologized for the bullshit and departed.

After the potential of violence was cleared away, I placed myself back on track in the lucrative tobacco and drug trade. Before long, I had created a clientele that only sought me out in business dealings. I believed in the philosophy of "A satisfied customer was a customer who'd return to spend another day". But I wasn't satisfied, and as the hustler I was, I wanted my hands in bigger plans and bigger dealings. Since it was already a known fact to me about The Mayor and his connections to the black market, I started working to place myself on his good side. Every day I would use some kind of psychological and subtle way to affect his opinion and outlook on me. Soon my relentless well thought-out maneuvers worked, as he started asking about me. After satisfying his curiosity about me and my gangster mentality, in which he liked, he put me to my first test.

In any environment, you will always have the good and the bad. The Mayor was considered bad due to his shady dealings, and his connections with the main shot callers were always questioned from the other deputies, who considered themselves good, as they were strictly by the book and looking for the chance to throw a big size monkey wrench into The Mayor's aspiration. To confirm rumors of The Mayor being dirty, they placed a white trustee named Troy in the module to seek out the relevant info. This is where I came in.

Since most of the black market activities occurred in the module 2600/2800, the good deputies gave the snitch trustee a job, demoting me from my lead man position. Right away, I knew something was wrong. Nowhere inside Men's Central Jail, especially on the 2000 floor had there been a white inmate lead trustee. It was unheard of. A few hours after Troy had been hired, The Mayor approached me inside the trustee dayroom, and what he did next threw a complete curb ball on my train of thought. "Take care of that white boy", he said. As the last of his statements slid off his lips, he tossed me a pack of tobacco. I nearly freaked out. "Did you hear me? Take care of the white trustee, he's a snitch." The Mayor's words sunk in and the challenge and mission he had placed into my lap, was right up my alley as I always planned for success on any military mission.

After the initial shock wore off, I cleared my head of all thoughts, so I would be able to bear my energy on the mission that was to put me in the good grace with The Mayor. An immediate war counsel was summoned to set the pre-emptive agenda into focus, and to assign roles to particular players, who were somewhat of specialists. No-Name from the Mad Swan Bloods was selected for his brute size and strength to knock the white boy out. G-Sta from the Pueblo Bishop Bloods was our eyes and ears during the proceeding of putting the snitches' lights out, and Reese from East Side Pain Bloods was the back-up unit in case the plan needed an urgent emergency improvising plan.

With everything in place, we waited around to allow the events to unravel naturally. It wasn't long before the snitch bee lined into the interior of the dayroom looking to check in on his personal property he had left behind from earlier. No-Name stood in the distance twisting cornroll braids into Sad Dog's hair, looking unimportant. As Troy prepared to make his exit, I blocked his departure with a question that should have roused his suspicion. He wasn't even close to comprehending the danger swerving around his head, and since he lacked the background experience that we had from our harsh environments, his guards weren't even up or tentatively aware.

"What's your name again?" My sudden request received a friendly oh-I'm-Troy-type reply, and even though I stood directly in front of him, he had completely failed to notice the subtle green light approval I sent to No-Name, who was approximately six foot five, and weighing in around three hundred pounds plus. A second later, I witnessed the biggest slugging in my life: "Pop!" The sound of the impact on Troy's face sent saliva flying through the air. All in one motion his eyes rolled in the back of his head, his body went limp, and he fell over like a hundred years old California Redwood tree freshly cut: "Boom!" His body hit the floor with a fleshy thud and lay motionless. I went down on one knee, placed my lips into contact with his ear, and whispered "Leave the building; it's not safe for you." After my words, we departed into the air, blended into the buildings interior not to be seen until the smoke had cleared.

The fruits of labor were thus rewarded: Troy was removed off the floor completely, I was given my lead man position back, and more importantly, I made progress on my quest to establish myself in the echelon of the black market. I also received the blessing and good grace acknowledgements from The Mayor. After the mission, I was officially a part of the inner crew. My name started gaining respect from all quarters on the mainline. The same philosophy I implemented on the streets in which I knew made the governments function properly, I also used inside the County. Our military was strong and second to none on the 2000 floor, meaning at least seventy-five percent of the Bloods were heated. With each day passing, the Bloods were maneuvering and monopolizing all the important jobs on the floor. Since we were always the underdogs in almost every jail setting, we held to the strict philosophy of: You fuck with one Blood; you have to fuck with all Bloods; and soon the other groups were reluctant to give us problems or issues.

By being the official Blood spokesman on the floor, I now was working over-time on my goal of monopolizing the entire market. My economical agenda with Rusty went from the first phase of tobacco dealings to include drugs such as marijuana and meth with the result that my clientele subsequently grew. I was climbing the ladder. With rampant drug selling floating around, soon came the relentless deputies' day and night raids descending on the Asian row with Deputy Andrade, a.k.a. Superman, who possessed a deep seated hatred against the Asian inmate population, and at every turn of events, he was sure to make his presence known.

With the winds blowing the news of the Asians having prohibited tobacco and drugs, Superman declared an unconditional war against Rusty, his variety of Asian comrades, and their supplier Deputy Mayor.

Superman and The Mayor were sworn enemies to each other. With every action taken by The Mayor to continue his drug and tobacco trade, Superman countered and wrecked havoc on the train of goods. As the battle lines intensified, it became clear to The Mayor that he was in trouble, and now under an intense investigation. Superman and his large assortment of buddies were winning the war front; soon declaring victory on the arrest of The Mayor, who had been busted coming to work with a large amount of drugs, rumor had it that it was heroin. Immediately after his arrest, Superman annihilated the entire Asian row. And to add security to his victory, he had them relocated to the 2100/2300 module, which had a conglomerate of single man cells. Superman had won his battle against the Asians and The Mayor, but in the process of knocking them from the theater of activities, he subsequently created a vacuum that I had every intention of filling with the mental and practice of a true hustler.

GOOD TIMES ROLLING
(2001-2002)

Before my partner in crime Lil Ken-Dog from the 60's Crips and I could fill the vacuum by locating a deputy willing to risk his job, the Cholos beat us to the punch. Frijo from the East Side 36th Street Cholo Gangsters, secured and convinced a deputy, who we'll call Deputy Youngster, to work for him. The vacuum that once was, was now filled. Frijo was one of the few Hispanic trustees, and since I was a trustee, we had a respectable and decent rapport with each other, thus making it easier for me to work out economical agreements with him. On our first dealing, he sold me an entire can of tobacco at the wholesale price of eight hundred and fifty dollars. It was a deal to me, as I could retail it into packs thus racking in an easy sixteen hundred dollars.

But I wanted the first position on the totem pole. So I sought out a deputy who would be down to open up a second drug and tobacco front. The winds of change blew, and Frijo only held the top position for a short period of one month. He was transferred to Delano State Prison, the Southern California reception center. As I watched the vacuum materialize again, Lil Ken-Dog and I moved in to influence Deputy Youngster, and take advantage of the greed he still possessed from the black market trade. Soon agreements were reached for the delivery of three cans of tobacco. Relentless work and continuous maneuvering had finally paid off, as Ken-Dog and I were now on top of the food chain.

With the top position firmly secured, the large benefits made things easier and better for me. For every delivery Deputy Youngster performed, he charged a flat fee of five hundred dollars, and it was then, I realized on how royally I'd been fucked by paying eight hundred and fifty dollars per can. I gave the Bloods the first opportunity to buy the brown gold at wholesale prices; that way they could monopolize the second position by retailing the product to those on the bottom. Initially my game plan worked out perfectly, but only temporarily.

After one too many bad and counter-productive deals, I quickly shook most of them because they were literally bullshitters. I eventually took my business endeavors to the vast mainline population who in turn sucked up the brown gold as fast as I could supply it. Business was booming and everybody was making money: an ounce of marijuana sold for five hundred dollars; a regular pack of Camel cigarettes for a hundred dollars; a regular lighter for fifty dollars; and the meth for a variety of prices being it was a heavy drug with the demand often time fluctuating. Soon I had the clientele bee lining from all quarters of the County, looking to place a buy with me. The Cholos became my best customers when it came to the meth and the Blacks when it came to the brown gold.

After awhile I received requests for such drugs as heroin and cocaine. I devised up a brilliant plan that would literally save me money, and in the same breath, it would make me lots of money. Instead of me spending my money on large amounts of drugs, I cut other people in. For instance if a person wanted me to smuggle an ounce of marijuana inside the County through my connection, they in return had to match it with another ounce for my payment. With this new way of procuring drugs, I ended up having loads of free drugs and tobacco at the expense of another. Within no time, I was making thousands a week, but as to be expected, with the large amounts of drugs, tobacco, and success also came the heat from the deputy squad. To me they were amateurs, as they reminded me of the street mob mentality. When they stormed a tier or row looking for drugs or knives, they often time passed it right up looking for it. Over a period of time studying their weaknesses, I soon found out the one vital mistake they made.

Every day as a trustee, I passed out small trash bags to each row and all cells, so the inmates wouldn't throw trash onto the tier. The one thing I always noticed during the raids was the deputies never removed the trash bags with its contents from the cells. That was their weakness, and I was aiming to take full advantage of it. Soon I had drug safe houses all around the module. The drugs were pre-wrapped in plastic, and then placed in empty milk containers that were squashed completely to give the empty box appearance. They were then placed into the trash bags along with all the other trash. Raid after raid my stash spot proved raid proof.

The main and most difficult problem the goon squad had in dealing with me was the desire of catching me dead bang with the goods that they knew I was faithfully pushing. But they were aware they had their hands full in smashing my operations. Just like on the streets of my neighborhood, I had multitudes of eyes and ears always seeking and finding out relevant information in which I paid for thru drugs and tobacco. Even some deputies, who admired and respected me for their own personal reasons, relayed important info to me. Those inmates, who were willing to assist or provide info against my system of shady dealings, were weeded out, disciplined, and merciless chastised to the degree of where they begged to be removed from the entire floor.

But then the cat and mouse game with the deputies began with earnest. They had snitches all around me trying to figure out my next move, and more importantly they wanted to know who my supplier was. The 2600/2800 module was soon under my complete control, along with the foot soldiers that helped me to keep my dictatorship in place. I passed out free tobacco and drugs to a host of individuals, this way I always kept them loyal and in depth to me. I literally believed in the Old Italian Mafia saying: "Keep people in depth, so they will owe you favors later." But the goon squad never gave up on their relentless attacks; they were always trying to punch holes in it with the hopes of the whole thing having a domino affect, thus crumbling little by little.

Their work of around the clock harassment started to pay off, as they eventually knew about the empty milk cart. Cell after cell they went through the trash checking and looking for large sums of drugs they were told that they'd find. They'd come up empty handed and lucky for me. Right before their raid, I had recently sold out of everything; but the trash stash spot was burnt. I had to find another one, something they would have a hard time in figuring out.

My foot soldier Sad-Dog came to my rescue with the best spot in the County. He discovered that the phone located inside his cell could be taken apart and put back together. At the bottom was a sizeable hollow area in which the drugs and tobacco fitted perfectly into. The hollow area was so signifying indeed that I also had five special made bone crushers placed inside. With this stash spot the worry of the goon squad stumbling onto my merchandise faded away, soon not worrying me the least bit until they were hitting close and nearly coming up on the goods that were depleted days prior to their raid. I knew the person who had given up the private info, had to come from within our rank and files. Immediately I set a vigorous plan of weeding out our weak and not to be trusted Bloods into motion, and one by one they were rolled up or departed on their own for fear of their safety. With me at the top of the food chain, I knew I would be the main one to blame for the violent and badly transformed inmates. But to that problem, I also had a solution.

Most deputies asked their trustee to deal with disruptive inmates who disrespected the deputies; and they often times asked for the discipline to be administered through beat-downs with the assurance that they would turn a blind eye on the requested situation. For every inmate a deputy wanted us to chastise, I would place that deputy in depth to me for the same favor later of me wanting to discipline inmates for my own reason. I had the Mafia motto working out itself. The respect I received from other inmates due to my large range of activities soon turned to fright as each day that passed I closed the grip tighter around my reign in the module 2600/2800. All the deputies, who were crooked to some degree, had some kind of rapport with me, on one level or another, and on the flip side of the coin, the goon squad took their attempt at trying to bring me down.

Regardless of our feud in the cat and mouse game, the majority of deputies gave me overwhelming credit and props on my handling of keeping racial riots off the floor. They believed I was just being a responsible trustee, but little did they know the real reason for what I was to save my black market business. If I allowed racial riots to erupt and to travel unabated, I would lose everything overnight.

On one particular day, the racial tension ran real high, and the two opposing groups nearly collided in a full-scale confrontation. My Hispanic friend from a Salvadorian gang appeared in front of my cell breathing heavy and hard, explaining that his people and my people were at war. "At war?" I shouted not understanding what had brought this about. "Yes we are at war, and I'm not supposed to be telling you this." I looked at him, and I could see the nervousness in his face, hoping I could somehow come up with a solution to the problem that arose so unexpectedly.

"Your people just jumped on two of my people, and they beat them down pretty bad." Before I could interrupt and ask a question, he hushed me and continued explaining: "The Cholo shot caller found out about the fights, and he immediately declared war on the Blacks and assigned me to go around and tell all the Cholos to prepare for war." As his words sunk in, the depth of what he had reported took me from my usual mind frame on a plain of blankness. I knew by him coming to me and informing me of the situation would without doubt get him stabbed merciless, if the Cholo shot caller found out, but I had to figure out a way to stop the war. "What cell did this incident occur in?" – "Cell No. 11, 2600 side, Denver Row." My movement was swift and urgent, and when I arrived in front of the cell all the combatants were bloody and exhausted. It was obvious who had won the altercation. The two Cholos had lumps and bruises all over their faces and bodies.

It was worse than I thought, and the only way a war could be averted now, was for the two Blacks to be completely innocent. If the Cholos placed their hands on the Blacks first, and they defended themselves thus winning, the Cholos would be in the wrong; and it would be ever more wrong, if the shot caller still declared war. Now on the other hand, if the Blacks laid hands on the Cholos, and the Cholos defended themselves and lost, then I could understand the shot caller's reaction.

"What happened here?" – "These motha fucken Mexicans are disrespectful!" – "What do you mean they are disrespectful?" – "Every time I'm on the phone they seem to get loud and shit, and every day they do this same shit." – "Who hit who first?" The question weighed in the air, and the thickness of this implication rained down on the perpetrators who had to confess up to the charges. "I started it, and I took off on them for their disrespect!" The words I feared and dreaded were out. While I stormed away from the cell, my thoughts flipped over the many ways I should deal with the problem at hand, but I was only slightly familiar with the two Blacks. All I knew for sure was they were Crips, and since that was the case, the problem of discipline fell into the Crip side of the fence.

I made a hastily exit from Denver Row, bee lining toward Lil Ken-Dog's cell. "Ken-Dog I need to talk to you!" The serious tone of my voice grabbed his attention. "We got a problem!" – "What's up Loko," without further delay I explained the situation in intricate details. After listening to the problem and my solution on the matter at hand, Ken-Dog demanded for me to get him out of the cell, so he could address the situation and right the wrong. Not only did I get him out, but also his little brother Head and another Crip from Long Beach named Wino. We huddled inside the trustee's dayroom and flipped over a multitude of ideas and solutions. It was already a clear fact that violence would be the means that would be used, but how much violence was the main topic floating back and forth.

Finally, we had reached a crossroad, and we all agreed that we would take the liberal route and settle for the usage of hands and feet on our intended target. But we had one problem on how we were going to get our two intended victims from the quarters of their cells to a location where we could wreck the havoc on them we had in mind. "Loko, you got to be the one to get them out, so we can do our thang." I stood there in silence thinking about which deputy owed me a favor of late; and that one was Deputy Superman, the asshole.

"Alright, I'll be back." I bee lined out the dayroom, and slid up the long hallway that led to all the other modules on the 2000 floor when I saw Deputy Superman with some of his comrades. I signalized for him from a distance. He immediately made it in my direction. "I got a problem." The words slid off my lips as he walked within ear range. "What kind of problem?" I took a deep breath and poured on my best-edited version. It was explained so overwhelmingly, with such horrifying vividness that he took a large chunk out of it, in other words, he had bitten, but he wanted to get approval from his senior officer. We shared a few more words before we departed. I headed back to the module and explained the developments to Ken-Dog and the fellows. All we could do was wait to see, if we would get the green light.

After about twenty minutes, I was summoned into the hallway corridor where at least six deputies were awaiting my arrival. A sergeant was there, Deputy Superman, and some other goons. After being giving the indication to explain the situation at hand, I once again poured it on, but this time a little juicier and thicker. Looking around me after my presentation all the deputies including the sergeant I had never dealt with looked to have been swayed completely. I knew I was good verbally, and manipulating words had become a major hang-up for me, but I held a slight doubt that I wouldn't be given the green light approval. I was wrong. The sergeant spoke directly to Deputy Superman: "It's your call; you can do it like you want." Then he walked away.

"Okay Old Man, this is what we gonna do." I hated it when Superman called me *Old Man*, but I refrained from my emotions as I listened to his plan on the dealing of the two Crips who were about to experience some hardship, all because an agreement was reached by the unholy alliance. They were told over the P.A. system that they were being moved to pack-up. Some time later, they entered the dayroom so unaware to the faith that lay seconds away for them. Deputy Superman gave his sternest orders for weapons not to be used, which we had all agreed on.

I learned a long time ago that most plans don't go according to plan, as our plan would soon take an unexpected turn. The dayroom door closed with a sudden and loud bang just as the two troopers stepped through it. Head from the 60's was on them immediately. "Ah Cuz, ya'll know ya'll put my life in jeopardy when ya'll took off on those two Mexicans." The younger Crip stood motionless and silent, but the older one defended his course of action and desperately tried to put some light on the events. "But Cuz…", it was obvious that Head was becoming angry, and the more he listened to the Crip's story, the more he was losing control over himself. "Look, if you'll had any beef with those two Mexicans, ya'll wasn't suppose to touch them first of all. Second of all if it's that serious, ya'll could have gotten at us, and we would have had ya'll move into another cell." The words he was speaking weren't having the desired affect. The older Crip still justified his attack despite the County Jail rules and regulations, which prohibited the touching of another race, especially the race of the Cholos.

Head had heard enough; he stood up from the table with the intent of bringing the drama we were there to deliver. I almost felt some sympathy for the two Crips, but the discipline they were about to endure would serve two purposes: The first would be a message to the general population of Blacks that disruptive behavior wouldn't be tolerated, especially at the expense of an unnecessary riot. And the other purpose would be to uphold and administer discipline to the perpetrators who were at fault. Before the older Crip realized what was going on, Head slugged him with a solid right across the mid section of his face. The other combatants jumped up immediately, and the discipline process commenced with Deputy Superman and his favorite side kick Deputy Sheehan, watching intently from outside the dayroom area. I hemmed up the younger Crip together with my foot soldiers Reese and Lil Hollywood from the Wilmington Bloods, who were unexpectedly invited to participate. And unlike his older compatriot, the youngster received a far lighter discipline. We only placed a multitude of bumps and bruises on him. His homey was over in the far side of the dayroom being introduced to brooms, feet, fists, and choke holds by Ken-Dog, Head, and Wino. He had two choices, either he would fight back defending his well-being or he would unquestionably succumb to the brutality he was suffering.

As the discipline drove to the next level of activity, Head blew a fuse that took all of us by surprise. He bee lined across the dayroom heading toward the front portion. It didn't registered to me of what his action implicated, but when he returned and stood over the youngster, an eight-inch long ice pick shined and reflected his obligated duty. Before I could intervene, he had already drew the weapon backwards; and like a deadly tomahawk cruise missile, he fired it not once, twice, or three times, but a multitude of times. My reactions were slow and of no use for the youngster, as he lay balled up in a fetish position. Head slithered away and made a beeline attack toward the older Crip who he wrecked havoc on.

The discipline had now gotten out of control, and if I didn't slow it down, or stop it altogether, there would soon be two dead Crips inside the dayroom. I grabbed Head and coaxed him back to his rational frame of mind. As I calmed him to relaxation, Wino lost his mind and grip on control, and was now raining uncontrollable damage on the two victims. After regaining control over the situation, I ushered the two victims over to the sink area where I encouraged them to wash up and clean themselves of the blood that poured from the holes that were eighty percent knife inflicted. This discipline had blown up in our faces, and any future discipline-approval from Deputy Superman would be placed on the back burner to remain there for a while. The two victims were subsequently removed and sent to medical, where they received the attention they needed. After all the smoke had cleared, Head was rolled up and sent to Wayside, thus covering the deputies' tracks, and we were told to lay low on any future discipline.

Soon things fell back into the norm, we continued to push our drugs; and the cat and mouse game picked up where it was left off. It intensified along all lines, as the goon squad commenced raid after raid on my infrastructure upon receiving the news through one of their snitches that I had hit for a large amount of drugs. The snitch was correct on every aspect on his information, as Ken-Dog and I had recently scored on more drugs than we normally would have. With the supply and demand in full effect, we ordered up a half pound of marijuana, three cans of tobacco, two ounces of crystal meth, and seven grams of heroin keeping them tucked away in the phone until the A.T.F. (alcohol, tobacco, firearms) style raids slowed or stopped. We still felt certain about the phone stash, and we knew for certain that only a hand few knew about it's existence; but even still we remained spooked as we watched trooper after trooper fall victim to the relentless raids that were eating away at the infrastructure from the bottom up.

I decided to give myself a break altogether, and promptly to sit on all the drugs until the eye of the storm blew passed. That way I could focus on the last of my court proceedings, which I tried to block out, as I knew without doubt I was going to be found guilty. The victims and eyewitnesses had placed me at the crime scene, my faith was sealed, and I expected the irreversible outcome. The day of my convictions I returned back from court with only one thing on my mind, to sell as much drugs and tobacco as I could; enough to make myself feel better.

When I exited from the bus, I was hemmed up by Sergeant Corina, Deputy Superman, and some other deputies who I wasn't familiar with. One of them snatched me by my shirt collar and shoved me against the wall with force. Sergeant Corina stood over my right shoulder and asked me a question that made my heart stop for what seemed an eternity: "Loko which phone is the drugs in?" I looked up at him, and although my voice rebutted the accusation, my eyes told a different story. My mind raced a thousand miles per hour. He knew he had dropped a bombshell on me, and he knew I would react the way I did, poorly.

After a few more questions and answers they cut me loose, leaving me rattled to the core. They watched me as I walked up the hallway, and I thought I heard laughter; they knew they had finally crawled under my skin. I bee lined to Ken-Dog's cell and immediately informed him of what happened. We rationalized they didn't know which phone the drugs were in because if they did, they would have hit the cell. We also rationalized that somebody had told them, but whoever that somebody was, he wasn't able to provide them with the information of which phone and cell. We were wrong!

The next morning on my way to visiting, I was greeted with the sight of Sad Dog and all his cellmates face down in the hallway. I didn't need anybody to tell me what was going on. Sad Dog looked up at me with eyes that confirmed what I already knew. Without doubt, they would all be going to the hole, and I knew I had to do some serious damage control. I went to my visit, but the normal enjoyment was wiped clean away. Bad luck had wrecked havoc on me; first my being found guilty, then my stash spot being raided. The latter sent me over the hill, and with the few remaining loyal Blood soldiers I terrorized the 2600/2800 module, nobody was spared who we thought was guilty of even the slightest minor infraction.

I only slowed on my military rampage after another deal was struck to bring in another shipment of goods. But again, I had the problem of stashing it, a problem that would worry me day and night. The next shipment was like the one I had recently lost, and there was only one for sure secure measure to guarantee that I wouldn't lose out like last time: I had to sell it right away. Deal after deal was made, and before the A.T.F. raid could impede my goal, I had sold out completely.

Not soon afterward, the goon squad came on through with a vengeance. Just when they thought they had wrecked irreversible damage on me, I was back in business the next week, and not only back in business, but I succeeded of ridding myself of all my goods. After the raid they knew they had arrived too late, and to show their contempt of my relentless hustling, they did something that spoke they were now tired of the games. They rolled me up and all the troopers from my neighborhood. They literally barred us from the downtown Men's County Jail, kicked us out, and spread us out to different parts of the county system. Some of us were sent to Wayside, while others were going to spend the rest of their jail time in Lynwood. March 28, 2002 signaled the official end of my domination of the drug trade on the 2000 floor in the Men's Central Jail.

Rolled Up
(2002)

After being in the county facilities some twenty-one months, I was finally on my way to the penitentiary to begin my new journey on the unending chain of events that spoke of my scarred and futile life. For one last time I went back to the Men's County Jail where I was prepared with all the other inmates for transportation to the reception center at Delano. When we were hauled off the bus and placed into a multitude of cells, I recognized the familiar face of Baby G-Kev in the midst of a crowd of inmates. "G-Kev," I dashed toward the front of the holding cell trying to wave for his attention. He recognized me and instantly felt a sign of relief as his youthful features beamed his delight.

Since his arrival from the juvenile facility, and his transfer to the Men's Central Jail, I took him under my wing to protect him from all elements that even contemplated hurting him, verbally or physically. Actually before we were all rolled up, I was over protective of him. He was eighteen years old; approximately four foot eleven and weighed probably a solid hundred pounds. He was still a kid in heart and had to be looked after, as some men with irrational thoughts would try to take advantage of him. Now here he was on his way to the reception center, convicted with a life sentence for a robbery that became botched and subsequently turned into a homicide robbery. I knew he wanted to be in the holding cell with me, as I was the main person who had made all his fears vanish.

When the transportation officers arrived performing their monotonous routine, I was able to get in a quick chitchat about the going on's, and the whereabouts of other homies. The transportation K-9's emptied cell after cell, cuffed us and marched us to the awaiting buses outside in the cool Los Angeles night air. As luck would have it, G-Kev was placed on the same bus as I was. My heart went out to my little homey, as the worries were written on his face. He always spoke of his grandmother whom I knew well, and whom I had made a promise that I would take care of him on the inside. As the bus departed, we embarked on a conversation that would last for hours, only ending when he talked himself to sleep. I watched over him when he slept, before I finally began to doze with thoughts of his homey Big G-Kev on my mind.

When I awoke some restless hours later, he was still sound asleep; the grey goose rocked back and forth as it made its way down the endless road that ran the entire length of California. I wondered did Interstate 5 continue thru Oregon, Washington, and up to Canada. A little later, we finally pulled over for a pit stop. It was lunchtime, and we were fed some dry, but highly desired sack lunches: peanut butter packs, jelly packs, bread, fruit, and drinks. I scoffed my lunch down as the stress build-up from my being bound by heavy chains and packed on a bus like sardines gave me a large and empty space in my stomach.

Once back on the road, the transportation officer instructed us with stern rules about not talking while the bus was in motion. Most officers were assholes, always looking to demonstrate on an inmate. If they believed an inmate had gotten out of hand, he would be manhandled which was technically an ass whipping. He would then be hog tied and placed into one of the three small size holding cages on the bus. If he bowed down and submitted his submission, he may be lucky enough to be cut some slack; but if he had a strong spirit and a strong enough will not to give in, then undoubtedly the K-9's would leave him stranded in his uncomfortable position; and depending on how long the ride to the destination would take, the inmate might need some medical attention upon arrival.

As the grey goose slithered up the dusty dirty road toward the reception center, the vast Delano complex grew larger and larger. The bus pulled to a stop at the perimeter gate where the transportation officers unloaded themselves of all the automatic weapons they had during our ride; the handguns, Mini 14 rifles, and shot guns. They were safely located inside the multitude gun towers that formed a perimeter encircling the entire prison institution. After a thorough check of identification and an inmate body count, we were finally motioned through the prison gates where most of us would remain from some sixty to a hundred and twenty days before being put up for transfer to another prison based on our points, enemy status, and prison terms.

At R&R, they marched us off the bus piling us into a number of holding cages, similar to the ones in the L.A. County. Baby G-Kev and I huddled in a far corner of one of the cells, and kicked up old times now past. Kev had question after question sliding off his lips, as he wanted to know what lay ahead for him. His biggest concern was whether he'd be housed with me, and would he become my roommate. To these questions, I had no answer. We were finally separated, as he ended up on D-Facility, and I was placed on B-Facility. After my first thirty days, I was hired as a dorm porter being responsible for the Blacks who always had an endless amount of demands for assistance. Immediately after, I placed my hands right into the black market trade that boomed all around me.

Just like the County Jail, the reception center inmates were prohibited from having cigarettes, but the mainline inmates were allowed to attain them, which in essence created a booming black market business for the mainline regular population. They charged us an arm and a leg for the tobacco, and we in return charged the retail buyers an arm and a leg when purchasing from us. The system was set up completely different from the County where the revenue was Dead Presidents (cash); whereas in Delano it was the typical postal stamps, which were then traded for more desired goods from the commissary. For example: Ten stamps would buy you a tootsie roll candy size of tobacco which approximately made eight to ten thin size tobacco sticks selling each for a dollar; which in the ending brings back the money originally spent and a profit with a small margin for overhead. The seller, who bought a tobacco pouch for no more than a couple bucks from the main commissary, made a killing, literally. He could make an approximate fifteen tootsie roll size pack out of that pouch, selling it to the desperate newcomers who are addicted to tobacco. This left the top seller, who accumulated the stamps, in the position to convert them back over to more desirable goods like noodles, can goods, or any other items to his liking. And just like in the County, the A.T.F. raids were carried out to try and put an end to the black market trading.

Immediately I established myself a clientele. Since our money on the books from the County took anywhere from and up to thirty to sixty days to be transferred to us, my initial hustling of tobacco balls helped me to keep up a limited supply of cosmetics and food.

After spending some three months at the reception yard, I was finally interviewed by my counselor; his only job was to put me up for transfer to the proceeding prisons. Although we were allowed to choose the prison location, there weren't any guarantees that we'd be sent to there. I chose Tehachapi State Prison, which was somewhere in the Mohave Desert, but more importantly three hours away from L.A.; and Lancaster State Prison, which was within forty-five minutes distance even closer to L.A. My paperwork was sent to C.S.R. (classification staff representative) who had the final say so over where I would go, and how soon I would leave. Some ten days later I was told that I was transpacking to Sacramento, which had only two prisons, and I've served time in both of them: Old Folsom and New Folsom.

I was headed back again to New Folsom, the terror dome, the gladiator school, the place where the weak are weeded out and made to feel less than a man. My first time arrival in New Folsom was May 12, 1989, and some thirteen days later on May 25, 1989 a major race riot erupted on the B-Facility prison yard. It's been reported that dozens and dozens of inmates were stabbed with prison made knives; one particular black inmate was victimized twice: a Mexican Cholo was stabbing him repeatedly and wouldn't heed or stop despite the massive barrage of bullets flying in all directions. Subsequently to the Mexican's relentless attack, one of the gun towers tried to intervene and fired off a shot; but instead of the bullet impend the aggressor, it missed its mark and slammed into the black inmate's head killing him instantly. That was the Folsom I knew. And now, here I was back on my way to the dungeon, some ten years after I paroled from there.

FRIEND OR FOE
(2002)

On July 30, 2002, I was shipped off state bound to the home of the lifers who were making up about eighty percent of the general population. They weren't too much into race riots, which were few in comparison to lesser levels. But because lifers were more serious in nature and more organized in military endeavors, they were chaotic and desperate when riots did occur. To me my first stay at Folsom had left a deep impression.

It was in Folsom where I first learned of an East African language called Kiswahili that's spoken in Tanzania, Malawi, and Kenya, and where I was exposed to Black History. On my book traveling experiences I met Malcolm Little a.k.a. Malcolm X, became a pupil to some of his ideology, and especially admired his courage to speak about the wrongs perpetuated by the American government in a time when it was considered political incorrect. It was in Folsom where I learned about Martin Luther King Jr. and his Ghandi influence. I met the Freedom Riders who faced the racist odds opposed to their movement and their equal opportunity provided and in theory guaranteed to the citizens of the United States of America. It was in Folsom where I met the Jamaican born Marcus Garvey who led many African-Americans down the path of independency, and instilled in them pride and the goal of being self sufficient.

It was in the same environment of Folsom that I embarked on my new education goals by taking such college courses as Political Science. A course, in which I learned about the three separate branches of government, the check and balancing system, and the amendments that were added in time to correct and smooth out the problems that came with the change of times. I took up Philosophy, which confronted me with my unbending mind frame of past teachings and made me learn to open up and to be more receptive to other opinions and solid premises. It also taught me that nothing in the world remains the same, and everything is bound to change. Philosophy in the end became me, and I became entrenched in its depth.

It was in Folsom I traveled the road of Physical Geography, being exposed to the seven continents and the oceans of the world. I learned that Australia was the only country-island-continent in the world, and that the earth we lived on was approximately consisting of two third of water. I also traveled to the far lands of the Orient: India, Cambodia, Vietnam, and Japan. I visited the largest populated country on earth: Red China, and the small island of Cuba to meet with its leader since 1959, Fidel Castro. It was there in Folsom I was first introduced to English 21; to the difference of descriptive, narrative, objective, and subjective writing, and how to use such words as 'an' correctly. It was Folsom Prison where I was now headed to again.

The ride from Delano Reception Center took a long body wrecking eight hours. I couldn't wait to stretch out and allow my legs the freedom of movement. As the grey goose pulled up to the double gates that released me a decade ago, most of the inmates, who had been asleep, awoke from the sudden charge of energy in the air. They were happy to be at the place that would hold some for life and others for a great period. They were tired of the bus and eager to exit it. After the routine check like many times before, we were finally waved through. We drove to A-Facility R&R where we were to endure another monotonous routine. The moment I stepped off the bus, the air filled my lungs, and I remembered being trapped.

    The reality of being back in Folsom again gave me instant claustrophobia, I felt congested as if some imaginary bars were already restricting my movement. I needed to do some serious self-reflecting, and I desperately needed to recharge my mental batteries, as they were completely depleted. After being fed another dry sack lunch, the processing routine began and ended with a serious of questions that had to do with my mental state of mind. "Have you thought about killing yourself?" – "Do you hear voices in your head?" – "Are you on any psych medication?" For every question that was asked, I answered no. But the reality of my prediction was I really did hear voices before; I have thought about hurting myself every now and then, and maybe I needed some psych medication. Maybe my ill experiences stemmed from all the wrong I've done to people, and maybe all the mental problems I was having at times been God's way of repaying me back, or maybe I was really crazy and hadn't realize it.

    We were escorted for orientation to B-Facility, which was reported for its ruthlessness, mass riots, and brutes. My cellmate was a fellow soldier from the Black P. Stone Bloods. He received a life sentence for a crime, which I thought was a misdemeanor: He had failed to yield on a traffic stop, and since it was his third charge, he was struck out under the minority targeted three-strike law. After a light chitchat, sleep came with no delays or impending. The following morning I was awaken by the breakfast being passed out which was warmly welcomed as it was a drastic change from the food in Delano. I complemented the food the entire time I was taking it down.

A few hours later, we were tested on our school standings, as it was required to determine whether the inmate should be placed into school, or in case his education level was up to part to immediately clear him for work. I was given the highest test the teacher had which I scored with 11.5 out of 12.9. I stayed in the orientation building for eight days, before I was transferred to building number 4, C-Section, cell No. 221. My new cellmate was the well-known Big Herm from the Athens Park Bloods.

When I arrived at Folsom, it was still on lockdown for a black inmate stabbing a correctional officer; but the population was already allowed to go out on a mini concrete yard that was part of the slow process of coming off altogether. On the way to my building, I got the opportunity to talk to Herm and Lil Loko-Dray who I hadn't seen since 1998 in the County's Blood module. After a twenty minutes chit-chat through the gate, the C/O ushered me into C-Section to lock me away in my cell that would probably be my new home for months, even years. The first thing that jumped out at me when I stepped through the door was the tidiness of the cell. The floor was buffed and waxed to a shiny self-reflecting image. The entire cell was spotless clean and well decorated in every way and without doubt, it was a Blood cell, as the red and black trimming confirmed.

I began making myself at home. The coziness of the cell made it easy for me to relax and to become comfortable. I tightened up my bed and placed the few items I had into my locker. After finishing the settling process, I was flipping through the T.V. channels looking for something of interest until loud noise from the dayroom area drew my attention. In seconds, the television was off and I was pretending to be into something else. Herm was returning from the yard, and immediately I geared myself to leave my first impression on him. In the gangster's world it was imperative to always leave the first impression as a solid impression, this way people gave you respect right away.

When Herm entered the cell, I sized him up; as it was a habit, I always performed. He was approximately six foot one, weight some two hundred and fifty pounds and his body structure was athletic and that of a person who worked out occasionally. "What's up Blood?" When he responded, I automatically analyzed his voice tone, his pitch level, and body language. I knew from experiences that most men put up fronts, and in the deeper realms of themselves, they were cowards or busters, and/or reactionaries, and I liked neither. It was a rare occasion that I met a man who I could place on the same level as me. But Herm was a different story: He was like me in a few aspects, easy going, possessing a sense of humor, and he was into politics and military endeavors. We clicked right away on a lot of things, and before we realized it, we were more compatible than I initially thought possible. Herm immediately updated me on the politics that buzzed in and around Folsom, and more importantly on all the main players who controlled each political group.

Two weeks after my arrival the administration resumed everything back to normal. It was fine with me, as I wanted to get to the yard to see how many familiar faces I would recognize. I knew hundreds and hundreds of inmates due to my extensive traveling up and down the California coast doing time inside a multitude of prisons: Pelican Bay, San Quentin, Old Folsom, New Folsom, Tehachapi, San Diego, Mule Creek, California Men's Colony, Avenal, not to mention all the county facilities and reception centers. "Yard release" – "Yard release" – "Building 4, prepare for yard release"; the building speakers blurred throughout every section. Herm was already out the cell roaming about somewhere, as he was a building porter. The control booth officer had released him for work like every morning, and I had the cell all to myself.

The prison program was still new to me, and regardless on how hard I tried to be prepared, I was caught off guard. Level IV (maximum security) jailing is different from any other jailing inside the California prisons. In most level IV's, inmates as a rule of thumb extend and offer courtesy to all; they are very much aware of their histories as individuals and their peoples' history. They are also the most intriguing inmates, as they are forced to make due with their harsh and mental depressing environments. The men in level IV prisons practice *The Art of War*, the ancient Chinese book written by Sun Tzu. They run through religions and ideologies like the passing winds until they find the one that fits best their actual mind frames.

I headed to the yard looking forward to confronting and reacquainting myself with the old train of thoughts that held me captive from 1989 to 1992. I still continued on my personal journey of refining my many ideologies and outlooks. Unlike the men I was about to encounter on the yard, I had been home and back to jail many times. To them time had stood still since their arrests in the 1990's, the 80's or even in the Black Panther – Vietnam era. They were left with fragments of freedom as the time of departure from the outside world had been chipped away at what they once knew to be.

I stopped in line waiting to be frisked by the C/O's who greeted us the second we exited the building's front door. They considered this measure a tactic to check inmates for knives before yard release, although they knew from experience that they were losing an uphill battle trying to impede or stop them from doing what they wanted to do. They learned a long time ago that inmates went around every obstacle the C/O's set up to impede them. In a deeper sense, there was no stopping a determined creative level IV inmate.

After the light frisk search the inmates bee lined toward the main yard where they gathered in their respective section. The Bloods' spot called 'Damu Alley' (Blood Alley) was located in the handball area whereas the Crips depending on their allegiance and clicks hung in various parts of the yard. The Blacks from Northern California cities, who called themselves 'Kumi' (which represented the Northern California 415 area code), hung on the 7-block mini concrete outer wall. On the other side of the yard one could find the White population, away from the American Indians, Asians, and Pacific Islanders. The yard was one big piece of real estate that was owned by a multitude of groups.

Through squinted eyes from the sun's warm rays, I eyeballed the central tower above me. I knew the gunner inside, most likely a trigger-happy white boy, possessed a Mini 14 assault rifle that had the capacity to slide right through the first victim and easily smash into another target. In fact, the guns were so powerful, they had initially replaced them in 1989 with some black colored rifles that shot nine-millimeter hollow points into its intended target and exploded inside with death as the outcome more than often; which again forced the Federal Government to scrape them altogether. The new policy trained the gun towers to fire alternative weapons, but in dire situations where life and death weighed in the balance, the Minis would be brought to life releasing a loud thunderous sound unlike none I've ever heard in my war battles on the street. I held respect for the power of the Mini, and if I were to do any wrong like the past, I knew I would have to move like a thief in the night, undetected.

Inmates were pouring out from all buildings; I watched and eye fucked every face looking for someone vaguely familiar. As I neared the Blood Alley, I recognized a Y.G. foot soldier named Speedio from the Nickerson Garden Bloods; he stood on the handball court pavement talking to some other Bloods. I blended into the midst of them, listening for familiar names of soldiers and their prison political allegiances. Some minutes later, my homeboy Lil Loko-Dray bee lined in my direction with a full cup of hot coffee steaming the air around it, and it smelt good. "Let me hit that." Loko-Dray slid the coffee to me. "Who are all the homies?" I was asking him to place names with the faces, as I wanted to know who each individual was, before they were to become over familiar with who I was.

In any setting, information is truly valuable, and I took the knowledge of knowing the names of the Bloods serious. Anyone of them could be an enemy to me due to some past incident that I may have been involved in. My name was a part of plenty dirty work in L.A.; and in the process of my life travel, I've made a multitude of enemies along the way, Crips and Bloods alike. "That's P-Nut right there from Carson

Bloods; the one with the blue beanie on is Bo-Bo from San Diego Bloods; the fat one with the tattoos on his face is Sir-Me from the Blood Stone Villains." Lil Loko-Dray named and identified everyone for me; I was sure to compute it permanently as I knew Folsom would be my home for a while.

As we walked the yard heading for the jogger's track, I took notice of enemy locations, its members' count, and the security measure of each group, and with Loko-Dray's assistance, I was able to identify the shot callers, the second-in-command, the lieutenants, and even more importantly the hitters. They were always packing the knives and stayed ready for action. Their jobs held a multitude of responsibilities, and their first obligation was to protect the main head of their particular group at all cost. They had to read the yard at all times to be vigilant against attacks from other groups, and they had to prevent the over running of their perimeter by making sure their security perimeters were always formed and enforced thru physical presence.

Besides the studies on the outside groups, I analyzed the Bloods as well. I had to distinguish between the ones who were truly my friends, and those who were potential enemies. B-Facility was packed with a lot of various conflicting ideologies amongst every group. The Crips always kept some form of tribalism going in their camps, and as of late, the Bloods also had become a victim of this bug. Tribalism is only a good thing when everybody within the tribe is working together as a collective toward goals that are beneficial to the whole. But when it is laced with mistrust, back biting and contempt for other members of the group, the inevitable is bound to occur. The Blood Lines, a more political minded group, were the first who were to experience the tribe bug, as my cellmate Big Herm ended up having an avoidable situation.

Rick Rock from the Swan Blood Gang and my homeboy Lil Loko-Dray had been waging a low-key war against Herm. They held little, and in some instance, no respect for him. Each day their actions grew bolder until the battle lines were drawn and a confrontation erupted. The morning it occurred started out normal. Herm went to work as usual, I had the cell to myself as usual, and the program we performed every day went along as usual. That was until Rick Rock screamed at Herm to get him out of his cell for a ducat (a prison appointment) that was scheduled for that morning. Herm informed Rick Rock that the C/O was in the bathroom, and as soon as he returned he would get him out. Somewhere in between Rick Rock was becoming belligerent and disrespectful over the tier. Soon a multitude of threats was flying all around. Herm was concerned, as he knew as a B.L. he wasn't allowed to get into confrontations with other B.L.'s period! "You go be my witness Loko." He wanted my assurance in case Rick Rock was about to get at him in an aggressive combat manner.

When Rick Rock and Loko Dray finally exited their cell and made a straight beeline path for Herm whom they intended to harm by launching a barrage of lefts and rights onto his facial area, all the rules and regulations went out the window. With no choice and due to his self-preservation Herm drew his heat out of his pocket and all hell broke lose. For every solid face-connecting blow Rick Rock delivered to Herm, he retaliated with well-calculated counter measures with his inmate-manufactured knife. The outcome of the battle soon became clear as Rick Rock was bleeding from a full dozen or so deep tissue wounds. Herm's attack was only interrupted slightly when Loko Dray entered into the fight and slugged Herm with a solid right, which drew a response call at his facial area with immediate results.

The melee went on unabated, and soon Herm was gaining the superior position over the whole situation. For what seemed to be a long time, it appeared to me, Rick Rock had froze up on his attack as it dawned on his psyche that he was being butchered, literally. "Get down! Get down!" The gun tower officer began repeatedly yelling for the combatants to halt their fight; he barked a third order; by this time, Loko Dray was already up the tier lying on his stomach, waiting for the cavalry of C/O's. The gun tower officer barked again, but this time it was a different order. He fired his 37-millimeter block gun, "Boom!" I immediately ran from the cell's front window, thinking the tower had fired his Mini 14 and the bullet would come through the window or door, and accidentally slam into me. After collecting my initial fright, it dawned on me the noise level I heard wasn't consistent with the nerve racking noise of the Mini 14. "Get down! Get down!" The gunner was screaming a loud defiant order for everyone to lay face down.

I cautiously inched back toward the front door to see the damage that was done by Herm's knife and the block gun. "Get it Loko, get it!" Herm slid the knife under the door crack. It was completely bloody. I took it and flushed it down the toilet just as the storm troopers paraded through the door with their batons poised for some action. The entire area where Herm was lying spoke the gruesome details of the matter; blood was everywhere and on every person. Immediately Rick Rock was carried out on a stretcher. Seconds later Loko Dray was led out in cuffs suffering from his deep tissue wound and his bruised ego. He was hyper and prided himself on his capabilities, but when he decided to launch his attack against Herm, he'd never foreseen this outcome. After his departure, the goon squad C/O's cuffed Herm and that's when I first noticed his wound to his left arm. It was deep indeed and wide open. Somewhere in the mix of the melee, he inflicted himself.

After all the combatants were cleared of the dayroom area, a C.S.I. (crime scene investigator) team took to work, photographing and collecting evidence. Every crack and crevice was searched for the unknown weapon. I was standing at my cell door front window, when two C/O's bee lined into my eye vision and ordered me to prepare to be handcuffed. They wanted to search my cell. After donning myself with the appropriate wear, I allowed them to cuff me and to lead me into the shower that had a locking bar gate to confine me until I was allowed to be placed back in. When I returned, it was like stepping into another dimension, as everything looked different. The cell seemed hollow, as half of the items that once were there had been hauled off like Herm had been.

I remained without a cellmate for at least a week. My next roommate was fifty-two years old, twenty-five of which he had been spent in prison, and at the rate of trouble he stayed in, he probably would end up spending another twenty-five years on the inside. His name was Rob and he claimed to be from the East Side 20's. Initially he was cool, but as the days came and went, his internal problems started to have their effect on our slightly built relationship. After realizing we had too many conflicts of interests, I hastily made arrangements to find myself another cellmate who I would have more in common with. My search wasn't long, and by then I figured anybody would be better than Rob, as I believed his quarter century in prison had affected his train of thought and somewhere along the line, it had made him anti-social.

My next cellmate, who eventually became my comrade, was a Blood from the 120th Street Miller Gangster Bloods. His name was Sneak and he had been in prison since '95 for a murder charge. We clicked instantly, as we both had a lot in common. I was a few years older than he was, which probably was the main reason that we got along so well, and he was a dreamer like me. Despite the harshness of the Folsom environment, he still held on to his objectives even when everything around him was bleak and dissolute. He didn't have any visible hang-ups, and fortunately, he didn't have any cell affections. In prison you could be around a person all day on the yard kicking it, laughing together, and straight chilling, and he was an alright person, but the moment he walked back into the confines of the cell, his attitude swayed completely; he suddenly and unexpectedly became anti-social, and his anger and aggression levels went up a notch or two.

Sneak didn't allow the cell to alter his mental, not even a slight bit. Besides him, my association was limited to Lil Pooh from the Black P. Stones, Ed from the Mad Swans, Red Bull from Pacoima Bloods, Bugs from the Fruit Town Bloods, Tyman from Athens Park Bloods, and Q-Ball from the Miller Gangsters. My friends were few and none as the politics and internal conflicts kept me with a warily eye. Just like I have done in any other environment, I had to place myself into a strategic position that would give me the leeway and freedom to guarantee my first step up the totem pole. I eventually landed my first post as a prison M.A.C. representative. M.A.C. stood for men's advisory counsel, and the M.A.C. reps role was to ensure the well being of the entire inmate population in general, meaning to make sure they received their fair share of things that were coming to them: appropriate yard time, canteen items, laundry, visiting hours etc.

With this position I learned of the free and unrestricted movements I now had. I bounced from building to building, and soon my face was recognized as the one who conducted business on behalf of the inmates' general population. I maintained this position for a short time before I was elected as an executive body M.A.C. member, who possessed a little more privileges than the general did. With this new position, I set about to establish myself firmly into the echelon of Folsom prison; but it wasn't to be, as my timetable would be hampered again and again, due to the repeated continuous lockdowns ranging in all magnitudes.

THE CONFLICT
(2002)

The first lockdown after my arrival was announced on September 28, 2002 when a dispute involving prison politics exploded between the Cholos and the Skinheads. The Cholos were trying to pressure the Skinheads into doing a stabbing against one of their fellow comrades, supposedly due to an incident that had occurred in Pelican Bay Prison. The Skinheads asked the Cholos for time because they wanted to do an investigation as they felt it was only an appropriate measure. But the Cholos became infuriated due to the difference of procedure and prepared silently and secretly for a pre-emptive attack against the Skins. The outcome of the dispute became clear when numerous Skins received serious injuries, and the Folsom alliance between both parties was severed forever.

Usually when two groups collide over issues politically motivated, the prison institute's procedure is to keep them apart and confine them to their cells for a minimum of ninety days, or even up to a year, depending on the severity of the situation. But this time it was different. The prison officials, fearing for a long drawn out war, tried to broker a settling between the groups' representatives. While the Cholos flat out declined a diplomatic solution, they opted to settle through the end of a knife; the Skins down played the problem and convinced the administration that they were ready to program. About six weeks later, it would become clear that the administration had been outsmarted by the Skins, and the Cholos had placed themselves into an inferior position by refusing to negotiate, thus exempting themselves from any activities.

On November 9, 2002, the Skins were ready to launch a military move against the Cholos, who had the disadvantage of being moved restrained and under escort of correctional officers wherever they ventured. That Tuesday the yard looked simple, normal, and even peaceful. But some few hours into the recreation activities, a dozen or more hardcore Skins caught my attention. They were up to no good: Their body language, rapid moving back and forth on the yard, but more important them passing around knives made them suspicious to me and the black population that was placed on the highest alert status for fear of a racial war. Without delay, many black gangsters and militants began passing and securing their prison made knives. Little did we know that we were about to get a front row seat to a mass butchering of some Cholo soldiers.

The Cholos were being ushered back and forth to the medical area all morning. Building after building was under escort of their protectors bee-lining to receive some medical attention of one sort or another when a well known female correctional officer named S. Curry, and another less known correctional officer exited building No. 5 with five Cholos under their escort. The Cholos chitchatted back and forth, displaying their arrogance and toughness through every fiber of their bodily actions. They gave the Whites little or no credit when it came to a military maneuver; they viewed them as a group that was still disorganized, lacking courage, and frankly speaking they believed the Whites didn't have the mindset to launch a well organized beginning-to-end pre-emptive attack, period.

The moment I noticed the Cholos and the C/O's entourage, I also noticed the movement of the Skins who held a quick and last minute meeting, and then broke off into groups of two, heading to their predestined picked location. I counted ten of them thus covering all angels of attack by following the Sun Tzu strategy: although competent, appear incompetent; although organized, appear disorganized; and although effective, appear ineffective. Most were fooled completely by the Skins' lay back relaxed nature, including C/O Curry and her colleague, who didn't notice anything amiss. If they were trained in the detecting of impending violence, they had failed completely. The entourage group had now passed by the central control gun tower. Two of the hitters, who had been standing by the water faucet, were now closing in from the flank side. The entourage passed two more hitters on an empty handball court; that was the unspoken secret cue for all the hitters to close in from their respective side and launch the guerilla style attack. They jumped up, withdrew their knives, singled out a particular target, and started the butchering in earnest. The other teams of hitters closed in thus making any attempt of escape impossible.

The two C/O's began a hastily retreat desperately trying to avoid the danger and violence, but they weren't successful at all. Quickly the five Cholos were completely and totally over-runned and literally overwhelmed by the ten aggressive Skins. Desperation, struggle, violence, mayhem, and destruction exploded with each team of hitters picking and selecting one of them. From where I stood, the hitters as well as their victims looked like large fish flipping and flopping out of water. Some ten seconds into the butchering the gun towers finally opened up with their various assortments of weapons to stop the on going mayhem: "Boom!"

As the crucial seconds ticked away with the reality of the scene in front of them, they realized that the rapid evolving events were more severe in nature than originally perceived; reason enough for them to replace their block guns with the military issued Mini 14. The melee entered into its second phase as all the hitters went through adrenaline rushes just taking away their rational mind frames from death and destruction that swerved around them and their victims. "Boom," the central tower opened up again with the unmistaken and explicit sound of the Mini 14, "Boom!" Building No. 6 demanded my undivided attention to the right, as one of its gunners signed his signature across the space looking to exploit one of the hitters: "Boom!" Building No. 5 had now joined in on the barrage of fire, as the melee went on unabated and escalating: "Boom, Boom, Boom," round after round was expended into the kill zone with the combatants ironically not fazed by any of the bullets. The panic alarm blurred throughout the compound, and it seemed to blare on for a long time as the butchering lasted longer than I thought it would.

Finally, correctional officers swarmed the yard from all quarters. A few more rounds were exhausted, and only after the C/O's ascertained some kind of plan, only then did they beeline in with their batons swiping and swinging. When the smoke had finally cleared, two of the five Cholos bordered on the middle plain somewhere between life and death. Three medical gurneys were used to carry away the two critical and badly wounded; and a third who would be okay, but who seemed to be in shock from the experience, his mind was rattled literally. The word in the air had it that one of them had succumbed to a lethal blow to one of his lungs.

As the C/O's began their crime scene investigation, we began placing our knives into the one place that's been a traditional and only secure stash spot for most hard-core convicts, and for a long time to come, our ass. We knew without a doubt that we would be strip searched completely naked before we were allowed to enter back into our respective buildings. It took at least an hour for the process to be completed. And some twenty minutes after being back in the confines of my cell, I replayed all the drama and violence over and over again with the result that the Skins of today were nothing like the Aryan Brothers of yesterday, they were much harder, brutal, and most important for me to note, more organized.

The Whites and Mexicans were completely separated from all activities, when some thirty-six days later the control booth officer, who was responsible for opening and closing the cells, made a grave and irreparable mistake by accidentally opening a Cholos' cell during the Whites' shower period. The Cholos were confused initially; but when the same officer made a move that questioned his ulterior motive by walking away leaving their cell wide open, they didn't waste a second. They retrieved their massive bone crushers, headed downstairs and butchered the only one skinhead in the shower.

Soon after the C.S.I. conducted a thorough investigation of the entire C-Section, looking for any evidence that could possible assist on the impending attempted murder charges. Due to these severe life and death encounters, the prison administration decided on a mass movement that would separate the two races altogether and completely ended the war for the time being, whereas all other races inherited the entire prison program, including benefits and privileges. But it would be short lived as the administration would merciless slam the prison for all minor or serious infraction like the one that occurred on the morning of December 28, 2002.

It was a typical morning, tray slots unlocked at 6:00 a.m.; coffee at 6:30 a.m.; breakfast at 7:00 a.m., and finally yard release at 8:45 a.m. Sneak and myself went to relax in the area on the prison yard known as Blood Alley. We stood in the company of other Blood soldiers who were doing what we loved to do, watching and eyeballing the yard for any signs of anything that might be out of place. In prison, you can never be not concerned about the atmosphere around you, as it may appear calm and relaxed in every aspect, but after further analysis and observation, you would soon discover that the entire yard is actually laced with tension and violence, and ready to explode.

O-Shay, one of the Northern California spokesmen walked up and asked for a second of my time. Instantly I made a straight beeline in his direction, as he was the person who I was conducting a heroin deal with, which was scheduled to take place early the following week. As we slow trekked around the yard, I couldn't help but think that he was about to bless me with the drugs that I had already paid for. Instead he fed me some drama about why my package was going to be delayed; and due to the delay, supposedly because his connect on the street went to jail, he pulled four caps of marijuana from his pocket and gave it to me, to make up for it. The four chap sticks equaled to approximately forty dollars on just any prison yard in the State of California. I took the marijuana thanked him for being straight up, and excused him for his untimely business mishap. After a few more shared words, we departed in different directions on our separate missions. I sought out Sneak to tell him that we now had some marijuana for the New Year's, which was only four short days away.

Some twenty minutes later we were on the far side of the yard blowing a fat marijuana stick like there was no tomorrow. The first one led to another one, then another one, soon we were blown out our wits, and watched the yard intensively, but from the marijuana affected state of mind, when a commotion to our right drew our immediate attention. Four correctional officers were in the distance harassing and frisking a young black inmate who looked to have no desire of being touched. Within seconds, the area exploded, and the four correctional officers were pouncing on him like some mad men, who had no control over their actions. "Get down!" – "Yard down," the central control tower screamed over the P.A. system for all the inmates to lay down where they were standing.

Soon more C/O's arrived on the scene adding their assistance to their compatriots, who were having an obvious difficult time in containing and controlling the now breathless, exhausted, and fatigue inmate. With their help he was overwhelmed and eventually manhandled, soon subdued, when unexpectedly an unknown C/O walked to the now restrained inmate, and in view for all to see, punched him two or three times in his torso area. The inmate was screaming and twisting, still putting up a struggle with the little leeway he had. From the second the C/O had took upon himself to assault the bound and gadget inmate, the black population voiced their disapproval in unison, drawing the correctional officers' attention, who immediately reframed from their nervousness, and opted for a softer approach to dealing with the inmate, who was now marched down the track.

Some ten minutes after he was removed from the yard, the central control tower blared over the P.A. system that yard could be resumed. Immediately some Crips began to gather and voice their discomfort about the C/O's ruff handling of their homeboy, and in seconds words of revenge and retaliation were sliding up and down the yard. The Bloods in general held a quick meeting of the minds to see what the majority felt and believed would be the best course of action. Some Bloods were with the drama against the C/O's, and others who still harbored tribal animosity against the Crips flat-out declined their help into a Crip related problem. I on the other hand was down for the drama, but I wanted to see what the Crips in general were going to do. Some of their hard core groups from Los Angeles, the Rollin 60's, the Compton and Watts Crips, the Hoover Criminals, the Long Beach Crips, the East Coast Crips, and for the most part ninety-five percent of the Crip car weren't even thinking about getting involved in the impending situation. In fact, only ten Crips from here and there decided to make a statement to the administration.

Following the majority we made a collective decision that we were not going to be no sacrificial lamb for no group that wasn't going to stand up for themselves. To make our statement clear we validated our stance by distancing ourselves to different parts of the yard that were out of harms way. Sneak, Ed, and I went toward the canteen area where the C/O's were conducting the close custody count of certain inmates. Immediately after, we bee lined up the track to a location safely away from where the drama was about to evolve.

Our entourage sat in the cut watching from a distance as a staged chunkum between two Crips proceeded: "Yard down! Yard down!" The central control gun tower ordered all the inmates to lay down where they were. Sergeant Murphy and a black sergeant, whom I've held friendly chit chats with, began a quick beeline run in the direction where the two combatants continued to fight. In seconds, C/O's from all sections began a hastily mad run with their batons in hand toward the area of action. Just then and unexpectedly the whole area exploded with violence that caught all the C/O's off guard, they were totally unprepared for the mayhem trap that they'd blindly ran into.

The moment Sergeant Murphy focused on the two combatants, an inmate, better known as Harlem Marv, suddenly assaulted him. Marv was an O.G. from the Harlem Crips, and the entire scheme of the plot and planning was his original blue print. He pounced on Sergeant Murphy from the backside, knocking him to the grassy area, promptly burying the knife into his bullet proof vest, thus making it a useless weapon, and saving the sergeant's life. All around inmates began bouncing up and striking down all the correctional officers around them. A group of knife-wielding inmates bee lined into the direction of where the black sergeant was standing and wrecked a reign of terror through their blades onto the helpless and now ambushed sergeant. A large dust cloud soon blanketed the entire area as the struggle for life and death swung back and forth. "Get down! Get down!" The central control tower blurred orders left and right over the P.A. to the inmates who kept popping up and turning into flight risk against all the C/O's in the kill zone.

With the reality that the inmates had ambushed some correctional officers, the central control gun tower implemented his military issued Mini 14: "Boom!" The shot echoed throughout the compound, and the noise bounced off every empty space throwing the vibration from section to section. "Boom," another gun tower had opened up, and as on cue, the other gun towers added their assistance to the situation. It was hard to tell who was gaining the advantage, but there was one thing for certain, the two opposing groups collided with enthusiasm. Each side threw themselves into pitched battles, desperately trying to attain the slightest edge in the on-going melee.

"Boom – Bling!" Tower No. 8 fired off a round, which struck a nearby workout bar. The bullet slammed into the pole, and its loud echoing sound made me duck my head down further with the fear in my mind that the flying bullet might slam into me. "Boom," another loud sound was discharged from my right, but the sound had less intensity to it as compared to the Mini 14. "Boom," the central control fired the same gun again, and this time an inmate, who had been sprinting across the yard, suddenly and quickly lost all control of his footing and slammed head first into the field. He had been hit and was lying squirming in the dirt, rejecting the unbearable pain that was forcing itself into every fiber, muscle, and tissue throughout his body. Fortunate for the fallen inmate, he was only hit with the block gun, which packed a powerful and lethal punch. The melee continued for a few more minutes, and its forward progress soon began to slow with the arrival of dozens and dozens of correctional officers, who seemed to be materializing from all sections and doors throughout the prison. They were quickly fanning out to place complete control over the violence that had erupted like a volcano spreading its hot lava in all directions.

As fast as the melee had started, it was over, at least ninety-nine percent of it, when an inmate named M.C. suddenly jumped up off the ground and made a mad man dash toward a group of correctional officers; he literally threw himself into the pack of them, falling to the dirt. The C/O's squirmed a little, thinking they were being attacked again, and as quickly as they regained their composure, they brought their batons to bear down on the knifeless inmate, who they were drilling merciless.

The black sergeant, who had received a multitude of stab-wounds from his neck to his lower torso, was quickly carried off the yard. Harlem Marv was also rushed away bleeding profusely from his entire facial area, as he had taken a severe and brutal beating from the C/O's. In fact, he had so much blood on his face and neck he was almost unrecognizable. Sergeant Murphy exited from the melee like a rising phoenix emerging only with a fast swelling black eye. He was pumped up from the altercation, stomping around the prison yard screaming to each gun tower: "If any of these mother fuckas get up off the ground, shoot him!" He repeated his executive order over and over again, and it was obvious to me that he was having an adrenaline rush. I soon counted a total of ten Mini 14 rifles hanging out the gun towers all across the yard watching, waiting, daring an inmate to jump up, and forfeit his life to the hail of bullets that would undoubtedly mow him down like a wild dog.

As the tension and danger subsided, I took inventory of the inmates that were lying prone in the kill zone: P-Nut from the Cabbage Patch Bloods, Spook-Ru from the Modesto Bloods, and Bo-Bo from the San Diego Bloods. Each were participants in the melee, and besides themselves, there were about a dozen Crips, who also lay proned out. The C/O's were all around the prison compound, in teams of ten. Each team cornered off a group of inmates, striped them, frisked them, and placed plastic restraints on them. Some half hour later, the whole yard was restrained, and building by building, we were marched into our respective housings.

As Ed, my cellmate Sneak and I neared the rotunda area to enter our building; Sergeant Murphy stepped away from a crowd of C/O's, and barked an uncompromising order to the escort sergeant: "Take them to the hole, they're B.L. shot callers!" By now, his left eye was closed shut and bruising every second with the dark colors of black and purple. "There were some B.L.'s in that shit, and ya'll going to the hole!" I was at a lost for words, how could he be so wrong in his accusations he was throwing around. As I prepared myself to suffer my faith, Ed from the Swan Bloods spoke up to down play the charges against us: "Sergeant Murphy, there wasn't any B.L.'s in that shit." Murphy quick counter argued by naming some Blood members who hung around the B.L.'s, and to him, any and everybody, who hung around the B.L.'s, was and had to be a B.L.

Ed promptly set the records straight with the result that Sergeant Murphy retraced his original statement, leaving us with one parting shot: "I'm going to take your word right now, but if I find out that they're B.L.'s, then I'll be sending for ya'll." As we were escorted to our building, I couldn't help but think of how the hell he spoke with such convictions that we all were B.L.'s. The thought bothered me, and one person kept coming to my mind over and over again. That one person had left the yard under mysterious and irregular conditions. Later it would be confirmed undisputedly that this person did in fact P.C. (protective custody); it was Lil Pooh from the Black P. Stones. He ended up on the New Folsom A-Facility mainline, a place where snitches, gang dropouts, and stabbing victims were placed for their own protection.

Once back inside the cell, Sneak and I went through the unwinding stages of relaxing ourselves from the danger and violence that we had just witnessed. We immediately rolled up another marijuana stick, and blew ourselves into oblivion, with the hopes that its chemical effects would drown out the high anxiety we were experiencing. New Folsom Prison had not changed since my decade old departure, in fact it remained its same old self in every aspect, the dungeon, the gladiator school, the compound of thuggism, and now it had another name added to its long reputation list, a name that I was so over familiar with, the home of the body bags.

Epilogue

At the time, I'd finished writing this book, New Folsom Prison would remain on lockdown from the bloody melee, and it would be a long time, before the program returned back to normal. In the course of those months, I've learned to adapt, adjust, and conform into a product of my new environment of being a convict. The day-in and day-out confinement to my small cell had altered me, and I became a part of the monotonous routine that I was forced to endure and accept. The Skinheads, although they remained on lockdown, had literally butchered two of their own due to internal conflicts. They call it "cleaning their house up."

My highly decorated foot soldier Sad-Dog, who performed remarkable well in the County Jail war, had arrived in New Folsom some three cells down from where I was. Big-Herm from the Athens Park Bloods had also returned to the mainline, after he successfully beat his attempted murder charges against my homeboy Lil Loko-Dray and Rick Rock from the Swans.

But my journey didn't end in Folsom. After I served time in the S.H.U. in Corcoran State Prison, I was transferred to the Corcoran S.A.T.F., right across the street, and about three hours away from Los Angeles, where I will stay for a little while.

To all my dogs in the Folsom S.H.U.:

Mad Moe and Sad-Dog from Denver Lanes,
El-Banger from Pasadena Lanes,
Pueblo Tae from Pueblo Bishops,
Sick Mike from Black P. Stones,
P-Nut from Cabbage Patch,
Tiny Loko from Inglewood Neighborhood,
Krazy-Ant from Sky Line,
Lil Loko-Dray from NHB 20's,
Red Bull from Pacoima Bloods.

APPENDIX A
Homeboys incarcerated:

OG Syke	27th Streets	murder
OG No Brain	29th Streets	murder
OG T-Dog	27th Streets	murder
OG D-Bop	29th Streets	murder
OG Lil Tray-K	27th Streets	murder
Lil One punch	2nd Avenues	murder
Lil Loko	29th Streets	murder
OG Karate-D	27th Streets	3rd strike - life
OG Zig-Zag	29th Streets	3rd strike - life
Lil Time-Bomb	29th Streets	robbery
OG Mouse	27th Streets	robbery
OG K-Dog	29th Streets	3rd strike - life, credit union robbery
OG Lil Reese	27th Streets	credit union robbery
OG Bo-John	27th Streets	credit union robbery
Baby Jimbo	27th Streets	murder - life
G-Nose	BZP 27th Streets	murder - life
Tiny Tray-K	27th Streets	stolen car
Baby G-Kev	27th Streets	robbery/murder - life
Shadow	2nd Avenues	murder - life
G-Boy	29th Streets	robbery/ murder - life
OG Tall-Dog	27th Streets	credit union robbery
Lil Jimbo	27th Streets	murder - life
Tiny Loko	29th Streets	robbery
OG Big Tray-K	27th Streets	robbery
OG Bolasko	27th Streets	drug poss.
OG Herk	27th Streets	3rd strike - life, assault
L-Dog	2nd Avenues	assault
OG Paradise	27th Streets	murder - life
Baby Timebomb	29th Streets	robbery
Big Timebomb	29th Streets	murder - life
Shorty Kapone	BZP 27th Streets	attempted murder
Sad-Dog	27th Streets	robbery/murder - life
Eddie Lane	27th Streets	robbery
OG Big Loko-Dray	2nd Avenues	robbery
Lil Loko-Dray	2nd Avenues	robbery
Big Snake	2nd Avenues	robbery
Solo	29th Streets	attempted murder
Devil	29th Streets	murder/attempted murder
Baby Insane	2nd Avenues	attempted murder
B-Brazy	2nd Avenues	attempted murder/robbery
Lil Sneak	27th Streets	attempted murder

Big Sneak	27th Streets	attempted murder
OG Cellous	27th Streets	federal cocaine case
Tramp	27th Streets	federal cocaine case
Big Tippy C-K	27th Streets	robbery
OG Big Nut	27th Streets	robbery
Lil Nut	27th Streets	poss. of cocaine
OG T-Bone	27th Streets	robbery
Le-Roy	BZP 27th Streets	credit union robbery
OG West	27th Streets	robbery
Baby Krazy-B	27th Streets	drug poss.
Baby Bosko	29th Streets	no info
OG Big Rock	27th Streets	murder - life
Baby Monster	2nd Avenues	spousal abuse
Baby Gangster	27th Streets	attempted murder
Baby Krazy-Boy	29th Streets	drug poss.
Tazz	BZP 27th Streets	robbery
Plunky	BZP 27th Streets	murder - life
OG Kay-K	27th Streets	robbery
OG Snipe	29th Streets	robbery/drug poss.
Junebug	29th Streets	robbery
Lil Bosko	27th Streets	robbery/murder - life
Big Gangster Dee	27th Streets	robbery
Lil Syke	29th Streets	robbery/murder - life
Lil Red	2nd Avenues	murder - life
Dollar Bill	BZP 27th Streets	murder - life
Jugalis	BZP 27th Streets	attempted murder
Baby Tray-K	27th Streets	credit union robbery
Ta-Ta	BZP 27th Streets	murder

APPENDIX B
B.I.P. (Bloods in Peace)

OG Saw Dog	27th Streets	1984	ran over by a bus
OG Stoney	27th Streets	1986	murdered by 30's Crips
OG L-Bone	29th Streets	1987	murdered by East Side Crips
OG Dopey	25th Streets	1987	murdered by 30's Crips
OG Don-Don	27th Streets	1988	murdered by 30's Crips
OG Thunder	27th Streets	1988	murdered by 30's Crips
OG Sweaty Teddy	27th Streets	1989	suicide
OG Mr. Rollin 20	27th Streets	1989	murdered by 30's Crips
OG Dez	29th Streets	1990	murdered by some jackers
OG Lace Dog	29th Streets	1990	murdered by Broadway Crips
OG Dipps	27th Streets	1991	murdered by 30's Crips
OG Lil-Man	29th Streets	1991	murdered by 30's Crips
OG Tee	29th Streets	1991	murdered by dope pushers
OG Santa Klaus	27th Streets	1993	murdered by a Jamaican
OG Insane Wayne	2nd Avenues	1993	murdered by Mid City Stoners 13
YG Smurf	29th Streets	1993	murdered by 30's Crips
YG Wino	BDS Avenues	1993	murdered by School Yard Crips
YG C-K-Man	27th Streets	1993	murdered by Geer Gang Crips
YG Baby-Krazy-K	2nd Avenues	1993	murdered by School Yard Crips
OG Moe	27th Streets	1995	murdered by a homeboy
YG Lil De-Kapone	29th Streets	1995	car accident
YG Kay-K	25th Streets	1996	murdered by 18th Street
YG Tiny Spook	29th Streets	1996	murdered by 40's Crips
YG Belizean Jerry	BZP 27th Streets	1999	murdered by an Inglewood Blood
OG Fatman	27th Streets	1999	died of natural causes
OG G-Kev	27th Streets	2000	murdered by 30's Crips
YG M-Dog	BZP 27th Streets	2000	murdered by 30's Crips
OG Big B-Rock	2nd Avenues	2000	suicide
YG G-Nipples	BZP 27th Streets	2001	suicide
YG Ant-Dog	27th Streets	2001	murdered by West Blvd. Crips
YG Tiny Evil	29th Streets	2002	murdered by 30's Crips
OG Iceman	27th Streets	2003	murdered by 30's Blood Stone Piru
OG Big Evil	29th Streets	2003	murdered by 18th Streets Cholos

Printed in the United States
40880LVS00002B/226-240